TRUTH ALWAYS KILLS

Jeff Prentiss's life is a mess. As a homicide detective working in St. Petersburg, he knows he's made too many mistakes and made too many enemies. When his wife's ex-husband, Roy Lee Evans, is released from prison and threatens his family, Jeff does what he must to keep them safe. Now fighting for his career, his wife Lori believes he knows more about Evans' whereabouts than he's willing to say. With his family life strained to the breaking point, a "celebrity" thief is found dead, and Jeff and his new partner find themselves roasting in the media spotlight. There's a disc that ties the dead man to a political bigshot in Tampa, but the link doesn't make any sense.

Everything keeps coming back to Lori's missing ex, even as the case points to an organized crime operation. Jeff compounds old mistakes with new ones and as the investigation continues, he begins a slow descent into his own darkened version of Hell. Should he share everything with his partner, be honest with Lori? Only she's disappeared and Jeff is a man in search of the truth, but he knows that if he finds it, it just might kill them all.

Rick Ollerman Bibliography

Turnabout (2014)
Shallow Secrets (2014)
Truth Always Kills (2015)

"All the slam-bang
anyone might want."
Booklist

Truth Always Kills

....

Rick Ollerman

STARK HOUSE

Stark House Press • Eureka California

TRUTH ALWAYS KILLS

Published by Stark House Press
1315 H Street
Eureka, CA 95501, USA
griffinskye3@sbcglobal.net
www.starkhousepress.com

ISBN: 1-933586-82-6
ISBN-13: 978-1-933586-82-3

Book design by Mark Shepard, shepgraphics.com

First Stark House Press Edition: December 2015

"Easy to Read: A Story of Rick Ollerman"
by Ben Boulden

You know Rick Ollerman. His name has graced more than a few Stark House covers. It generally reads something like this, "Introduction by Rick Ollerman," and, if the byline were completely accurate and honest, it would include, "Terrific…" "Wonderful…" "Brilliant…" "Introduction by Rick Ollerman." He has a way of putting context to the novels he introduces with a perceptive, informed, and lucid flair. His introductory essays clarify and set the stage for the story to follow by explaining why the story, and the writer are worth the reader's time. Author Bill Crider, in a review of a recent Stark House title, wrote, "[T]he additional material included with [Stark House] novels is worth the price of admission on its own." And I'm pretty sure he was mostly speaking of Rick's excellent work, which is why writing an Introduction for his third published novel, *Truth Always Kills*, is intimidating. He would probably do a better job with fewer words, and a higher standard of execution, but here I am not only in awe of his essays, but also of his fiction.

Mr. Ollerman's first two novels—*Turnabout* and *Shallow Secrets*—arrived in a Stark House trade paperback double published in September 2014. The book received critical praise, including a telling comment from Don Crinklaw in his *Booklist* review:

"Remember those old Ace paperbacks, with two actioners in one volume? Stark House is reviving them, with [*Turnabout / Shallow Secrets*] holding all the slam-bang anyone might want."

Mr. Crinklaw's comparison with the old Ace crime novels is spot on, too; except the length. Ace liked them short—closer to novellas than novels—and Rick's are full length. Otherwise *Turnabout* and *Shallow Secrets* would have made sterling additions to the Ace line up; perfect partners to the work of its best writers. Harry Whittington, Robert Bloch, J. M. Flynn, Robert Colby. In a phrase, and I am borrowing here, the old Ace Doubles (at their best) and Mr. Ollerman's first two novels, are *easy to read*. This is the very phrase Rick used to describe the work of Ed Gorman in his essay, "Cruising the Literary Strip with Ed Gorman." It originated, for Rick at least, when his father told him Dick Francis's novel *Proof* was easy to read. Rick had recommended *Proof*, and as he explains in the essay, he was disappointed with his father's seeming dismissal of the novel. At least until he understood what the phrase meant:

"Easy to read is not a bad thing for a book to be. It is actually a very good thing. It means the book has clear language and a good pace, it means it has interesting characters, and means the single most important thing to the average reader: they want to keep turning the pages. 'Easy to read' is good."

Easy to read is good, and a compliment worthy of only the most skillful writers; no matter if the writing is category fiction or literature, "easy to read" is the single most important element a novel or story can have. It means it is accessible, interesting, and the story never stumbles over the writing. It means the reader can identify the novel's subtlety and nuance without wading through gaudily self-aware prose.

It also perfectly describes Rick Ollerman's latest novel, *Truth Always Kills*. It is easy to read, but complicated and dark. It is something of a character study. A study of the protagonist, Jeff Prentiss. A self-destructing homicide detective working in St. Petersburg, Florida. His life is idyllic; a good job, a loving wife named Lori, an adopted daughter named Roxy, and a house on the water. It begins to fold when the investigation of a brutal murder goes sour—Prentiss taking the blame—and Lori's ex-husband, and Roxy's biological father, is released from prison. His name is Roy Lee Evans, and, at first, he makes himself known in small ways, but his appearances become more brazen and frightening. Prentiss, being a cop, knows stalking is often a prelude to murder, and when Roy disappears Lori is scared Jeff was involved. She takes Roxy and runs; afraid of what Prentiss likely did.

Roy is the catalyst of the story. He is the beginning, and while he never appears on page, his shadow is long and familiar. It is something like a sequel to John D. MacDonald's *The Executioners* (filmed as *Cape Fear*)—what happens after Sam Bowden kills Max Cady? Do the Bowdens return to their idyllic life, or does Sam lose everything? His family, and, at least figuratively, his life?

Jeff Prentiss knows, but he gave everything he had to learn it.

It begins with a corpse in the bay. The dead man is a celebrity thief named Randy Shawcross: "The King of the Cats." He was tied, beaten and drowned. The only evidence is a computer Shawcross's wife gave the police with a single suspicious website in its browsing history. A porn site where the actors are amateur, their faces blurred, but the filming standards are professional. The investigation leads Prentiss into unlikely places; the murder of a Tampa political bigshot, prostitution, and Roy's name, from a thug in Ybor City, keeps surfacing. As the case builds and pressure increases, Prentiss begins to make bad choices. He keeps information from his partner, investigates far outside his jurisdiction.

The plotting is complicated, but everything revolves around Jeff Prentiss and Roy Lee Evans. Lori and Roxy, the investigation, Jeff's partner, and his career. Its success relies on Prentiss's self-concept as an honest man. It is a brutal, self-destructive honesty, but it is who Jeff thinks he is. The irony is that Jeff's overt dishonesty—about Roy, the investigation—destroys him. In the beginning he is self-righteous and angry (honest with the world, but dishonest with himself) and at the end he feels guilt for his actions (dishonest with the world, but honest with himself), which, in a dark and brooding way, is his redemption.

A redemption that is hinted at in the title with three simple words, *Truth Always Kills*. A title that seems odd at first, and as the novel unfolds begins to make more and more sense. It is a story about truth and deceit. The title is similar to a phrase from Robert Penn Warren's novel *All the King's Men*:

"…the truth always kills the father."

And though I know Warren's prose did not influence the title of this book, and the meaning does not crossover perfectly, it is fitting because, at least figuratively, the truth did kill Jeff—father to Roxy—and his death made life possible for his family.

Truth Always Kills is all this, and more, but simply put, and all you really need to know is, it is easy to read.

—August 2015
Cottonwood Heights, UT

Ben Boulden is a crime fiction writer and editor of the renowned website, *Gravetapping*—gravetapping.blogspot.com.

Sources

Ollerman, Rick, "Cruising the Literary Strip with Ed Gorman," included in *The Autumn Dead / The Night Remembers* by Ed Gorman, Stark House Press, 2014.

Crinklaw, Don, book review of *Turnabout / Shallow Secrets* by Rick Ollerman, published in *Booklist*, September 15, 2014.

Justus, James H., *The Achievement of Robert Penn Warren*, Louisiana State University Press, 1981.

An Introduction. . .

I'm old enough to have bought all those old Gold Medal and Dell Originals right off the wire racks of dime stores, drug stores and grocery stores. This gives me a certain arrogance when I decide to pick up an article or even a book about those old novels. I was there, right? Doesn't that give me a special insight not only to the historical context in which they were sold but also the material itself?

Nope. I have on my bookshelves a number of histories of Paperback America that put my knowledge and perception to shame. Geoffrey O'Brien, Richard Lupoff and Lee Server have written classic takes on the times and the writers that produced the paperbacks we cherish and value today.

Now I need to add a new name to the list of people who have brought extraordinary work to the subject of Paperback America. Rick Ollerman. The introductions he's written to various Stark House two-fers stand as exemplary takes on not only the material but on the lives of the men and women who produced that material. I don't believe they have any equals as introductions to genre material. I'd liken them to Phd dissertations but they're too damned much fun to read. I reread each of them at least twice a year especially if I have to write an introduction myself. I want to learn from the master.

And now Rick's proven as fine a novelist as he is a historian. I remember receiving his first two books *Turnabout* and *Shallow Secrets* and having no idea what to expect. No, correct that. I felt a certain *dread* about the books I was about to read because the cover copy lead me to believe that they might be the kind of bad hardboiled mutations that infest the ebook original market. Because I respected Rick so much I wanted to be able to say something not just positive but effusive about his work. But what if I had to lie? He'd know it.

Whew. No lies were necessary. Rick is as good a novelist as he is a critic. His first two novels salute the books of the Fifties but bring a new energy and (to quote ole Two Gun Ernie Hemingway) a whole new angle of vision to the work. I thought *Turnabout* should have been nominated for an Edgar Best Paperback Award.

And the new one, the one you're holding here? *Truth Always Kills?* This is a major stride forward, a richer, cleverer and even more rewarding journey down the meanest of streets. This one has the power to hurt you.

I don't know how many more introductions Rick will be writing now that he's proven to be a fine novelist himself. I've warned him about all the temptations that are put in the way of writers—you know, the money, the fame, the prestige. He's assured he'll be able to handle it.

—Ed Gorman.
September 2015

TRUTH ALWAYS KILLS
by Rick Ollerman

For Pat Frovarp and Gary Shulze
Because One More Book Never Hurt….

Chapter 1

I tried to get her to stay, to at least wait until I got home to decide anything, before she did what she said she would. I told her she couldn't go, she'd at least have to talk to me. In a quiet desperation I told her that she couldn't do this over the phone, for god's sake.

But of course she could.

I could hear the crying in her voice, could imagine the tear-streaked face wetting the phone as she struggled to maintain enough composure to tell me what she was doing. My wife was leaving me? She was taking my daughter? Why? Where? Why now?

"Lori," I said, the fingers of my right hand death-gripped to the steering wheel of my car. "Is Roxy okay?"

A loud sniffle. "She's fine, she doesn't know anything. Just that we have to go…."

"Doesn't know anything about what, Lori? Damn it, just stay there. I'll be home in fifteen minutes—"

"I won't be there, Jeff. I'm already gone." She paused. "I love you."

And then she quickly hung up. I threw the cell phone across my body into the passenger seat where it bounced up into the panel covering the air bag and ended up somewhere else.

What the hell was I supposed to do now?

Leslie Alcaro called just after I'd lost the phone. I let my hand follow the ringing and leaned hard to pull my phone out from between the passenger door and the passenger seat.

"Prentiss," I said, barely aware of the phone, the road, the traffic.

"Hello, Jeff, it's Leslie." She sounded awkward, probably since I'd just left her office.

"More lawyer stuff?" I asked.

"No, nothing like that. Your wife just called here. She didn't sound well. I told her you'd gone. Was that okay?"

Was that okay. I'm meeting with my union lawyer to try to save my job and my wife calls to tell me she's leaving. Only she's already done it. Of course everything's okay.

"That was fine, Leslie." At a loss for anything else to say, I added, "Thank you."

"That's— that's fine, Jeff. I wanted to say, you know you could come back. Here, I mean. If you wanted. We could—"

"No thank you, Leslie. I have to get home right now." Or did I? I didn't really know.

Quickly, "Okay, Jeff, that's fine. I just— well, if you need to talk to someone…."

"And everything we say is confidential, right?"

She gave a small laugh. "Something like that."

"Another time," I said, no feeling of grace in my voice. I just hung up, feeling cruel and mean and having no other place to let it out. She didn't need me reminding her what an ass I was. Especially when she had only been reaching out. I knew she was lonely over the state of her own marriage and I liked her. But there were lines, always lines.

I sat pulled over in the car for as long as I dared. The sky outside was an effervescent sort of black, a state that passed for darkness these days in central Florida along the Gulf Coast. Too many streetlights, parking lot lights and warehouse and home security vapor lights have obliterated all but the brightest objects in the night sky. There was no moon over St. Petersburg and I sometimes thought it didn't need one anymore.

The caller ID on my cell phone had showed that Lori had been using hers, which meant that what she'd said was probably true, that she'd already left the house. I had no doubt she was gone. I could feel it. Maybe in some weird psychic way I'd even been expecting it. She and Roxy were out there, but like the missing night-time stars, I couldn't see them through the haze. Yet I felt no surprise, just a sense of deep loss.

Yes, there had been a rough few weeks—months?—but were they enough to make her leave? Why didn't she tell me anything about it beforehand? Why didn't she try to talk it out? Isn't that what husbands and wives are supposed to do with each other?

I'd been giving her space because I knew she was troubled. She'd been that way since Roy disappeared. She didn't bring it up, and I couldn't, but it was clear that she was having problems. I didn't know what to say to her, I didn't know what she needed to hear, or what she could handle. Roxy could tell something was wrong too, but she was smart enough to leave us both alone.

In the end, neither of us said anything. Anything at all. And that silence that turns to darkness can kill any relationship ever forged.

But what could I do? Roy Lee Evans wasn't coming back, I knew that, and that was what Lori wanted, I believed. It was what I knew. It had to be. Even Roxy wanted that, and Roy was her biological father. They weren't safe with him coming around again. They couldn't be at peace and they knew that. There was real danger with him around. As a husband, as a father, as a cop, even just as a man, I had to do something. Ultimately it was up to me to keep them safe.

I checked my watch. Now I had to get moving. The M.E. was waiting for me at the crime scene and my lieutenant was waiting for me to call him. Goddamnit to hell. Every last stinking bit of it. Why couldn't I get a few hours alone to try to pull my own mess of a life together? I didn't need Leslie offering whatever it was she was offering, I didn't need more crap from the department, and I didn't need to work a new case in the middle of the night. What I needed was a way to keep from exploding from the inside out.

I put the car into gear and pulled back onto the road, heading south on Fourth Street. The interstate would be faster but I kept driving past the cross streets that would take me to an on ramp. The hell with 'em. The dead body wasn't going anywhere.

Breathing deeply, trying to hold it together, to not think, I noticed my hands were trembling on the wheel. Starting with my neck, I tried to concentrate on each muscle, each muscle group, force them to relax. I couldn't let them see me struggle. I couldn't let them look at me that way. That's what they were all looking for and I wouldn't let them win, even if they'd earned it.

I just drove.

The corpse was a male, dressed in black, elegant yet non-descript. No jewelry. Both shoes were missing and one sock was gone. A piece of frayed rope was knotted around the man's chest, the loop set tight under the arms. His hands were tied behind his back with a piece of what looked to be the same type of rope.

He had been pulled up on to the rocky sand beach so that the head was out of the water, pointing up the gentle slope toward land, the feet still bobbed gently in the tiny waves. The area had been taped off and a tech was setting up a pair of portable lights to illuminate the scene. Tiny crabs scuttled along the edges of the shadows.

Wally Steener, the county medical examiner, was waiting outside the cordoned area, taking notes. "Jesus," he said. "Take your sweet time, why don't you?"

I didn't respond. Steener looked at my face and then let it drop. Besides, my partner wasn't there, either. I walked over to the tape and peered down at the body. Headlights flared in the lot behind me and I turned and saw Moran's banana yellow Monte Carlo pull in next to my Jeep.

Steener's voice came from my elbow. "You okay, Jeff?"

Jesus. "Everything's grand, Wally." To Moran I yelled, "Get down here, Terry."

The portable lights blasted an unforgiving arc across the body on the beach. The face was swollen and bruised. The eyes were open and didn't look—normal.

We asked the officer controlling the scene who had found the body. Sweeney, I think his name was. "Don't know," he said as he wrote my name on his clipboard, then Moran's. "It was called in, sounded like a kid, was what I was told." Moran and I ducked under the tape and followed single file along the existing footprints to the water's edge.

"Who moved him?" Moran called back to Sweeney.

"I did. It was floating about three feet out. I pulled him in and flipped him over, left him there."

"Cool," Moran told him. Then to me he said quietly, "You look like shit."

"You have no idea. And you can't see that well in the dark."

"Yeah, well, take my word for it and stay out of the light."

I listened through the raging background wash of my mind, saw images of my wife and daughter, the inevitable growing but still unseen image of a house, formally a home, without them in it, as my partner did the job and asked all the right questions of those around him. I could see the beach wasn't the murder scene. There would be no evidence here. Had someone called for a boat?

I shined my light across the inky flatness of Tampa Bay. A lone sailboat seemed stuck to the surface about fifty yards out, hull paint peeling, uncared for. Probably abandoned, now likely home to some junky or group thereof. Beyond and to the east the lights and orange-yellow cable-stays of the Sunset Skyway bridge rose 190 feet above the water. Architecturally brilliant light pollution.

"We should probably check the bridge."

"You think he could have been a jumper?" Moran asked.

"That wouldn't explain the rope," I said. "More like an involuntary flight job. What do you think, Wally?"

Steener shook his head. "I can't tell. If he jumped or was thrown off the bridge, I'd say someone had already worked over his face. His body too, to some degree. I'd have to get him on the table to tell you more."

"Time of death?"

"I'll take his core temp now. But if this guy came from someplace else it's going to be a guess with half a dozen asterisks behind it. The water temperature's too inconsistent with all these flats to factor in accurately."

I grunted and pointed out the pieces of rope to my partner. "Look at this crap," I said.

"Clothesline?"

"Nothing you'd expect to find on any self-respecting boat."

Moran was a big fisherman and would know about these things. "Not on my mine, anyway."

"There's something else," I said. Steener stepped up to do something to the body but I stopped him with a touch on the shoulder.

"What?" Moran asked.

"I think I know him."

"That what's eating your shit?"

I ignored that. "You know him, too."

Moran walked around the body and shone his light on the lightly disfigured face. "Sort of looks familiar...."

"Shawcross," I said. "The King of Cats."

"No shit," Moran said, leaning closer to the damaged face. "I think you're right. Damn. Lot of cops gonna be disappointed they didn't get to him first."

"They still want him behind bars."

"No, they want to do something like this to him."

I stared at my partner. He stood up and flicked off his light. He finally caught me looking at him. "No. That's not what I was saying...."

"Hm," I said. With the forbearance of Steener, I knelt down and went through Shawcross's pockets. There was nothing there.

"Think he was working?" Moran asked.

"Dressed all in black costume, clean pockets, could have been."

"That's going to upset a whole lot of people."

I turned around and ducked back under the tape. Lori's voice was getting louder in my mind. I was starting to lose the small amount of focus I was working with. I couldn't concentrate anymore.

Moran stepped up beside me. "Seriously, what's going on, man?"

"It's raining shit, Terry."

"I thought you had this job crap handled. The brass getting on your ass again?"

I'd had some trouble on a case and it came out in a bad way in court. Moran had drawn the short straw after my suspension and transfer and been made my partner. We were friends despite all of it. "No," I said. "Lori."

"She okay? How's Roxy?"

"They're gone, Terry. Lori took Roxy and left." I told him about the phone call.

"I am so sorry. What're you going to do?"

"Listen, can you ride this in? Greene's waiting for a call but I've got to get out of here. I'm going to lose it all over this place." Part of me wanted to add, *And I can't afford to do that*. The lawyer in Leslie Alcaro would have been proud.

"Go," Moran said. "I'll call the lieut. I'll make up some bullshit if he wants to talk to you."

"No, don't do that," I told him. "Don't get yourself in trouble on my account."

He said, "Man, all you are is trouble," but there was concern in his voice.

"Yeah, but they're just waiting for it. Tell him I've gone to see Darlene Shawcross."

He jerked his head toward the beach. "His wife?"

"Yeah," I said, walking away. "Someone has to do the notification. And maybe she knows what Randy was up to."

"She'll talk to you?"

"We'll see."

I left the shore and drove slowly out of the park along the shell road. I picked up my cell phone and dialed Lori's number. I don't know why I hadn't done it already. I guess I would have been surprised to hear her voice answer back.

And I was right. No answer. Not even voice mail.

I hit pavement and took a left at the first light and headed north to 54th Avenue. Before I did anything else, I was going home. A quick stop, I told myself. Tears began rolling down my cheeks. Darlene Shawcross would just have to wait a little while.

Chapter 2

She was certainly gone. Clothes, jewelry, anything personal. Everything personal. Lori had obliterated herself from the house. There was nothing left of Roxy's, either. The floor of my daughter's closet was clear, the western saddle I'd gotten her last Christmas was gone. She wouldn't have willingly left the house without it. Lori must have used a truck or van. I wasn't in there for more than five minutes before I had to leave, too.

Clearly the move had been planned for some time. More than a day or two. Lori'd known I'd be gone for most of the day though she couldn't know I'd be called to see the body on the beach.

There was a knot in my stomach that formed after her phone call and it had only gotten worse. And when I realized that this was the second time she'd run out on a husband, I had to sit down and think it through. As much as I might hate it, I would forever be linked to Roy Lee Evans, maybe for the rest of my life, for good or for ill.

Evans had been Lori's first husband, a smuggler running dope from Mexico across the Texas border. When Lori had met him, she had no idea what he really was and she'd been overwhelmed by the charisma and presence of a man who danced in country bars better then anyone she'd ever seen. And he was one way to take her away from a father she'd grown to fear.

He got her pregnant, and they got married. When Lori found out not only the truth about Roy but also became acquainted with some of the more violent tendencies hiding behind those outward charms, which were considerable, she fled to Florida. She was lucky, too: Evans got busted before he could follow and was sent to prison. She left his ass his first year in and got an annulment based on fraud before the baby was born.

I met her when I was a patrol fresh in town after moving down from Ocala. We went out on five or six date before she'd told me about her past. When I didn't cut and run things got more serious pretty quickly. At a picnic at Lettuce Lake Park, I decided I'd fallen in love with both Lori and the three-year old Roxy. We were married after I joined the force in

Tampa and we bought a house on the water in St. Petersburg. We were a family, we were happy, and we were perfect.

Or so I thought. At least until Roy Evans was let out of Huntsville early and decided he was still interested in Lori and the little girl he'd never seen. He wanted them back. Maybe he really did love them, maybe it was something else only he could understand. I wasn't sure he was capable of being interpreted in the same way as other people were. He may have wanted them back simply because Lori had had the gall to actually leave him. He was just the kind of asshole sociopath that would find that fact impossible to accept. In any case, he came for them.

He came for my family.

My watch told me it was nearly eleven o'clock as I pulled over in front of the modest Pinellas Park home of Randy and Darlene Shawcross. The light was on next to the door and I could see the flickering glow of a television through a gap in the front curtains.

Darlene pulled open the door before I made it up the steps. She looked at me for nearly a minute, her face going from questioning to recognition to something sad and ugly as she held open the screen door and stood aside for me to enter.

"It's Randy," she said. "Isn't it?"

"I'm so sorry, Darlene."

She stumbled backwards before I could catch her but she kept her feet until she slumped onto the living room couch. A desperate hand clutched at a box of Kleenex from an end table.

"What happened?" She wouldn't look at me.

I didn't reply right away. At that moment the two of us were sharing a bond of grief, although of two different types, not that she had any idea about that. I focused myself and walked around the couch, stopping in front of her.

"Was it cops?"

I lowered myself onto the same couch but stayed a cushion over. I didn't want to get too close, and I didn't want to hover over her. "I don't know yet. First blush, doesn't look like it."

Darlene leaned away from me and lowered her chin down to her chest. She began to sob and weep and when she didn't make any moves toward me I stood up slowly and went into the kitchen. I'd been to that house before and knew where some of the things were. I stayed in there while I made coffee, pushing out the troubles in my own life with the news I had just brought Darlene Shawcross. I thought about how I'd known her cat burglar husband and how he'd made public fools of the legal system and nearly gotten away with being one of the most prolific thieves of all time. When the coffee was ready I brought a cup out to the living room.

Darlene was sitting up, face red and puffy, but the tears were under control. I offered her the cup but she pushed it away. "I don't want it," she said.

I sat down on the couch again, this time even further away.

"Please tell me what happened."

Beginning with how Randy was found in the water, I told her gently that he had been bound and possibly beaten. I told it to her that way because I felt that was how she needed to hear it and if so, that was how she deserved to get it. The details seemed to calm her down, which surprised me.

"I knew something like this was going to happen," she said. "I just knew it. I think I always did."

"I'm so sorry, Darlene."

She looked at me through bloodshot eyes, disheveled brown hair framing damp, puffy cheeks. "Thank you, Jeff. I think you probably mean that."

I wanted to reach out to her, touch her, but ultimately that distance was too far to cross. "You know I need to ask you a few things, don't you?"

Darlene blotted her nose with a fresh tissue and nodded. "I'm glad you're the one who came, Jeff. You were always different from the others. All of them. You and Randy could have been friends, I think."

"I think we were, in a way."

She nodded. "Randy did, too. It bothered him what they did to you after that trial in Tampa, especially after the same people tried to go after him when his trial was over. He didn't know how you could still be a cop after all that."

I didn't know what to say. I had my own past that affected my life, my career, in negative ways and I had made almost as many enemies as Randy had, at least among the Hillsborough County prosecutor's office. But I was a cop, not a career criminal and I wasn't certain how much of my sympathy for Randy had been misplaced. "The move over to St. Pete helped," I said.

Darlene nodded, lost in her own mind.

"Was Randy working again?"

She took her time answering. "I knew if he ever got arrested again it would be bad for him, real bad. But you never hated him the way those animals from Cleveland do. Did." She sniffed again, wiped her nose.

"He was a thrill criminal, not an evil man. He did what he did because he couldn't get away from the rush of it, not because he wanted to hurt people."

"But he still belonged behind bars."

"He still broke the law. And he did hurt people regardless of his motivation. Aside from all the stuff he stole, he took away his victims' ability to feel safe, in many cases to feel secure in their own homes. Those aren't good things, Darlene."

She nodded. "I know. That was always the most awful part. For me, anyway."

"So was he on a job, Darlene?"

"I— I don't know. I think he might have been."

"What does that mean?"

"It means I never asked him. I never wanted to know. I didn't want him to start again but I don't think he could help himself. He missed it, I think, but I never specifically tried to find out. All the time he was— working, you know, back in the day, I never really knew what he was up to. I guess I didn't want to know. At first I thought there were other women, but...."

"Do you know where he went tonight?"

She shook her head. "He's been gone since lunch time, maybe just after. I don't know where he went, just that he said he might be back late."

"Do you think he could have been working a job?"

"Stop asking me that, please, Jeff. I didn't know. I don't know. I was just afraid—"

"It's okay," I said, reaching over and patting her knee.

She picked up her coffee and we talked about what would happen to the body and what she would have to do to identify it. What needed to happen afterwards. "I could send someone over to be with you, if you'd like."

"No, that's all right, I think." She gave an almost kind of laugh. "I can call my sister. She's not in town but she'll help. I don't think Randy'd like it if you guys were with me too much."

I smiled a little, too. "You're probably right." I asked her about Randy's wallet and cell phone. She went off to check their bedroom and when she came back she said she was sure he must have taken them with him. She gave me the details on his car; I was hoping we'd find his effects when we located it, which might at least help us narrow down the area he was interested in.

"Did Randy have a computer?" If he was casing a place he would have done as much research as he could, probably a significant amount of it online.

Darlene left the room again and brought out a black and silver laptop. I took out a pad and hand wrote a receipt which she dropped carelessly on to the table. After a few minutes' more awkward conversation, I left her dialing the phone for her sister, a fresh wave of grief washing down her face.

I felt as empty inside as I ever had in my life. I should have called Moran but my cell phone was too damned heavy. I put the Jeep in gear and drove slowly home. The world could live without me until morning. I just had to find a way to hold myself together that long.

Chapter 3

The night was hell. The knot in my stomach grew firm and I couldn't eat. I could barely sip a glass of ice water. For some silly reason I couldn't stop looking at the phone. I couldn't stand the thought of being in *our* bedroom: I'd walk in, close my eyes, then back out by feel. I tried sitting on Roxy's bed for a while but it didn't have her presence any more, her essence having already passed on. The longer I stayed the stronger the physical urge to get out of the house became.

I needed out of my own home.

How could I have that feeling so quickly? *Because it's real*, I answered myself. Because it *feels* like she's gone, like they're both gone, and like they're not coming back.

When I started pacing the hallway faster and faster I finally left. It started as a walk, it turned into a wild run. Then I'd walk some more, my body taut with tension and sorrow, and soon I'd find myself running some more. I ran faster when I wanted to scream and pound my fists into the ground. When the eastern sky showed signs of lightening I made my way back home and fell asleep on the living room couch, exhausted.

I went in late to the office the next day, a Friday, with Randy Shawcross's laptop computer under my arm. Moran was already at his desk and when I walked in he steered me to the break room and over to the coffee machine.

"Greene was looking for you," he said.

"Of course he was." I rubbed my eyes and thought about how much I was struggling to stay on top of all the crap. "Did you tell him anything?"

"I told him that you were out to see the widow last night and that it went long. She broke down, was a mess, wouldn't let you leave."

"He buy it?"

"Seemed to. You just be careful."

Moran was a good friend and a good man but I didn't know how to tell him that. He had been a football star in Bradenton before he tore up his knee and failed his physical at Florida State then had to forfeit his scholarship. He tried a comeback at a community college but couldn't make it go. He'd had his whole life taken away with that injury but never quit working at it until he had built himself a new one. I wondered if I could learn from that. I told myself that if I was any smarter I would at least try.

"Thanks, Terry."

I told him about the time spent with Darlene Shawcross as we walked back to his desk, gave him the information on the Shawcross car we wanted to find. He filled me in on what had happened in the park after I'd left. There wasn't much I couldn't have guessed. A police boat made a run between the bridge and Maximo Park but didn't find anything, which wasn't surprising. It was scheduled to be back out this morning. Moran was still waiting for an update.

I processed the laptop and took it down to the computer techs. I told them we had a dead burglar but I didn't tell them who it was. They'd find out for sure soon enough, especially if they were anywhere near a news broadcast in a few hours. What I wanted to know, I told them, was what he had been looking at on the internet. Was he researching anything, local places, people, celebrities, special events, anything like that. They said that as long as he hadn't cleared out his the cache, history, temp files and registry, they should be able to come up with a good list.

"Don't talk to me like that," I told the tech, a fresh faced kid named Darren. "I don't have any cash, didn't study history, and you can stick the rest of that stuff in your ear."

He laughed and I left the room. There were still a few guys around that I could talk to like that but they were mostly various techs and support staff.

When I got back to my desk my lieutenant was there, looking down at the papers I'd left on my blotter. "What's up?" I asked.

Lieutenant Lucas Greene looked at me with a set of loose, slightly sagging features that seemed to project a sense of constant displeasure. He may have been a good cop once and maybe even a good human being, but he had been sticking it to me for the sake of brownie points from above and he hadn't bothered to take the time to try to know me. I'd come to St. Pete after the union worked out a transfer from Tampa following the problems I'd had with the Safrenza case. The brass in Tampa wanted me gone immediately but the union stood up and after my suspension worked out the transfer across the bay. The problems hadn't ended there, they'd only changed.

Greene made me update him on the Shawcross murder when I knew full well he'd already gotten everything from Terry Moran. A press conference had been scheduled for two o'clock and he didn't want me anywhere near it. The King of Cats had been too much the celebrity criminal, too much a symbol of futility in the legal system, to not warrant substantial news coverage. Throw in the new department black sheep and you had a public relations nightmare.

"Listen, Lieutenant," I said. "I'm not feeling very well today. I was hoping you'd let me take a sick day and head home early."

"Done," Greene said and turned away abruptly. Wasn't supposed to be that easy. I guess we understood each other. Problem solved, I suppose.

From eight feet away, Moran's head popped up like a prairie dog. "What?" he said when Greene had left the detectives' room. "Dude, you giving in to them?"

I walked over and sat in the chair next to his desk. It was suddenly hard to look at him.

"Your wife?" he asked.

I nodded.

After a moment he said, "You do look like shit."

"Hm," I told him. "Ever thought about being a cop?"

"Damn. You know, if I were a man…."

"Yeah, Terry. I know. You'd kick my ass." I swatted his knee and stood up to go.

I signed out and went home. It was easier in the daytime. There were no new messages on the machine in the kitchen. Big surprise. Not knowing what else to do and not wanting to stay inside, I went out the patio doors and across the lawn to my dock. I lowered the cradle lift holding the twenty one foot Donzi into the water and tossed the remote control unit into the boat. Now that I was away from work, my guts began clenching again and I still didn't know how to face the emptiness inside.

There was no place I knew of that was more centering, more peaceful, than being on a boat somewhere adrift at sea, out of sight of land and Jet Skis. I stepped lightly into the boat as the cell in my pocket went off. The display showed the number for my favorite lawyer. I thought about it and then answered anyway.

"Jeff, hey, it's Leslie."

"More trouble? It can't wait?"

"It's nothing new. I just thought I should check in on you."

"I'm getting ready to skip town. Can you file some sort of motion, get me a head start and a chance to get away?"

"How long do you need?" she asked.

"I don't know. It's not a well-thought plan. A few hours anyway. How far away is Cuba?"

"I think you're okay without involving a judge."

"Good, then," I told her. "My boat awaits."

"Are you alone?"

"Not quite. I have a cooler named Larry that needs filling and I'm trying to make that my biggest problem of the day."

She laughed and it was like a drip of icy water beading down the back of my neck. "I wish I could say the same thing," she said.

"Come on down," I said, wondering immediately why I'd done it. But I continued, going with the momentum. "Throw on a bikini and make my boat look better than it should."

"Almost tempting," she said. "Maybe another time."

That was potentially confusing. So I didn't think about it.

"Well, then," I said, "thanks for calling. I appreciate the thought. The boat's in the water and I'm going to clear the bay and head west. That's about all I know at this point."

"You be careful."

"We'll see." We both said goodbye and I would have thought more about it but I wanted to get moving. Leslie had left me with the feeling that there was something going unsaid.

I stopped at the pier at Demen's Landing for fuel and beer and away I went.

I followed the markers for the Intracoastal Waterway over to and under the Sunshine Skyway bridge, imagining as I often did what it would be like to see an actual body plummeting downwards toward the water. Around a hundred people launched themselves over the railings every year. I cut back the throttle on the other side and looked off to my right at Maximo Park, the site of last night's body recovery. I didn't see the police boat and I kept going, not really caring.

There was only a light breeze and the water was just a little bumpy. All this meant was that I could get to where I was going faster. A pod of dolphins broke the surface off starboard but I didn't stop to watch them like I usually did. I moved out past Egmont Key and its turtles and lighthouse, went past Anna Maria Island and headed straight out into the Gulf of Mexico following a loose compass heading. The water was rougher out here and I reduced speed a little bit as the cushions started jumping off the seat bases. The rushing air and flecks of spray that exploded over the bow and windshield were both distracting and wonderful, even down to the salty sting in my eyes. After twenty minutes I throttled down to idle and finally killed the engine. Let me drift where I may.

I hadn't taken the time to put the bimini top up so I pulled some sun screen from a compartment and covered myself with a thick layer. Then I folded out the cushions on the sun deck and lay back with a cold beer dripping condensation on to my chest.

Now what, I thought. What the hell was I supposed to do now?

The gentle bobbing motion and the internal stress I was fighting encouraged sleep and I gave in after gulping down two of the beers I had stuffed into my cooler. Lori's face was never far from my mind and I couldn't keep from wondering where she would have gone. Nothing came to mind but it I knew it could have been anywhere. As I surrendered to the sucking unconsciousness the last cohesive thought I had was how strange it was that out here, cradled by the gently moving waves, you could actually feel the wind but not hear it.

It was like passing through a constant stream of ghosts.

The boat and I bobbed for hours. The alcohol wasn't doing anything to me other than prompting periodic streams over the side of the boat. I tried not to focus on Lori but the more I tried to think of other things, the more her face kept creeping in at the edges of everything I came up with.

I didn't want to beat myself up for what had happened—it was far, far too late for that—but that notion only went so far when I considered the size of the truckload of shit I'd been carting around for as long as I had been. It made me sad and morose. I thought about people I knew who were truly happy. It wasn't a long list. Moran seemed to be that way. He had a lovely wife, Sandra, who sold real estate and came from a well to do family. In fact, Moran could quit being a cop tomorrow and find himself in a higher social circle just by staying home.

He seemed to have everything I didn't, except children, but that had been their own choice so far. Moran had a subtler personality than I did, whereas I didn't seem to know when best to keep my opinions to myself. Somewhere along the line I'd decided that I could call a spade a spade and not piss anyone off as long as I did a better than average job as a cop. How I could be so naive for so long I'd never know.

I thought about my troubles in Tampa and how they seemed to relate me to the late Randy Shawcross. He'd been almost too clever for himself, getting busted in Detroit when for the first time in his career he'd taken on someone for help on a job. When his accomplice was picked up on some bullshit charge later on, he got himself off the hook by dealing away Randy, a much bigger fish.

He was prepared, though. You had to give him that. The physical evidence they had on him was weak enough that he could possibly have gotten off with a good attorney and a reasonable doubt, but he played a different game. He surprised everyone and agreed to plead guilty.

And not only for that heist. In exchange for immunity he'd tell the prosecutors everything he'd ever done. He promised the prosecutors they'd be able to close at least a dozen cases that had gone unsolved, that he'd be completely forthcoming and they'd look good for taking a person like himself out of circulation.

They'd had no idea that a thief like Randy Shawcross had even been operating on their turf and they readily agreed. Seemed easy enough work to them and a big win for just a little effort. Little did they know.

Randy used disguises, electronics, ropes to rappel from rooftops to balconies, and had made quite a career out of ripping off the rich and careless. After making sure the language of his deal was what he wanted, he spilled everything, his entire criminal career, and the prosecutors couldn't wipe all the egg off their faces with beach towels. Sure they were able to recover some of the jewelry and even a bit of cash, but they couldn't touch the mastermind behind the crimes themselves. At least a dozen cases? More like five times that number.

Shawcross became a minor celebrity, the crook who beat the system, and was photographed like a movie star everywhere he went. But the Detroit cops weren't finished with him. He'd made monkeys out of the whole system and the judge did what he could by sentencing Randy to the maximum penalty he was allowed, fifteen years in prison. Because of the prior agreement the jail time portion of the sentence was suspended but what Randy hadn't realized was that the judge was able to put him on probation for that same length of time. He wouldn't be going to prison, but he was subject to a curfew and all the other restrictions that went along with carrying that punishment. He'd escaped imprisonment but they still had him on a leash.

When his mother got sick he petitioned for and was granted the ability to move to Florida. That was when I got to know him a little. Every time a burglary happened in the area, a warrant could be written allowing the cops to burst into the Shawcross home and toss it, ostensibly looking for the stolen goods, even if the crime had been a convenience store robbery across town. After all, stealing was stealing.

I'd had my own trouble with warrants but I hadn't been anywhere near as clever as Randy Shawcross when I dealt with it. No, I had probably behaved in the worst way possible, and that had the Tampa brass calling for my head and had gotten me tucked away in St. Petersburg, at least temporarily. A union grievance had been the only thing that had saved me. It had fallen to Leslie Alcaro as the union appointed lawyer to forestall the execution.

My trouble started with the Safrenza case, also known as the College Park fiasco. A Cuban meth dealer and his family had been beaten to death with aluminum baseball bats while eating dinner in their apartment. While working that case my partner and I came across the name of a petty criminal named Diego Safrenza. We stayed with him for a few days but couldn't turn anything up that could justify taking him in.

The local Cubans were putting pressure on the department and posters made from the crime scene pictures that had been printed in the *Tribune* were appearing on telephone poles and night club walls from Ybor City north to New Tampa. The brass wanted to arrest anybody with the slightest connection to the case in order to calm things down. They didn't want the sort of ethnic strife that had plagued Miami to surface up here.

Without much to go on, we got a judge to give us a search warrant for Diego Safrenza's bungalow out by Lowry Park Zoo. The judge limited the warrant's reach to the closets, garage area, or "any obvious location that could reasonably be expected to serve as storage for one or more aluminum baseball bats or other sporting goods related paraphernalia." Not exactly what we wanted but sometimes you just have to take what you can get. Occasionally it even works out.

I was lead investigator on the murders and I led the search on the house. One of my guys found a padlock key on a silver chain. There weren't any padlocks on the property so we bagged it as potential evidence. People lock up sporting goods equipment in other places, right? Starting with the house as the center of a circle, we worked our way outwards until we found a self storage facility with a padlock that was opened by none other than Diego Safrenza's key.

Bingo. Not only did we find the bats but we had equipment for a fully functioning meth lab, complete with finished product just waiting to be carried off into the streets. Enough means and motive to put Safrenza away for a very long time.

What I didn't know at the time was that this would be the beginning of my end as a detective with the Tampa PD.

Chapter 4

I maneuvered the boat back onto the lift in the canal behind my house in St. Petersburg. The sun was nearly down and the evening mist was beginning to coalesce above the water's surface.

Briny residue mixing with sun block covered my body and I rinsed myself with the cold water from the hose on the dock before I flushed the salt water from the engine. Then I headed for the house and picked up the phone. I'd had an idea while coming in from the bay but that didn't mean I was looking forward to it.

I dialed the number for Lori's mother in Houston.

Her name was Catherine and she'd always liked me, possibly because I was someone who wasn't called Roy Lee Evans. I had no idea if she knew that Lori and Roxy had left me and if so, if she'd even want to talk to me.

I didn't want to make her uncomfortable but that didn't keep me from acting like a high school kid and dialing and redialing every ten minutes until she answered. The more times I did it the more I felt that I would *feel* Lori if I could only get her mother to pick up. The feeling was almost desperate when Catherine finally answered. At that point I knew she'd been home all along.

"Catherine," I said, instantly downbeat. "It's Jeff Prentiss."

"I knew who was calling."

The tone of her voice made it clear she also knew all about what had happened with her daughter.

"She's not there, is she."

"No, Jeff, she's not. And don't ask me to tell you where they went because I don't know."

"Can you at least tell me, Catherine, is she okay?"

"She'n Roxy are fine. But that's about all I could get her to say." Her voice was low and quiet and filled with her Texas drawl.

Once again I realized I had no idea what I was doing.

"She didn't want me to lie to you, Jeff."

"Yeah, okay," I said, feeling as bad as I ever could. "It's all right, Kate, it really is. I just wanted to call. It was good to hear your voice—"

Catherine sniffled at the other end of the line. "I hope it works out with the two of you," she said. "That's what I want."

"Me, too," I told her. "Take care of yourself, and if— Never mind. I'm sorry I bothered you." I couldn't put the phone down fast enough. I said a quick "Take care" and hung up.

"Damn it!" I yelled. I never should have called, but something inside me told me I had to. It was a way to keep trying.

Like the night before I left the house and sprinted along the sidewalk and around the corner, burning myself out in three quarters of a mile. Later, bathed in sweat and swatting at mosquitoes, I walked back home, reconnected the hose to the spigot at the dock and washed the rest of the salt water from my boat.

The next day was spent in useless motion: walking, running, swimming. Any kind of movement was better than sitting still, wondering about Lori and Roxy, waiting for the phone to ring when I knew it wouldn't. I wanted to turn my mind off, take a pill and wake up in a few years when the pain wouldn't hurt so much. I tried drinking but I didn't want to be blitzed if Lori did actually call, so I made myself stop.

With all the problems I had at work, the one thing keeping me sane had been the presence of my family. When the sudden return of Roy Evans had begun to erode that security, there was very little left that was right in my world. Work certainly didn't fill the gap.

It's hard to describe the overwhelming stress and tension, the constant and unrelenting pressure, that came with being a cop when it felt like all the higher ups wanted me gone. I'd lost them a high profile case, put the community at risk (they said), and gave a black eye to the department.

I don't know. Maybe I had. I also wondered if I had just tried too hard to deliver what they wanted and that failure was what had cracked me up. I thought back to the Safrenza case and how it was still taking up far too much space in my life. I could think of very few ways to make it end in a way that I could accept.

When they'd excluded from evidence the padlock key from Diego Safrenza's house, and so by extension the self storage unit containing the murder weapons as well as an entire meth lab, there was literally nothing left of the case. One of my guys had gone into the master bedroom and on the nightstand next to the headboard had found the key. Not in a "closet, garage, or other location that could reasonably be assumed to hold sporting goods paraphernalia." Safrenza, murderer, drug producer, drug dealer and who knows what else, would walk.

I lost my composure on the stand. The defense attorney asked me if I knew where the key had been found. He wanted to know why one of my men had gone into the master bedroom if not to look in the closet. He wanted to know why I thought I could disregard a judge's clear instructions on the search warrant.

This case isn't about police procedure, I told him.

Of course it is, the attorney said. Sloppy police procedure. The arrogant attitudes, the casual racism that leads you to persecute an Hispanic man because of the color of his skin, the accent of his speech. That's what this case is about.

I looked him in the eye and asked: Did you ever notice that everyone in a courtroom is sworn to tell the truth but the lawyers?

There was stunned silence in an already quiet courtroom. I was warned by the judge and my question was stricken. But the lawyer smelled blood and moved in for the kill.

So, Detective Prentiss, he said. Is it your contention, then, that this was in fact a proper search? Carried out in full agreement with the search warrant signed by Judge Halleck?

The bastard had me trapped. I could admit to either a sloppy search or an illegal one, and I didn't believe that either was strictly correct. Now that the evidence would fall in his client's favor, he was going to bury me once and for all. Blaming the accuser can be a solid strategy if you can get the jury to buy it. It would also have the effect of keeping me away from his client for good. I knew what he was doing and in the end I said what I believed, in a public court room and on the public record. Big mistake.

I started by saying it was all bullshit. The judge picked up his gavel, ready to start gaveling.

Now the lawyer knew he had me. Is it, Detective? How so?

If the search was illegal, then prosecute *me*. If I broke the law, I'm a criminal, too. We can't let this scumbag go. There's not a person here who doesn't know beyond a reasonable doubt that Diego Safrenza is guilty as hell.

This drew a loud rap and a contempt warning from the judge but the lawyer was smiling. He didn't mind this at all.

So the ends justify the means? he asked.

I'm saying that if there is clear evidence that the man is guilty, why shouldn't it stand? If the law was broken somehow when the evidence was discovered, then prosecute the person who broke that law, too.

The district attorney tried to object but the judge beat him to it. The defense lawyer was admonished and I was finally cited for contempt and excused from the stand. The defense entered a motion for dismissal of the trial, the judge granted it, and I served three days in isolation in the county prison. And then I was disciplined by the department. They tried to fire me but the union wouldn't let them. At the time I didn't want to go without a fight. One of their lawyers suggested the arrangement with St. Petersburg and it seemed tenable so I took it. The brass approved because it took me out of Tampa, away from Judge Halleck, and away from Diego Safrenza. But it didn't end anything.

Ever since, every thing I'd worked on, every case, every piece of paper, had been scrutinized six ways from Sunday. I was watched and double checked, questioned and second-guessed; all of this is what I found myself having in common with a convicted burglar named Randy Shawcross.

Around dinner time I heated up a frozen lasagna in the microwave. Why even go back, I kept thinking. The department didn't want me there, so why keep fighting it? I asked myself this over and over again, but it was always followed with the question of what the hell would I do instead?

Anything else, I told myself. But it didn't stick.

Two bites into dinner my cell phone rang. The display told me it wasn't Lori, it was Darlene Shawcross. And when I answered she was hysterical.

"Jeff! Jeff! You have to get here! Please! Right now!"

"Calm down, Darlene. What's wrong? What's happened?"

I could hear some deep breaths over the line. "Two men, they were just here. They wanted Randy's computer."

"The one you gave me?"

"Yes," she said. "It was the only one he had."

"They're gone now?"

"They just left."

"Okay, you sit tight, I'll be right there."

Chapter 5

"Did you call the police?" I asked her when she opened the door.

"I called you," she said.

I nodded; what was I going to say? The bags under her eyes and the disheveled clothes told me how she was doing. "What about your sister?"

"She's still at home. She couldn't leave this afternoon. I'm still alone."

I walked through the house with Darlene following me. Everything looked normal. "They didn't look for it, they just asked where it was?"

"That's right. One of them walked through the rooms of the house but he didn't stop for long. The other one kept me in the living room."

"How long were they here?"

"I don't know. Five minutes, ten."

"Did you see how they got here? Did they have a car?"

"I was afraid to look. I didn't want them to come back inside—"

"That's okay." I led her over to the couch and we sat down in nearly the same positions we had been in before. "What did you tell them?"

"That I'd given it to the police."

"What did they do then?"

She shook her head. "Nothing. They sort of looked at each other and then they left."

"And you've never seen them before?"

She shook her head again.

"This is important now, so please think. Did they ask if he had a computer, or did they ask *for* the computer?"

"For it," she said. "They knew he had one."

"You're sure?"

"Yes, yes, I'm sure." She was starting to shake again.

"Okay, Darlene. I'm off duty right now. You should call the cops, get them out here, cover your bases. I understand if you don't want to, but I'm saying this in case those men do come back."

"Oh my god." She looked sick. "Do you think they will?"

I shook my head. "I don't know why they would."

She thought about it and said, "I think the police may be more likely to let the men do what they want."

That may be a fair statement, given the official feeling toward her late husband.

"Are you going to do anything? You, yourself?" She reached out and gripped my forearm.

That was the question. "It does look like Randy was working on something, doesn't it? You're sure you don't know what it could have been?"

"I would tell you, Jeff. I really would."

"Then I guess I'll go back to work. You be careful, Darlene." I squeezed her hand and she let me go.

I got back into my Jeep and pulled ahead, then parked in front of a hydrant near the corner. On foot I went up and down the street, stopping at each house, asking if anyone had seen anything unusual at the Shawcross house. Most of the people said no, nothing, but a few took the opportunity to rail against known criminals living in their particular respectable neighborhood. Two came up with a vague description of an SUV, black, no model. Not a lot to go on.

I was at my desk the next morning when Moran came in, did an exaggerated double take, and came over and shook my hand.

"How you doing, man?" he asked.

I knew what he meant. "I still haven't heard from her."

"You will, you will. You just have to give it some time."

I turned away. I couldn't look at him; he just didn't know enough. I filled him in on what had happened to Darlene Shawcross the night before.

"So they wanted to know *where* the laptop was? They didn't show up to *look* for it?"

"That's what she says."

"Interesting."

"You're full of shit. Either they guessed she no longer had it or they somehow knew she didn't. When she told them we had taken it all they did was a quick walk through of the house."

Moran fiddled with a packet of Splenda and his coffee. "What do you think they really wanted?"

"I'm waiting for the tech to come in, the one who's working on the laptop. He may have an idea."

"But you don't know what we're dealing with here?"

I shook my head slowly. "I'm not sure. I think the King of Cats may not have been all that retired."

"You're thinking he was working and got caught?"

Before Moran arrived, I had been scouring the internet for news of any Shawcross-style burglaries or attempts that had been reported the past week. There was nothing. "Maybe. If he was, it wasn't against guys who call cops."

We talked about what to do next. Moran was going to pull Randy's cell phone records; if he were working something I wanted to find out who he had been talking to. I went on my way to find the computer tech, a kid named Kelly, downstairs. On the way I passed Lieutenant Greene, a meeting I'd rather have avoided. He gave me a curt nod and kept moving. Fine by me. He didn't say anything about my being back at work and I had the feeling he was going to keep himself busy by checking on my paperwork.

To hell with him, I thought. If they keep looking they'll find something eventually. Not even Leslie Alcaro with whatever resources the union's willing to expend can save everyone. The politics involved always got bigger and the people like me got smaller, ground down into nubs. The hell of it was that we did most of it to ourselves.

The thought made me angry but I pushed it back as I entered the computer lab and found Kelly at a workbench table in front of half a dozen computers, including Randy Shawcross's laptop.

Working with the reports I had gotten from the computer tech, I was back at my desk trying to make sense of Randy's internet usage. I started with his e-mail accounts but there wasn't much there other than some correspondence about some golf clubs Randy had been trying to buy.

The websites he had bookmarked in his browser were mostly mundane. I spent some time entering their addresses in my own computer but there weren't many surprises. Again, there were some golfing and sporting goods sites, a used bookstore, a few odd science related sites like space.com and the official NASA site. More hobbies? I had no idea. I didn't know him on that kind of level.

There was one protected site but I couldn't get into it without a login name and password. Darlene had given us the password to Randy's computer and I tried his laptop credentials on the site itself but those didn't work. I started up Randy's laptop, opened the browser, and navigated to the site from his bookmarks menu.

The computer had retained his user ID and password, though the latter was represented as a line of nine asterisks. Standard stuff. I clicked on the button that said "Log In" and was presented with an error message: "Invalid user name or password. Please try again."

I was tired of walking so I called Kelly and asked him to come upstairs. While I waited I jotted down the ID name, "maleman." It had a kinky sound to it that I wouldn't have associated with Randy but you never know. It might be something to run past Darlene.

Kelly appeared at my desk, reeking of cigarette smoke, and I showed him the login screen to the site. "May I?" he asked. I scooted my chair backwards across the plastic mat and left him room to work. Moran called out that we should have Randy's cell phone records that afternoon, then came over to watch Kelly work his magic.

"The first thing to do is to find out what we can about the site." Kelly opened another browser window and went to a "whois" utility page. He entered the URL for the protected site and clicked a button. Up came a screen's worth of information that included the site's registrar, a company called Little Y, Inc.

Moran jotted it down on a pad, said he'd look it up, and went back to his desk.

"What else can you get?" I asked Kelly.

"Well, let's see." He opened another window and entered more commands. After a number of screens filled with cryptic numbers and elongated words with multiple periods he said that their ISP was local to the Tampa area. Kelly used another command to track the server's IP address back to a block controlled by a specific service provider. He knew by looking that it belonged to a company name First Call Internet.

"You want the password for that site? It looks like the account's been shut down but you might want it for something."

"Couldn't hurt," I told him.

He navigated to the browser's security settings from the Tools menu option. There was a button labeled "Show Passwords."

"Too easy," I said.

"You just gotta know where to look, is all."

"Could there be cached web pages from that site that we can see? I'd like to know what the hell it is they do."

"Let's see." He opened a window to the computer's Control Panel menu and clicked on the "Internet Options" item. He found the location for the cached files then opened up another window and navigated to it. He clicked on the address bar title to sort the files by their website address and scrolled down until he got to the name of the protected site. "There you go," he said, and double clicked on the listing for the first file.

Kelly and I watched for a few seconds, and I called to my partner. "Terry, come here. You'll want to see this."

Moran put down his phone and came back over. "This is from the site you were trying to access?"

"Hm hmm."

"Shit. That's just porn."

"Why's her face pixelated out like that?" Kelly asked.

I was suddenly irritated. "How the hell should I know?"

Kelly was peeved but I didn't care. "Do you need me for anything else?"

"Not right now," I answered.

Moran added, "Thanks, man. We'll let you know if we need more help." He reached toward my desk and began clicking on more of the file names.

"Everyone's faces are blanked out," he said.

"Isn't that odd?" I asked. "If you're paying to have access to a private porn site, why wouldn't you be allowed to see their faces?"

Moran opened still another file. "You're sure the hell seeing everything else."

My extension rang and Lieutenant Greene's secretary told me the man himself wanted to see me before I left for the day. I hung up and answered the inquiring look on my partner's face.

"Might as well go now," I said.

"Keep your head down, man."

"Like an ostrich."

"That's what I'm afraid of. You know they don't really stick their heads in the sand, don't you?"

I walked out of the room and down the hall to the elevators. I rode up to the fifth floor and walked slowly to Greene's office, trying to stay calm.

I was so much on edge it was my only defense against myself, and I did-n't want to blow up and end it all right now. Or hell, I thought, maybe I did.

"Sit down," he said when I entered his office.

"Thank you, sir."

He looked at me from across his desk as though he hadn't expected me to speak. The use of "sir" was a little on the formal side. There was a copy of the Randy Shawcross crime scene report spread out in front of him. "Why did you leave your partner at the Maximo Park crime scene on Monday night?"

Involuntarily I cleared my throat. "I recognized who the victim was. I knew his wife. Given all that they'd gone through, I thought it would be a good idea if she got the news from me."

"You working public relations now, Prentiss?"

I didn't say anything.

"You are familiar with department policy. You do know the rules and regulations."

I concentrated on keeping a neutral expression on my face. All I could do here was get myself into more trouble.

"We have specialists who do this work, Detective. You should not have left your partner and the crime scene. You know that. If it had been appropriate for you to interview the widow you should have been ac-companied by an outreach officer. Because of that shithead's history all of the t's needed to be crossed and the i's dotted. It's possible his home could have been part of a crime scene. As far as I know it still might. This department does anything wrong with this and the media will crucify us." He paused for effect. "Just like in Tampa." Unexpectedly, he sat back in his chair and pushed the file away, waiting.

"I also wanted to find out if she knew anything about what her husband may have been doing. She wouldn't have talked to me about him in those terms with other police around."

"And you know that how, exactly?"

I didn't respond.

"Look," he said. "What is it about you that you think you can do bet-ter work than the rest of us? Huh? Is that the little special bond you ap-parently shared with Randy Shawcross? Something with his wife maybe?"

That was too far. I gripped the arms of my chair and started to get up. Something was coming out of me and we were both about to find out what it was.

"You do not leave that chair!" he shouted.

I stopped moving, halfway out of my seat.

"If you keep moving, mister, I swear by all that is holy that you are done. As of right now."

My heart was thumping in my chest but I lowered myself back down. This is not what I wanted to do. These sons of bitches were after my ass and sooner or later they'd get it. Now just wasn't the best time, not with the Roy Lee Evans thing hanging over me. Other than Lori, no one knew the asshole was even missing yet. At least as far as I knew. When they did, everything might change.

Greene was aware he'd pushed hard. "You toe the line, son," he said, keeping anger in his voice as though he'd been the one accused of impropriety. "I won't tell you again."

I nodded as an excuse to break eye contact then left his office without a word. I thought about calling Leslie Alcaro and then wondered what she could really do about Greene anyway. Still, it would have been nice to hear a friendly voice.

Chapter 6

Walk it off, I told myself, let it go. I rode the elevator down to the lobby then strode out through the door. I walked down the street, across the railroad tracks and down to the stadium. If there had been an afternoon ball game I might have bought a ticket and gone in.

After a while I grabbed a gyro from a shop with a window open to the sidewalk and made my way back to the station. Moran was at his desk but when he saw the look on my face he knew well enough to leave me alone.

I spent a few hours going through the rest of the stuff on Randy's computer; Kelly had burned CDs of the cached web stuff, both still pictures and video clips. The video files were all roughly the same size, which meant they were all about the same running length, twenty minutes or so. These weren't any more revealing than the pictures but they filled four discs.

Unless you had an interest in internet porn, there wasn't much to look at. There was the research on golf clubs, some used book orders, and the stuff on NASA and the space program to go through. I called Darlene and she confirmed the golfing hobby, and how Randy had become a reader during his housebound years when every time he showed his face outside it was followed by a Detroit PD squad car. She also said that Randy had wanted to buy a telescope but he wasn't sure he'd be able to see anything through all the light pollution in the city. I didn't mention the porn.

Moran got the cell phone records and we went over those as well. Shawcross didn't get many calls, which usually made things easier, but not always. The past two months he'd been receiving regular calls from a "B. Schoenfeld" and when we compared his number to Randy's outbound calls log, we could see they'd had a regular correspondence. We debated about whether to call the number but lacking any platform for questioning we decided to let it go for the time being. I told Moran I'd ask Darlene about it in the morning, and finally went home for the day.

I'd been hoping for some more distraction from work, something to keep my mind from turning back to Lori. Merely being home was still hell. I wanted to take the boat out again but there were thunderstorms building over the gulf and those would make it a bad place to be very soon. I sat in the lanai and popped a beer instead.

The hours crawled by, the bright of the sun reluctant to quit the day. Get dark already, I thought, angrily. I didn't want to see anything anymore. Flying things battered the screens and from time to time I'd slap and scratch at the invisible sand fleas that made it through the fine mesh unhindered. Can you squash a no-see-um? If felt good to try. Couldn't help it anyway. In the old days people would rub petroleum jelly on their screens to keep them out. I was wondering why people had ever stopped doing that when I picked up my cell phone and stared at it. Without any real reason, I dialed my lawyer.

"This is Leslie."

"Hey, it's Jeff Prentiss. I hope it's not too far past office hours."

"Jeff! Did something happen?"

It registered somewhere in my mind that she'd recognized my voice before I'd identified myself. It gave me a nice lift to my mood.

"Got called up to see the lieutenant this afternoon. No big deal."

I could hear her take a sip of something before she said, "It can be. Is he harassing you?"

"Always. That's the main quality these people look for when they promote. He wasn't wrong, though. I left a murder scene the other night to visit the victim's widow."

"Isn't that normal?"

"Sometimes. The department has a policy of having a community outreach officer ride along with the informing officer but I went without one."

"You can't keep doing whatever you want, Jeff."

I laughed a little. "I don't know how to stop. Anyway, I knew her and I was hoping that if she had any information we could use she'd be more willing to share if it was just me. Her and her husband didn't exactly enjoy a normal relationship with the police."

There was a long pause on the line. Another no-see-um found one of my legs but this time I didn't slap at it until I couldn't stand the itch any longer.

"We'll get through this, you know. As long as—well, as long as you want to."

I drained the rest of my beer. "As long as I want to," I repeated. "You alone tonight?"

"Don't ask. I'll tell you about that another time. How about you?"

And then it all poured out, everything about Lori having left and taking Roxy with her. Nothing about Roy Lee Evans, though. I wasn't that drunk. Or that crazy.

"That's why she was calling for you?"

"It was."

"How could she do something like that over the telephone?"

I shrugged. Talking to Leslie was making a lot of the tension in my shoulders dissipate. "At least she called at all. She could have just left. Actually, she already had by the time she called, but still."

"Jeff, I'm so sorry…."

I cut her off. "Not your problem, Ms. Alcaro. I just— It's been good to talk to a friendly voice. I'll let you go."

"No problem, Jeff, you realize you can call me whenever. You know I'm more than just your union lawyer."

"Um, yeah, Leslie, I know. Friends, right?" She didn't respond. "Look, I think I'm going to hang around out in the lanai and watch the light disappear." I felt a sudden urgency to get off the phone.

"Okay, Jeff."

"Leslie?"

"Yes?"

"Thanks for taking my call."

I hung up before I heard her answer.

At almost ten o'clock the phone rang. I had been halfway asleep, conscious but not aware, and the sound was jarring. I walked into the kitchen and picked up the cordless handset.

"Hello?"

"Dad," came the voice of my adopted daughter. "It's me."

"Oh my god, Roxy." I sagged against the counter and felt my heart rate double. "Where are you, sweetheart? Are you okay?"

"I'm fine, Dad. We both are. How are you?"

I laughed out loud in relief. "Get lost. I miss you guys so much. Where are you?"

Her voice was quiet, not much more than a whisper. "Mom doesn't know I'm calling you. You have to promise me something."

"What?"

"That you won't try to trace this call or whatever it is you can do. You have to promise, or I can't call you again."

"Honey, why? What's going on?"

She sniffled and my heart tore. "I promised mom I wouldn't try to get a hold of you until she said it was okay. She made me do it. She is so unhappy. Please tell me you won't."

"Okay," I told her, and just like that I couldn't think of anything else to say. The sudden silence was like a barrier slipping back into place. "Can you tell me anything, sweetheart?"

She sniffled. "I don't know what's going on. Mom is just so sad all the time. She's talking about finding a therapist or someone to talk to."

I wanted to tell her Lori could always talk to me....

"Do you know why she's like that, Dad?"

Oh, god. "Your mother's been through a lot, honey. I think maybe she just needed a break for a while. Or something." I tried not to ask, but I did anyway: "She hasn't told you what's bothering her?"

"What happened to Roy, Dad?"

No, I thought. *I can't do this.* I realized I had no idea how to answer her. I was still groping for the words when Roxy spoke again.

"Mom said not to worry about it. She said you're my real dad even if Roy was my biological one. But she seems so sad when she talks about it."

"I don't know what to say," I told her, and I didn't.

"Did you make him go away, Dad?"

What are you supposed to do when you can't tell the truth and you can't bear to lie, when either course hurts the ones you love?

"I'm just glad he's gone, kiddo."

"I guess I am, too."

"How are the horses, Rox? Have you been able to do any riding?"

"Mom's taking me tomorrow if it doesn't rain." She was quiet for a moment. "I wish you could see me."

I closed my eyes. "Me, too, honey."

There were some sounds in the background and Roxy said quickly, "I have to go. Remember your promise. I'll try to call again."

"I love you, Roxy!" I shouted.

"I love you, too, Dad," she said quietly, and I could hear the smile. She hung up.

The next morning I called Darlene Shawcross and asked her if I could come over and ask her a few more questions. We probably could have done it over the phone but it was a good excuse to stay out of the office for a few hours. I picked up Moran in front of the station after he parked his bright yellow beacon in the lot across the street.

"When are you going to outgrow that thing?" I asked him.

"What, the car?" he said, settling into the passenger seat. "You finally getting jealous?"

"Just don't give it a name and park it in your living room."

"I've had that car since high school, man. It's a classic."

"It's an eyesore. People know you're coming from four blocks away."

"And they don't mess with me, either. They see that lemon yellow shine and fall down jealous."

"Okay, Peter Pan."

"I'll grow up when you do." He laughed and tuned in an AM sports radio channel and we drove the twenty minutes out to Pinellas Park and then on to the Shawcross house. Darlene opened the door as we got out of the car and waved us inside. "It's been a zoo out here," she said. "The newspapers and cameramen have finally stopped coming around. I don't feel right about having the door open."

We sat down in the living room and Darlene brought out some coffee she had already made and poured it into porcelain mugs that had come from a matched set. They had gold rims and a filigreed pattern stamped on their sides. I wondered idly if they had been relocated from a previous owner as Terry expressed a stock message of sympathy to the widow.

"Thank you, Detective," she told him flatly.

I took out the copies of Randy's cell phone records and showed them to her. She looked them over briefly then said she didn't know anybody named Schoenfeld.

"Do you think it's important?" she asked.

"I don't know, Darlene," I told her. "It could be. If Randy was working on something alone, maybe not. If he was working with someone, it might mean a lot. Either way, it's the only regular correspondence we can find."

She was shaking her head. "Randy always worked alone. There was just that one time in Detroit, you know, and that got him arrested."

"Might have been a good thing," Moran said. "Got him into court where he could do that immunity deal."

Darlene fumbled with her coffee cup and looked at me as though she didn't know whether Terry was friend or foe. I nodded in what I meant to be reassurance and she took a sip from her cup. But she seemed to be reluctant to say anything else and we got up to leave. I was thinking I should have come alone. On a table near the front door was an un-opened *Tampa Tribune* from that morning. Moran picked it up and un-folded it as I was telling Darlene goodbye.

"Look at this," he said, holding out the front page. "They've got bad guys across the bay, too."

Under a caption that read "Mayoral Candidate Shot Dead" was a clear black and white photograph of a crumpled corpse, blood spattered across a white-shirted torso.

"Can I see that?" I asked the room, taking the paper. The dead man's name was listed in the first paragraph of the article. It turned out to be a well known one, too, one that had been a mover and shaker in the Tampa power structure for many years. His name was Barry Mervin Schoenfeld.

B. Schoenfeld.

Darlene repeated she'd never heard of him. I tried to place the name from my Tampa PD days but wasn't sure if I knew it or not.

"At least now we know where all the reporters went," Moran said as we walked out to my car.

Chapter 7

We were back in the office, each of us at our respective desks, waiting for a return call from Tampa. In the meantime I asked Moran if he'd found out anything concrete about the company that operated the password protected porn site we'd seen on Randy Shawcross's computer.

"Little Y, Inc.?" Moran said. "Still waiting on the feds to get back to me." Sadly that was not unexpected.

We watched a local news conference on the TV in the department break room that covered the death of Barry Schoenfeld. The wealthy politician had answered his doorbell and been gunned down with a twin shotgun blast to the chest. The shooter or shooters had then fled on foot, disappearing into the busy night life pedestrian traffic along Bayshore Boulevard.

"What do you think?" I asked Moran.

"I'm thinking we've got two bodies and one case."

A little after eleven we got a call from Isabel Marquez, the detective who had caught the Schoenfeld case. Moran had put a call in for her earlier. I knew her from my time at Tampa PD; she was a climber, a nose to the grindstone and follow the numbers officer. She was careful never to voice an opinion that hadn't first been given to her by a higher up.

"Ding Dong?" Moran sang into the phone. "Is that you?"

"Oh, Terry," she said. "Why do you have to call me that?"

"'Cause you Is-a-bell." He laughed. She didn't.

"What do have for me?"

He ran down the apparent phone connection between Randy Shawcross and Barry Schoenfeld. "That King of Cats guy was talking to the man who was probably going to be the next mayor of Tampa? What the hell for?"

"Million dollar question."

Marquez said she'd run down Schoenfeld's phone records and call Moran back. Beyond that she wouldn't commit to anything. Other than the shotgun pellets taken from the house and body there wasn't a lot to go on, and those weren't much.

"You still working with Jeff Prentiss?" she asked Moran.

"He's my partner."

"Lucky you," she said, and hung up.

Moran and I walked down the street to a sports bar and grabbed some burgers for lunch. Every time I heard a phone ring I thought of Roxy's call the other night. It was a constant struggle to live up to my word not to track back her phone call. I knew that if I did Lori would be furious and it would only make things—whatever they were—worse. After all, she'd left for a reason, and deep down I knew what it was. I may have lost her, I really wasn't sure yet, but I didn't need to alienate my daughter, too.

It wasn't helpful that Moran wanted to talk, but he always did when we took lunch together. He said that he was concerned about me. He asked me what had happened with Greene the other day and I didn't want to talk about it but I told him anyway.

"Damn," he said. "They're still after your ass. They're being careful though, aren't they?"

"Hmf," I said as I stuffed a bite of cheeseburger into my mouth.

"You'd think they'd get tired at some point. You're a good cop, a good guy. You just don't know when to keep your mouth shut sometimes."

I looked at him. He was only being honest. I wanted to say something in anger, tell him to piss off, but I didn't want to give up the only friend I had in the department. And really, he wasn't wrong. But was I so different from everyone else? That was something I'd been asking myself a lot lately. Was I that big of an ass, or did I get caught up in a colossal maelstrom of bad timing? The answer was probably some of all the above.

He let it lie for a minute, then said, "Tell me about Lori."

That shouldn't have been as unexpected as it was. I almost gagged on my coke. Terry was my friend and he had been giving me space but I was still very reluctant to keep him up to date on my personal life. I tried to figure how little I could get away with saying.

"Um," I said. "She left."

"Damn, man." He set down his own burger and wiped his fingers in the paper napkin balled up on his lap. "Have you heard from her? Do you know where she is?"

It was easier to give in to him than not and that way I wouldn't hurt his feelings. "I spoke with her mother in Houston. She knew that Lori had gone but said she didn't know where she had gone to."

"You believe her?"

I thought about it. "Yeah, I guess I do. It doesn't matter, though." This was making me tired.

"What?"

"If Lori was sitting at the bus stop across the street it wouldn't change anything. She wanted to leave. Me knowing where she is wouldn't make her want to come back."

Moran looked lost, like he'd been thinking of this as some sort of missing persons case. I told him about Roxy's call.

"At least the kid still loves you."

Yeah, thanks, Terry. I made a remark about the guano on his car and he went with it like I knew he would. Knowing how to distract people's line of thinking was a very valuable skill. Most cops, if they were around long enough, could pick it up.

"Dude, I was standing next to the Monte watching this pelican up on a light post. Suddenly he took off and flew right overhead. I was looking straight up at his belly and he just cut loose. I saw it coming and danced out of the way."

"And left the banana to take the hit? Surprised you didn't throw yourself over the hood of the car."

He leaned back and grabbed his belt buckle. "Didn't want to scratch nothing."

We ordered a couple more cokes than sat back and didn't talk about work. No Randy Shawcrosss, Barry Schoenfeld, pornographic websites, or my family. It was the best part of the lunch.

Before the end of the day we heard back from Isabel Marquez in Tampa, confirming that her dead Barry Schoenfeld was our "B. Schoenfeld." Moran gave me the news after he hung up.

"That's interesting," I said.

We also heard back from the FBI about Moran's request for information on the corporation that owned the domain name for the encrypted website, Little Y, Inc. A man named Roger Ferrarro was listed as the president of the private corporation, registered in the Bahamas. Ferrarro was indicted three months ago on racketeering and gambling charges and had not bothered to return to the States.

"Racketeering?" I asked. "What was he doing?"

"He was running some kind of illegal lottery game. Guess where?"

"No," I said.

"Yup. Right here in River City."

"Trouble with a capital T and that rhymes with B and that stands for bolita?"

"Lost me, chief."

"*Music Man*. Who'd this guy work for? He wasn't solo, not in this town. He was in Tampa?"

"Ybor City."

"Then he worked for Rudy Pope."

"You want me to call the feds back?"

"Maybe. Let's think this out first." I stood up and stretched my back and legs.

"What's this bolita thing?"

"Spanish for 'Little Ball.' The Cubans brought it over a hundred years or so ago when they were working the cigar business in Tampa. They'd put a hundred numbered balls in a bag, toss it around and take bets on what number they'd pull out."

"Was it crooked?"

I shrugged. "It was controlled by the mob in the '20s, so what do you think?"

"I think I asked a stupid question. How much money in it?"

"They played it in every saloon in town. The big boys owned it. Organized crime took the bets, ran the numbers. There were no honest elections in Hillsborough County for at least a decade."

Moran snorted. "There still aren't."

"Welcome to Florida."

He gave me a look. "Don't get started. You don't need to open any more fronts. How'd they fix the games?"

"The balls were in a velvet sack that they'd pass around among the player to mix them up. The winning ball was sometimes made of something heavier and when it came time for the catcher to select the ball it had already settled at the bottom of the bag."

"Why do you think this Ferraro guy would have worked for Pope?"

"Pope's the last man standing in Tampa, works out of Ybor, like his late father. Most of the rest of the big boys got cleared out in the Caya Bank scandal a few years ago. They either went to jail or ran away to Miami or New Orleans. They'd been trying to cut Pope out for years and he wasn't involved with the bank thing. He ended up outlasting them all and that left him around to pick up what he could."

"Why this bolita game?"

I sat back down in my chair and leaned forward on my arms. "I don't know. Because it's under the fed's radar? Bringing back the family business? That was how his dad made his fortune before he was offed in the seventies."

"What happened?"

"Unsolved. Someone rang his doorbell one night. Like with Barry Schoenfeld."

Moran said, "You're shitting me. Shotgun?"

"That was how they did it back then."

"Somebody's doing it now. How is old Rudy?"

"Got to be in his eighties at this point. Haven't seen him in a few years."

"You know him?"

"A bit. I used to work in that town, you know."

"And look what happened to you. How do you want to work this?"

I thought about it for a minute. "Why don't you see if you can get a hold of Ding Dong Marquez again? See if you can get her to take in Schoenfeld's computer and tell us about his internet habits."

"What, you think he might be a porn user?"

I shrugged. "Who knows? But maybe Rudy's got himself into a new line of business."

Moran reached for the phone and punched in a number. "Tell her to be careful," I told him. When he looked puzzled I said, "Remember Darlene had visitors after we looked at Randy's laptop."

Chapter 8

It was Friday and the weekend was looming large like a giant sucking vortex threatening to swallow me into a wallow of depression and loneliness. At least I was scheduled off for both days, so the pressure I felt by just being in the office wouldn't be there.

Moran and I hadn't heard back from Isabel Marquez before we left for the day. She said she'd check on Schoenfeld's computer but wouldn't commit to when. There wasn't anything we could say. My involvement with the case brought an extra layer of crap to wade through. Moran did all he could do, thanked her, and that was that.

I thought about old Rudy Pope and Ybor City. Everyone called the place "ee-bore," one-time center of the hand-rolled cigar industry, and it was named after one of the pioneering manufacturers. I considered driving out there, just east of downtown Tampa, but at this time of day the only way to get there meant sitting through a rush hour's worth of traffic and not a lot was worth that.

Rudy had taken over from his Prohibition-era father when his older brother Gianni was killed. Three cars boxed him in one day at high noon and they blew him apart with shotguns. Gambling was king of the day and the family had ties to New Orleans and Kansas City. By the time Rudy was installed, cocaine had taken over and the big boys had left Rudy on his own.

I pulled into my driveway and went straight through the house, through the lanai and across the short yard and onto the dock. Motion helps, I kept telling myself, any kind of motion. I climbed into the boat and lowered it into the canal, gently floating off the cradle lift as it hit water. The sky was mostly clear with some high clouds making a slight haze out of the waning sunshine. I fired up the motor, took her out to the Intracoastal, then around the peninsula and out towards open water. Out towards the great blue nothing. If I had to wallow I was going to do it out here.

There was a box of crackers and a half filled water bottle stashed in a compartment so I had something for dinner. The water was only just starting to taste bitter but I was lucky to have it as I lay on my back on the sun deck, contemplating the twinkling stars. Saltine crumbs accumulated on my chest and I was half expecting to be swooped by a pack of wild seagulls as my mind drifted over familiar ground.

Stalking, I knew, was the only precursor to murder that law enforcement has.

Its victims have very few protections under the law, mostly because the stalkers themselves don't take the laws seriously, giving much more weight to their own delusional emotions than to arbitrary rules set down by people who *just didn't understand.* Attention from the courts was often flattering. It legitimized their actions, their feelings, and unless they ended up doing time it often made them grow bolder more quickly.

So what can a stalking victim do? What happens when an emotional parasite attaches itself to you and simply will not let go?

You say something forgettable but nice to the wrong person at work and the next thing you know, you find a muffin on your desk along with the morning mail when you come into work the next morning. Then maybe there's a flower, a card or a note. Suddenly occasions for small talk arise when you start bumping into each other in new and unexpected places. The parasite has entered your life.

You begin to feel uneasy so you ask the person to stop, but now you've acknowledged the connection. This makes things worse. The phone starts ringing at home, you start to see shadows at the grocery store, at the coffee shop, outside your house.

What do you do about it? What can you do about it?

Confront your stalker directly? Then they really know they have you in their power and you've given them what they want: recognition. Go to the cops? Well, they really haven't done anything yet, have they? Not a lot they can do. Get a restraining order? Thanks for the paper. Get a new phone number? Quit your job? Move out of town? Change your name? How far do you take it?

I finished the box of crackers while still lying down and wadded the garbage into the smallest ball I could and stuffed it into a cup holder by my head. If you go to the cops, I thought, at least they'll know about a suspect if you turn up murdered. Too late to do you any good, but still.

I got up, stretched, and walked up to the cockpit.

And, unfortunately, I thought, the reverse is also true. If you go to the cops and something happens to the stalker instead, they still have a suspect, only this time it's you.

The engine turned over immediately and altered the atmosphere of what had turned into a quiet and peaceful night. The sound not only carried across the surface of the water but created a pocket around the boat that smashed the sense of isolation. It was time. I hit the running lights and turned the boat to follow a compass heading. There was only a small moon and it would take me a while to feel my way back home.

But it was good, though. It made me think different thoughts.

Chapter 9

Terry Moran called me the next day just after noon. I could hear his wife singing a tune in the background and it made something in my stomach jump. "Come on out," he told me. "I'll buy you a beer."

"What's up?"

"Can I lie?" he asked.

"Hell no."

"Then just come over. I'll tell you when you get here."

This can't be good, I thought. It might not be awful but it won't be good. I threw on a clean Tommy Bahama print shirt that Roxy had given me for Christmas and changed into a pair of khaki shorts. I didn't want to look like a complete derelict when I walked into my friend and partner's home.

The Morans lived in northern St. Petersburg in the Fossil Park area. I headed up Ninth Street and kept the Jeep just below the speed limit. I wasn't in a rush, and I wasn't in the mood for the noise and bustle of the interstate.

I parked on the street in front of the house and went up to the front door. When no one answered the bell I walked around the house and through the fence to the back yard. Terry and his wife, Sandra, were reclining on patio chairs on the deck of their pool.

"Hey, Jeff," said Sandra when she saw me. She had on a flattering bikini and across her lap was a stack of manila file folders. The top one was spread open with pictures of homes for sale printed from a digital camera arranged in a sequence.

"Working?" I asked.

"In this market, honey, that's all I do. Wanna buy another house?"

I laughed. "I'd have to sell the one I've got first."

"That's everybody's problem," she said.

Terry came over and clapped me on the back of the shoulder. "Welcome, sir," he said. "We have a beer with your name on it over here."

He led me inside to the kitchen and got me a cold one from the fridge. "Come on back here," he said, and I followed him down the hall to the bedroom they'd converted into Sandra's real estate office. Terry took the chair behind the desk and I settled into the love seat sofa they had placed beneath the outside window.

"So what's up?" I asked him.

"You are always so straight and to the point, man, aren't you?" He twisted off the top of the fresh beer he had brought and tossed me the cap. I caught it and pitched it into the garbage can next to the desk with the same motion.

I shrugged. What was I going to say?

"You know Greene wants us off the Shawcross thing."

"You mean Greene wants *me* off the Shawcross thing."

"You know them," he said, meaning the department brass. "They don't want any bad press. They're still living down the LeShaun White case and they're scared to death of you."

LeShaun White had been a juvie offender with an excessive rap sheet. After carjacking a Lexus from a doctor and his family in front of their own home, White led police on a high speed chase that ended when he was cornered in a strip mall parking lot. When officers approached him with guns drawn, White gunned the engine and dropped it into gear, grazing one cop and heading for another, who opened fire. White died behind the wheel.

A crowd gathered and before long someone started saying that White had been trying to surrender, that he'd been trying to get out of the car when the white officers shot the black teenager in cold blood. It was getting ugly and only an overwhelming show of force kept the situation from turning into St. Pete's third race riot in as many years. The obligatory lawsuits entailed and while the officers were acquitted of any breach of procedure, the city agreed to build a new community center in a reclamation area and name it after the slain felon.

Never made sense to me. Dedicating a public building to a petty criminal who was trying to kill police with a stolen car? It was all politics of some sort, the kind that smelled.

"What do they think I'm going to do?"

"They don't know," Terry said. "Which is part of the problem. They don't know what you're going to say, what you're going to do. They don't think you fit any more."

"Greene told you this? Why?" And then it became clear to me. I wondered how Terry Moran had become my partner. "They've got you watching me, don't they, Terry?"

Instead of answering he took a long, slow pull from his bottle. "Yes and no," he said eventually. "Kind of. After a fashion."

I waited him out.

"When you joined the department they asked me if I knew you. I told them we'd never met."

"Who's 'they'?"

"Chief Smith and Lieutenant Greene."

I nodded. Impressive, in a way.

"Look, all they wanted was for me to let them know what was up, how you worked, how we worked together. You know how they felt."

"How they feel."

Terry nodded. "Yeah, well." He took another pull from his beer. "I haven't really told them anything. There was never anything to tell them. You're a damned good cop. You just speak your mind whenever you want. What's that Shakespeare expression about suffering fools gladly? You don't do that."

"That wasn't Shakespeare. It's from the Bible."

"Oh. Doesn't change anything, though. They think you don't mind getting in trouble and you sure as hell don't care about how they all come off to the public and the press."

I sat back and thought about what he'd just said. I wondered if I should feel angry or upset or betrayed. Instead I just looked at my partner who wasn't looking at me.

"You're right, Terry. I don't care," I said.

"What do you mean? These guys are just political—"

"I don't give a damn. About any of it. Greene can go fuck himself. Marquez can—"

"Whoa, boy, slow down. This is no time for additional suicidal tendencies to come out."

"Oh, no? Why the fuck not, Terry? Can you tell me that? Do you know of a better time? 'Cause I can wait a few days if you think that works better. Whatever's more convenient. I'll turn over a new leaf and be flexible. I'll walk a beat. That'll show 'em."

I knew my voice was rising and I didn't want it to so I shut up. We sat there, being quiet, and I felt the tension in my body, the thud of my elevated pulse rate, the heaviness of my breathing. Of course I was overreacting. The problem was that I didn't think I could help it just then.

"What's really going on with you, man?" Terry finally said. "What's up with Lori and Roxy? That shit's eating you up. I can see it."

I made a gesture by spreading my hands out from my knees. For a moment I was tempted to tell Moran everything, empty out all the crap I'd been holding on to for months. I knew, though, that if I did it wouldn't really be gone. I'd still be carrying around this creeping, corroding poison in my guts and I would have slopped some of it over on to the one person who was trying to be my friend.

"She's just gone," was all I said.

He looked on the verge of saying something else but kept it to himself. Smart man, I thought. Smarter than me.

We sat there for a while, surrounded by plaques and photographs of Sandra in front of different houses, a broad smile showing large white, even teeth. "She needs the funny jacket," I said finally.

"What?"

"The jacket. With the patch over the breast pocket, material made out of your grandmother's drapes, color someone forgot about in the seventies."

"Hmpf. She's got a closet full of them. She only wears them to the office parties."

"Then what good are they? How are they supposed to make me want to buy a house if they're wadded up on your closet floor?"

We downed the last of our beers and stopped looking at the wall decorations.

"So we're officially off the Shawcross thing?"

Terry shook his head. "That's what's funny. They're too scared of you."

"They think I'll do what? File another grievance with the union?"

"That," Terry said, "or hold a news conference. Or punch Greene in the nose. Or something worse."

"Like solve the case?"

"They didn't mention that one. They want us to let Isabel Marquez and Tampa take lead for a while, see if the Schoenfeld thing points to whoever killed Randy Shawcross."

"Jesus Christ, Terry," I said and slumped back into the love seat. That could work out, I thought, who knows. But it wasn't right, it was just more politics. All the stress and tension of the past few months ran back into me like a train engine. "I can't take this shit anymore. I've been thinking I should probably just give them what they all want and finally quit."

"What?" He seemed genuinely shocked. "Just like that? After putting up with all this crap? You can't let these guys get at you. They don't deserve that. What the hell would you do instead?"

"That's the only problem," I said. "I don't have anything else to do. I can't afford not to work. And all I've ever been is a cop." I swallowed half my beer. "Shit. I don't know what to do."

After a few minutes he said, "You can't quit. You're the only one who likes my car."

Then we laughed, harder than we should, and it felt really good. I knew, though, that the feeling wasn't actually gone and soon it would flower again, pushing me to the edge of something rash or self harming. Thing is, I didn't think there was anything I could do to stop it.

We had some burgers out by the pool, Terry doing the grilling while Sandra kept filling out the paperwork spread across her lap. Unlike mine, their pool was covered by a mesh enclosure that kept most of the bugs away and they kept a propane powered grill with a sink stowed against the outside wall of the house. The annoying buzzing of gas powered yard tools polluted the air. Typical weekend stuff, ruining the peace of the moment.

For a while life seemed a whole lot calmer than it had been only an hour before. Sandra didn't mention Lori or Roxy so I knew Terry had kept her updated. Misery's just another kind of notoriety: eventually everybody hears about it and it affects how they deal with you. I drank another beer and then switched to cokes. Not only did I have to drive home I had a notion in the back of my mind to take the boat out again at nightfall. I wasn't sure how else I could relax.

At five o'clock I kissed Sandra on the cheek and Terry walked me out to my Jeep. "So where we at?" I asked him.

He knew what I meant. "Your call. You want me to tell Greene to fuck himself, say the word."

"You asshole," I said. "I'm the troublemaker, not you. Forget Greene for a minute. What do you want to do about our own King of Cats?"

We both leaned against the Jeep with our backs. If it weren't for the soft top we wouldn't have been able to take the heat from the sun-warmed steel body. "I can't see letting Tampa walk away with it."

"No?"

He shook his head. "No way. What kind of message does that send? What does that say about me? That I'm just Greene's yes-boy? I didn't sign up for that."

"You know," I said, "whether we agree to it or not, Izzy Marquez is going to take it and run with it anyway. That's her personality."

"'Izzy'?"

"Yeah, she hates that."

"More than Ding Dong?"

I smiled.

"Cool," he said. "Then let's keep on with the boogie."

"What about Greene and the chief?"

"Don't ask, don't tell. If they pull me in again, I'll tell them we're just doing the minimum to keep the widow happy. That way we can try to be sure she won't get upset and go to the press."

"They'll like that."

"Yes, they will."

We stood together for another minute, looking off into the faded blue of the afternoon sky. Why does the color get so much deeper up north? I always wondered. And the leaves and grass look so much greener, too.

I pushed off from the Jeep with my foot and turned toward Terry and hit him on the upper arm. "Thanks, man."

"For the burgers?" he asked, but he knew what I meant.

"Fuck you," I told him.

Chapter 10

I felt better about things after I left the Morans' house on Saturday but I knew it wouldn't last, and it didn't. On Sunday I tied a kayak onto the roll bars of the Jeep and took it down to the Myakka River and put in at the state park. I coasted downstream with the current for a few miles, passing alligators, turtles and some truly massive spider webs. I enjoyed that primal feeling of being on the same level in the water as the alligators, so near to being food for something that was so wild and potentially deadly.

It was just another short term fix, though, a way of keeping moving, burning off some physical energy and keeping my foreground thoughts busy. It worked better when I turned back upstream, tiring myself as I worked against the current. Poolside cookouts aside, I hadn't been eating very much since Lori and Roxy had left and despite leaving me feeling weak at least the workout gave me an appetite. The rest of the evening and night I spent on my lanai with quiet music fighting pernicious thoughts.

Monday found me back at my desk at seven o'clock, going over what we had on the Randy Shawcross murder, feeling that most of the weekend had been eaten by locusts.

I wasn't kidding when I told Terry that I would quit. All it would take would be a rub in the wrong direction from Greene or one of his bosses and I could see myself jumping at the opportunity to do something stupid. Hell, they were probably counting on that. If I had any kind of money in the bank or some other way to make a living I'd save them the trouble of waiting. The urge to act out, to strike out, was strong, even though I knew it would be against my best interests. Maybe. Probably.

I couldn't shake the feeling that Randy Shawcross had been working again when he was killed. It wasn't a surprise that Darlene didn't know anything about it but the tie-in with Mr. Barry Schoenfeld from Tampa was too much to be coincidence. Their phone records connected the two men and it damn sure wasn't because Schoenfeld wanted the endorsement of a notorious felon in the run up to the mayoral race.

Terry came in a little after seven thirty and we talked about the case as though nothing had changed; we were just careful to keep from being overheard. He had been following the press coverage on the story over the weekend but nothing new had been released. I told him I hadn't turned my television on or read a newspaper in a week.

He called Isabel Marquez who made a point to say she had been at her desk already for an hour. Good for her. She told Terry she'd taken in a desktop from Schoenfeld's study and a laptop he used for work. They hadn't been able to find a password for the laptop yet and hadn't been able to access it. The computer from the study had a different operating system and Schoenfeld had kept himself logged in, or at least had been at the time he was killed.

Moran asked her to hold for a second and pushed the button while she was protesting. "What exactly do you want me to ask her?"

"Tell her we want her tech guy to talk to ours. Make it sound like that way we can make sure she gets everything from our end. We can work it out with what's-his-name to get what we want out of them."

"Cool," Terry said and went back to Marquez, who told him she'd been about to hang up.

"You were talking to Prentiss, weren't you?" she asked.

"Never heard of him," said Terry. He brought up the tech to tech issue and after a minute she agreed. Knowing her like I did, I was sure it must have been hard for her as a control freak to agree to get information from another party but that was her problem.

Terry hung up and we talked about what to do next. He thought it would be a good idea if he popped in on the lieutenant and told him we were arranging a handoff from our tech to Tampa's. If Greene didn't press him he could make it seem as though we were turning the whole thing over to Marquez.

I went downstairs to the computer lab to find Kelly. He wasn't there. He was standing outside, taking his first cigarette break of the morning, one hand cradling a Marlboro and the other holding a liter-sized insulated mug from a convenience store. Living up to the IT nerd cliché. I was sure the cup held something like extra strength Mountain Dew; they had never gotten around to putting put Jolt cola on tap in most convenience stores.

Dragging him upstairs we began discussing Randy's laptop. "Tampa thinks they're in charge," I told Kelly. "They've got their own dead guy and his phone records tie him to our dead guy.''

"This that politician dude that's on the news?''

"Hm hmm. He had two computers, you'd have liked him.''

"Crap,'' he said. "I have two networks at my house. Three servers and thirteen computers in my apartment.''

"Yeah, you're a lucky man,'' I said with a straight face. We had arrived at his bench in the computer lab. "Listen, we don't want to get caught up in the departmental political situation here. Not at all. Tampa wants to think they're in charge, that's fine with us. We just need to find out if there's anything on that desktop computer that can link him with Randy Shawcross.''

"Like what?'' he asked, which was annoying. I tried not to let it show.

"You're the expert, Kelly. I'm counting on you to figure it out.'' I clapped him on the shoulder as a sign of camaraderie and got the hell out of there before he saw how pissed off I was getting. Too much stress leads to lack of patience.

Terry was back at his desk and he called Kelly and gave him the contact details for the Tampa side. Kelly asked him if he should offer to help with cracking the password on the laptop. Moran covered the mouth piece of the phone with his hand and asked me.

"Not if it will make him concentrate on that over working on the desktop. I don't want to lose any time.''

Moran repeated this into the phone and hung up. "Now what?'' he asked.

"Rudolpho Lopresti,'' I said. "We need to check up on the Pope of Ybor City.''

Rudy Pope had never been big time. His younger brother Tino had been a lieutenant with Santo Trafficante in New Orleans and that helped some of the other players leave Rudy alone, at least as long as he didn't create any conflict. The word on Rudy had always been that he wouldn't make himself a threat to grow too large and his longevity provided everyone a certain value. If left alone he'd make his payments, which weren't a lot in the grand scheme of things, but they were something, and that was especially welcome once the Caya Bank thing blew up and cleared out a lot of business. Keeping everyone's head down became that much more important.

As far as I knew, he didn't let himself be seen in public often. Maybe he had an unusual fear of shotguns. Most of his business was carried out by a series of lieutenants that probably couldn't make it with another, more traditional mob boss. Pope owned a number of bars and restaurants and floated from establishment to establishment, keeping several apartments in the upper floors of one or two of them, and in the past few years could often be found in the company of his protégé, Ralphie Wandorski.

We couldn't do anything like make an arrest or get a search warrant, not without going through Tampa, who had jurisdiction over Ybor, but there wasn't anything wrong with asking him a few questions. Moran wanted to wait until we at least got something from Schoenfeld's computer but I was feeling antsy. The shotgun murder smelled, and if something was really going on in the underworld, we needed to know what it was. Two people had been killed, and it was conceivable that if Pope thought we had a light on him things might slow down a bit. Assuming he was involved.

"How do we find him?" Moran asked.

We were in Moran's canary colored Monte Carlo, coming off the interstate and heading south into downtown Tampa. "We'll cruise his restaurants and look for Ralphie Wandorski's Escalade. If he's still schlepping the old man around we'll find the two of them together."

"How do you know Wandorski drives an Escalade?"

"Ralphie always drives a Cadillac, and an Escalade's the biggest model."

"Be our luck if he's gone Toyota."

"Then we'll have to think of something else."

We found the big SUV parked behind the Casa Amarilla on Seventh Avenue. Whether it was Ralphie's or not, it stood to reason that since not many people would have dared to block off the loading dock for one of Rudy Pope's restaurants, this was the one we wanted.

Moran pulled over in front of a meter a block away and raised his eyebrows at me. "Should be safe," I told him. "It's still early." He was worried about the Monte Carlo.

We walked back to the Spanish restaurant, Moran glancing over his shoulder at his car a few times, and I nodded to the bouncer when we got to the door. I badged him and kept walking. The host came out from behind his stand and tried to get in our way.

"Gentlemen," he said. "Are you here for lunch?"

"Stop it," I said. "We're here to see Rudy."

"Who?" he said.

"That's okay, we know the way."

If Pope were here he'd know by now we were looking for him. As we passed through the bar area a familiar face turned away when he saw me, his face staying low and close to his drink. I wasn't sure who it was but I didn't stop to confirm. Didn't matter.

I led Terry to the swinging door that opened into the kitchen and we walked through a cloud of spices, peppers and piles of steaming yellow rice frying on a grill. There was a painted wooden door at the end of the stainless steel countertops and we opened that and went up the stairs. Here there was another door, this one made of steel, and I knocked on it politely, ignoring the buzzer and intercom screen mounted next to the frame.

The door opened and Ralphie Wandorski stood there, a bit heavier since the last time I'd seen him, but still with the wispy mustache and goatee style beard that marked him with a style I'd always thought of as classic smarmy. He recognized me too, but he didn't let us in.

"Detective Prentiss," he said to me with a smirk. "Who's your friend?"

"This is my partner, Detective Moran." I kept my voice even and formal and it gave Ralphie pause. "We'd like to speak to your boss. Please."

Wandorski looked over his shoulder, then turned back and opened the door wider, taking a step into the room. Seated behind a small table set outside an unused kitchen area was Rudy Pope himself, a half eaten meal set on a restaurant place setting in front of him. Slowly he put down knife and fork and sat back in his chair.

He was a small, slender man with weak shoulders and most of his hair gone, his pink scalp covered by a skimpy comb-over. He was short, maybe five and a half feet tall, and had a way of looking up at you without meeting your eyes. Often he didn't seem to be listening to whomever was speaking to him and the only time you seemed to have his attention was when he was talking directly to you. Pope spoke quietly, with a tired voice, but still there was a presence. He was like somebody's grandfather keeping a secret he would never tell.

Moran and I approached the table and I said, "Hello, Rudy." Pope's attention seemed to be on Wandorski shutting the door behind us and I could see my partner turn to keep him in sight. "We'd like to talk to you for a minute."

Pope attempted to clear some food from the front of his teeth with the tip of his tongue, then pushed himself back from the table. When he stood up his shoulders rolled forward so his arms hung not just at his sides but slightly in front of him. It made everything he wore look like a cardigan sweater.

Without paying attention to us he moved to a small sitting area beneath an outside window covered with a set of vertical blinds. He took a seat in a chair set at a right angle to a small sofa and looked off somewhere in Ralphie's direction. I sat down on the sofa and angled toward him while Moran stayed on his feet, still watching Pope's man.

"Well? What do you got to say?" His voice was a dry croaking sound.

"We were wondering if you could tell us about a few things, Rudy." When I said his name his lips wrinkled in an expression of distaste. I didn't mind that a bit. "Bolita, for instance. I understand you're on a nostalgia kick or something. Bringing back the old days."

Other than a different set of wrinkles appearing on his face, there was no response.

"Nothing?" I asked. "We have a couple of dead bodies, Rudy, and it seems like we might be able to connect them to your operations."

Ralphie Wandorski cut in with, "You don't know what you're talking about," but that bought him a vicious look from his boss.

"I don't know, Rudy," I said. "Could be a gambling thing, maybe a pimping issue I don't know about." I wanted to push for a reaction, see if I could crack that veneer. "What I'm really wondering, though, is when did you get into the pornography business? That doesn't strike me as your style. The young buck's over there, maybe, but not a class gentleman such as yourself."

Pope swiveled his head around as if to see if more people had come into the room. I really wondered if the old man's marbles were still there. When he finally spoke, I wasn't sure at first to whom he was addressing. "Do you have anything else to tell me?"

I looked over at Moran. He looked back without changing his expression. I was getting the distinct feeling that I'd fouled something up, but I didn't know what it could be. Pope stood and walked around a corner and down a short hallway. We heard a door open and then shut, gently.

Ralphie Wandorski stepped closer, a smirking smile revealing a dis-colored front tooth. "Time for the old man's nap, gentlemen. He needs to save his energy."

I deliberately didn't get up. "Of course he does, Ralphie. You got any-thing you want to say?"

"About what, Detective? I don't know nothing about two dead bod-ies. Why you want to come here and talk smack like that? You're a little off your turf, anyway, aren't you?" He tilted his head and made a show of looking up toward the ceiling. "But you still have a job, though, don't you, Prentiss? Just decided to leave town, maybe go for a change of scenery, right?"

I started to feel like Terry had been right and that this trip had been a mistake. We weren't going to get anything out of Pope and now we were being hassled by a cheap punk like Wandorski. He wasn't anything but a kiss ass toady, a former juvie with a taste for designer suits, dark skinned women and cheap rum who'd been able to parlay a truly vicious streak into a career with a not quite washed up has-been like Rudy Pope.

Feeling a bit mean I stood up and brushed off the seat of my trousers as though I was disinfecting myself. "You've come a long way from busting up drunks and boosting cars, haven't you, Ralphie?" I nodded my head in the direction Pope had gone. "Aren't you worried about what you're going to do when the old man kicks it? Or are there a lot of sen-ior citizens out there looking for good little number one boys?"

Unlike Pope, Ralphie had no problem with looking me in the eye. I ig-nored his stare and stepped past him toward the door. "When you don't have a mommy I guess daddy will have to do, eh?"

Ralphie forced a laugh and I stopped and smiled back at him. Moran moved around me toward the apartment door. As I turned to join him, Ralphie spoke up.

"Say, you seen Roy Evans around, Detective? Been looking for him."

I froze. Why would this asshole bring up Lori's ex-husband?

"He was here somewhere but he seems to have disappeared. You know?"

"So file a report," I said. My voice sounded strange in my ears.

"I might do that," he said. "On the other hand, he was looking to bor-row some money from me and I said I wasn't sure I wanted to give it to him." He looked over at Moran. "Maybe now he doesn't need it."

What the hell was going on? Despite myself, I asked, "How do you know Roy Evans?" I couldn't help it.

"Oh, we been buds since way back. Fact is, we both come from the same state."

That was possible, I supposed. It wasn't necessarily that much of a coincidence. What he said next was what really got me.

"I was at his wedding, you know."

He was telling me he knew Lori? He knew my wife?

"Ol' Roy was back in town. He was a changed man, when I saw him. After he got out of the joint he wanted nothin' more than to make amends with his darling ex and his little girl. You know who I'm talking about, don't you, Detective?"

I took a step forward and I felt Moran's strong hand on my shoulder. "Don't you ever speak to me of my wife again, you rotten-toothed piece of shit. I mean it."

He just laughed and I felt pressure from Moran as he moved me a step backwards toward the door.

"Doesn't matter anyway, does it? She's done gone and left your ass."

I threw off Terry's arm and was on him in two steps. His right hand moved to his beltline and I grabbed it by the forefinger and bent it backwards until it snapped and then I threw him on the ground. Wandorski rolled on his side, screaming and cursing incoherently.

A harsh but commanding sound cracked the air and I looked up to see Rudy Pope standing at the head of the hallway, telephone in his hand. "Officer!" he said. "Leave this place now."

Ralphie Wandorski was cradling his swelling hand, looking up at me in obvious pain. "Go on," he said through his distorted face. "I'll be sure to tell your wife you were here next time she calls."

I'm not sure I remembered exactly what happened next. I know I grabbed Wandorski by his jacket lapels and pulled him to his feet. I think Moran was pounding on my arms trying to get me to let go as I duck walked the little prick toward the sitting area and set all my weight on my right leg and propelled Ralphie over the couch and through the glass panes.

Later, sitting in the Monte Carlo back on the street, my muscles were still shaking as Terry Moran told me I'd have been in deep shit if there hadn't been an old fire escape outside that window.

Chapter 11

After we left Casa Amarilla Moran headed east, the opposite direction of St. Petersburg, and then picked up the toll expressway out to Interstate 75. We headed south down the mainland and then cut back up 275 and drove into St. Pete the proverbial back way, heading north over the Sunshine Skyway. It added almost an hour to the trip. Moran didn't say so but I knew he was trying to get us and his conspicuous car out of Ybor with the least possible resistance. And I needed the time to cool down.

"What the fuck was that about?" he asked me during the trip.

"I don't know," I told him, which we both knew wasn't exactly true.

"Man, I have never seen a cop rip into somebody like that before. Ever."

"Wandorski provoked it," I said but I wasn't convinced.

"You threw him through a window! He didn't provoke that kind of shit."

There was nothing to say and we both knew it.

"I'm telling you, that fire escape saved your ass. Do not try to tell me you knew that thing was there."

I could have lied and told him I had seen it when we sat down on the couch. I'd only be disappointing him more.

"Damn it!" Moran said and pounded the wheel.

It occurred to me that the long detour would also give my partner time to calm down, too. After some miles of silence, I said, "I'm sorry about that, Terry. I didn't mean to bring you any grief." And that was the sincere truth.

He looked sideways at me, then flicked a knuckle at my knee. That trademark smile made its first appearance of the afternoon and in spite of everything else, I cracked one, too. "You're a good cop, man, but you can be a mite unpredictable sometimes."

"Yeah," I said. "Sometimes."

We drove on a bit before he brought up the topic I knew was coming. "So Ralphie Wandorski knows Lori's ex, huh?"

"So he says."

"You think he's lying?"

I had no idea. "Don't see why he would." Something else was bothering me and now that we were talking about my wife, it began to come clear in my mind. "I'm really wondering how he knew Lori had left."

Terry pursed his lips in thought. "What about Roy Evans? You think he had something to do with it?"

Oh, god, please don't go there. What could I say about Roy Lee Evans, the father of my adopted daughter and the man my wife had married ten years before she'd even met me? "Don't know," I said, hoping he'd take it.

"Maybe we should look him up, dude. Get his side of the story." He looked over at me. "Who knows, maybe he could tell you where Lori went."

"Watch the road."

"I'm serious man. You want help there, just say the word. If he's tied up with Ralphie Wandorski and Rudy Pope, he may even be involved with this King of Cats thing, and the dead guy in Tampa."

That was something I had to think about. I had no reason to doubt what Ralphie had said about his relationship with Evans but who I had no idea if that was all there was to it. What about this money Ralphie said Roy was after? Payoff for services rendered or a personal loan, like Ralphie had said?

I rubbed my eyes in frustration. Only bad things could happen for me if people started looking for Roy Lee Evans but I didn't know what I could do about it. Anything I tried would just make things worse.

"Look, man," Moran said, looking at me again.

"I told you to watch the fucking road."

He grinned. "Seriously," he said. "If there's a chance Evans is involved in all this we may have to get a line on him."

"We don't even know if Pope is involved," I said. "We don't even know what any of this is about, do we?"

"For us it's about two dead guys," Terry answered. "And making enemies out of punks like Ralphie Wandorski. You sweating that one?"

"Not really," I said. "Maybe if I'd tossed Pope. Ralphie's just a roach looking for a sink basin with a vacancy."

We got back to the station and there was a note waiting for me on my desk from Kelly, the computer tech. Moran and I turned around and we both went downstairs to find him.

"What have you got?" I asked him.

He had a stupid grin on his face and he stunk even more of cigarette smoke. I was suddenly irritated with him beyond reason. His expression reminded me of a child's who had just done something that only he could be proud of, too dense to realize the rest of the kids thought he was a schmuck.

"Beyond the many coincidences, using Google for a search engine, hits on CNN.com for news, and a few things like that, both the King of Cats and this Schoenfeld guy had the same taste in, say, computer recreation. And I'm not talking about gaming."

"What do you mean?"

"Well," he said, "they both went to that same password protected website, the one with the cached porn shots we took off the Shawcross laptop."

I looked at my partner, unsure of what that meant.

"Could that just be a really popular website?" he asked. "I mean, how can we tell how much of a coincidence it is?"

"Ah," said Kelly. "That's the good part. I couldn't get in because the account is still shut down, but, get this, both computers cached the same login name."

The word popped into my mind. "'Maleman,'" I said.

"That's the one," Kelly said, that silly grin forming again on his face.

"Who knows," Terry said, and winked. "Maybe he always delivered."

I didn't say anything to Moran but I spent the rest of the day waiting for the other shoe to drop. When nothing came in from either Tampa or Lieutenant Greene by four o'clock, I took off, justifying it with Terry by mentioning that I had been in an hour early. If Pope or one of his lawyers was going to raise a stink about Wandorski they'd have to wait to tell me about it.

"You don't want the overtime, that it?" he said.

"Like Greene would okay it. See you in the morning."

And I was gone, a full day's damage done behind me. More like this and I would be bringing the shovels to my own funeral. I felt the pressure squeezing inside my head and hoped I looked better outwardly than I felt inside. I felt like I needed a beer, or better yet, some scotch.

We'll see, I thought. The night is young.

Again at home I parked myself on the lanai, with the second and last beer that I had in the house dripping condensation on the patio table. My mind was going off in twenty different directions, randomly changing course like the track of some crazy firework. I'd think about Lori and wonder how she was feeling right now, at this very moment, and then I'd flash on Ralphie Wandorski and the sense of his weight pivoting over my leg and out into space. I'd see the almost dazed look in Rudy Pope's eyes, recall the aroma of the lunch he had left on the table in his apartment, and then think about Roxy and whether she had anyone her age to spend time with, to ride horses with.

I'd think about Randy Shawcross and wonder just what the hell it was he'd been planning on stealing. I'd convinced myself he must have been setting up some kind of score but there was no telling what it could have been. It popped into my head that maybe his target was Barry Schoenfeld but I couldn't see them talking so much on their cell phones if that was the case. Whatever the heist was, could Randy already have pulled it? Maybe he and Schoenfeld had been negotiating for the return of whatever it was Randy had stolen, or had been planning how to get rid of it. Schoenfeld as a fence?

Schoenfeld as burglary victim didn't seem likely. Randy had never gone back to his victims before, so there'd be no phone calls if that were true. He was anonymous, he was the King of Cats, in and out and no one the wiser.

Besides the calls themselves, the only thing they knew Shawcross and Schoenfeld had in common was that they visited the same password protected porn site using the same credentials. I'd done a search on the site's address after seeing Kelly earlier and found nothing. It wasn't a site intended for the general public. It knew how to hide itself from the search engines that used software robots to index them. Kelly had told me how those things work, and how there were different methods the search engines used to find and rank all the various websites. Even so, they only captured about fifteen percent of all the websites on the internet. It couldn't be that hard to hide—but they had to want to.

Which meant that it was more of a private site, or a "dark" site. Strictly invitation only.

The light of the day was gone and it didn't look like there was going to be a moon tonight. I couldn't remember what lunar cycle we were in and

I thought about taking the telescoping pole I used to clean the pool down to the sea wall and rake the water to see if there was any biolumi-nescence going on. I was tired of thinking of the case. A distraction would be nice. I'd make my own light show in the water. The pole was over—

A private site. Two people logging in with the same credentials. One of them had to be a legitimate user. So the other was—what?

Randy Shawcross was a known thief, a burglar. It had made him fa-mous enough so that if someone, say a Barry Schoenfeld, needed some-one to steal something, he would at least have an idea where to find some-one who could, in theory, do the job.

But why share the website? Based on the cached images, it was more or less standard porn stuff. If the two men were just friends with a shared interest then you'd expect to see other, similar sites cached on both men's computers. I told myself I needed to remember to check with Is-abel Marquez, or better yet, go through Kelly and the Tampa computer tech, to see if Schoenfeld had been a bigger pornography connoisseur than Randy Shawcross.

Darlene Shawcross had said that she had never heard of Barry Schoen-feld. I'd check with her again but I couldn't see why a thief like Randy would seek out a politician like Schoenfeld. It was a much better fit the other way around.

Maybe. It wouldn't hurt to ask Darlene if Randy ever took on any work for hire. Knowing how Randy kept his secrets, she probably wouldn't be aware but it would be a good excuse to spend an hour or so away from the office.

I realized that I had come to focus on a single train of thought. That'll never do, I told myself, not tonight, as I pushed myself up by the arm-rests of the chair. I took the cleaning pole down from its hooks, removed the strainer net from the end, then went outside the lanai and down to the sea wall. No more thinking about work.

This is something Roxy would like to do, I told myself. Play with the lights in the water. With my luck I'd probably poke a bull shark.

Chapter 12

I slept as poorly as I had every night since Lori had left, tossing around, slipping in and out of a narrow slumber. I had begun to craft an image of her, based on absolutely nothing, where she was calm and relaxed and even happy. I could see her that way in my quasi-dreams. Content. Free from the stress of the fears that had been weighing her down before she left.

Was she thinking of me, I wondered. Did she miss me? Did she ever think about coming home?

Whenever I got to this point I had to physically move, do something before thoughts like this drove me insane. She was gone, it was because of me, and that was that. Own it and move on.

But maybe she's coming back....

I rolled myself out of bed and into the bathroom for a shower.

In the back of my mind I was still nervous about the Ralphie Wandorski thing. That had been stupid, allowing myself to give it up like that, especially in front of Terry Moran. It's not the thought of losing my job that concerned me, I'd come to grips with that months ago. The real problem I had with it was the investigation they'd use to hang me with. What I did with Ralphie could give them the excuse to start one. Terry would have to tell the truth and there would be no union standing up for me.

Not that I'd want them to, not anymore. A few months ago I had been worried about going to jail, being separated from my wife and daughter, but that part had happened anyway. Obviously I'd prefer to stay out of prison, or some place worse, but I didn't feel like I had a whole hell of a lot more to lose.

Ralphie Wandorski, well-dressed two bit punk in an expensive suit and chief bounce boy of Rudy Pope, had known my wife had left me. How? As far as I knew, I hadn't had any contact with Ralphie for the past two or three years, not since before I'd come over from Tampa. But he knew Roy Evans, or said he did. But he did know Evans was gone. Had Ralphie been looking for him, had he tried to find him through Lori? Why would he do that, I wondered. What value did trash like Evans have for

Ralphie Wandorski? And Lori was married to me, had my last name. How difficult would it have been for Ralphie to track her down? Probably not very, but I couldn't believe she would have been having these contacts behind my back.

Unless Roy for some reason had put Ralphie onto her. But again, I couldn't think of a reason why. Was Roy recruiting Ralphie's help for something?

Anyway, all this was a circular conversation, speculative thoughts wrapping around their own legs. It didn't feel like Ralphie was completely full of crap but there was no way I was prepared to take what he said as pure gospel, either.

The only thing that I knew was that Roy Lee Evans had been interested in a reunion of sorts with my wife and daughter. His was a compulsion born not of love but of obsession and possession. The woman he thought of as his had taken up with another, his daughter had found a new father, his ego had been scorned, his own self rejected. This wasn't something the sad, pathetic mind of Roy Evans could accept, nor did he seem much inclined to try. After his release from prison he had tracked Lori and Roxy down, had tracked us all down, and begun to slowly make his presence known.

It annoyed the hell out of me at first, but it wasn't anything I thought I couldn't handle. I'd had no doubt, especially when I braced him outside of a hotel bar in St. Pete Beach. He was an ex-con, a career criminal, and he should have at least had a show of respect for someone with a badge. But he hadn't, not even a little, and when I saw he had no fear of my station I grew concerned, maybe even a little afraid. But not for my person. Roy's vengeance would take the form of single-mindedly reclaiming the property he thought of as his own.

The visit at the bar hadn't gone the way I'd intended and I'd been diminished by it. That was the time when I first started to realize the damage that Roy Lee Evans could do to my family, and it left me cold. Deeply, bitterly cold. That was the time when I first started to realize what I was capable of.

I called Darlene Shawcross from the station and she sounded relieved when she recognized my voice. I didn't ask her why. She said that we were welcome to come over anytime in the morning.

"Anything from Greene?" I asked Moran.

He shook his head. "I told him we're staying on our side of the bay, running down the Shawcross thing. Tampa can take care of their own guy."

"He happy with that?"

"For now. As long as the TV cameras stay over there I think he is."

We drove out to Pinellas Park in the Monte Carlo, stopping at a convenience store on the way so Moran could get a cup of coffee. The morning sun had burned off the pockets of fog that had clung to the stands of trees alongside the roadways, allowing another intensely bright, washed out day to emerge. Moran pulled his car into the driveway of the Shawcross house and we walked over to the front door. Inside, Darlene had been busy packing.

"Leaving?" I asked, not surprised.

"What's there to stay for?" she asked. "We'd been trapped here, trying to hide, but now—" She shrugged and I wanted to reach out and touch her. "I don't want to do it anymore. I need it to be over. I don't want to keep feeling ashamed of things I never did."

She put some folded clothes on a table and looked at me. "Does that make me a bad person?"

I shook my head. "No, Darlene, of course not."

"None of this is easy," Moran added.

We took the same seats on the couch that we'd used before and I asked her about the things that had occurred to me the night before. Had Randy ever done any work for hire? Had he had any interest in politics or in Tampa, especially in the weeks leading up to his death?

She looked weary as she told us again how little she had known of Randy's illegal activities and I still had no reason to not believe her. To all appearances Randy had led a double life, handyman by day, cat burglar by night. Part of his thrill was to keep his two lives separate, to pull one over on the rest of us so completely that even his wife wouldn't be able to tell where the line was drawn.

And as for politics, there was nothing, especially local ones. If her husband had even known who Barry Schoenfeld was, or even that there was an upcoming mayoral election in Tampa, she'd have been surprised. In other words, I thought, she had nothing new to tell us.

I wasn't sure why but I gave her a quick hug and a kiss on the cheek when we left her house. She said she was probably going out west, back to San Diego where she'd grown up. I wished her well and she waved goodbye as we walked out the door.

Back in the car Moran asked, "Think she's got any of the swag?"

"I don't know," I said. "I wouldn't think so. He didn't want her hurt."

"She's got to be living on something."

"If it was something that could have been taken away, it would have been. Randy was too smart for that. He took chances with his way of life, but he didn't believe in putting Darlene at risk."

"I hope he believed in life insurance. Seems like she deserves a break."

"Or at least a book deal. She'll be all right. We just have to find her the right ending."

Once back in the car I suggested to Terry that he call Ding Dong Marquez and see if she had anything new. I wasn't sure what else to do at that point.

"What are you thinking?" he asked.

"So far no burglaries have been reported, on either side of the bay, that fit the King of Cats profile. We've got nothing on the boat that was involved with his killing, no witnesses have come forward. All we've really got is some sort of connection between Shawcross and Schoenfeld and this porn site thing but I don't know how to go after it."

"Think we can go for warrants?"

I shook my head. "On who? The porn site? We don't have anyone suspected of doing anything illegal. I can't see any grounds."

"We've got murders."

"That we can't connect to the site, assuming a connection exists. We have to sit on it for a while."

Moran fiddled with the air conditioning controls and drove on. After a while he said, "We do have something else."

"What's that?"

"Roy Evans."

Jesus Christ. My blood turned cold. "What the fuck are you talking about?"

"Listen, man, hear me out. We go and talk to Pope about his little website and that goes nowhere. Ralphie Wandorski decides to push your buttons and brings up your wife's ex-husband."

"So? Look where that got him."

He ignored me. One of the things that made me so lucky to draw Moran as a partner was his willingness to treat me as a friend, outside the department. Too often I overlooked what he did for me.

"Well, Ralphie lets on that he knows something about you that you say he shouldn't. Unless the news had actually come from Roy Evans, like he inferred. Which means we might have another connection to Ralphie and Pope through Evans."

I said, "You're wrong." I thought about what he was telling me. "We should let that one go."

He was looking at me as he said, "I think we should at least talk to the man."

I tried to choose my words carefully. "I don't know that I can do that."

"You mean after what you did to the Flying Wandorski? You don't trust yourself?"

"Maybe. Something like that."

"Okay, then," he said, finally. "If you don't think we should look into it, we won't. It is curious, though, isn't it, that Ralphie brought him up."

I took a deep breath and exhaled slowly. "He was just trying to piss me off."

"Did a good job of it, didn't he?"

"Sometimes it's not all that hard to do."

He looked at me again but I kept staring ahead through the windshield, wondering just how long I could keep this up.

Roy Lee Evans. I prayed Terry Moran would never find him.

Back at the station my partner put a call into Isabel Marquez but was told he'd have to wait for a call back. I busied myself with paperwork for a while and then headed out for a walk. More motion, more movement, better to think. As soon as I left the building breathing was easier; there had been a pressure sitting that close to my partner after the conversation we'd had in the car. Being out of his sight for a while made me feel less wound up.

The muscles in my legs were wooden, as though I was exercising them under protest. I kept them moving mindlessly, subconsciously heading away from the busy streets and toward the more quiet ones. Of course these were the ones with the bad smells, the leftover spoor of the city's homeless and disenfranchised. The stench of stale urine clouding the areas around the recessed doorways of storefronts that had seen better days. Much better days. Fecal smears marked the insides and outsides of commercial trash dumpsters lurking in alleyways. It was too distracting and I turned more towards downtown, pushing my sunglasses further down on the bridge of my nose. The brightness in my vision was at odds with the squalor of the shadows.

After a while the distractions stopped crowding out the thoughts I was avoiding and the crept into the foreground. So Ralphie Wandorski knew Roy Evans. Hell, Ralphie Wandorski said he knew my wife. And Ralphie knew Roy was missing, gone from whatever circle of hell the two had in common.

I turned this over in my mind. Roy had been living in a shabby rental house in south St. Pete with painted cinderblock walls and a lawn that had more fire ant mounds and sand spurs than it did blades of grass. I'd look up Ralphie's address when I got back but I was sure it had to be in Tampa, probably near Ybor, or else he wouldn't be so close to Pope. If Ralphie and Roy had some sort of friendship, it had to be Roy that had sought out Ralphie. Roy was fresh out of prison from Texas, Ralphie was established with Pope here in Florida.

The more I thought about it the more I thought Ralphie was probably telling the truth; it was logical that if Roy needed money he would think to look up his old buddy from hicksville. Whether or not they were that close or if there was some other reason Roy thought he could get money from Ralphie I had no idea. Maybe Roy had just been after a job with Pope.

I was getting near the Baywalk shopping area and it suddenly occurred to me how far I'd walked. I crossed the street to my right and started back in the direction of the station, no closer to figuring out what all of this meant. As I grew nearer to the 1st Avenue North police headquarters building I wondered if it was really important. It seemed like it should be but I still couldn't see the connection. What I really needed to know was the precise relationship between Ralphie and Roy but I didn't know how to get that.

Until I reached the concrete steps of the station. I'd been thinking that I'd done a terrific job of getting in good with Ralphie, that breaking his finger and throwing him through a window would make him feel like opening up and confiding in me. Sure, if I asked politely he'd tell me what he really knew about his childhood friend. Right. And I couldn't talk to Roy if I'd wanted to.

As I made it to the steps leading to the entrance of the station, it hit me. Ralphie may have given me the key to the whole mess after all. Someone else may know what the relationship between himself and Roy Evans had been: Lori.

Oh, god, I thought.

There was a cement bench just outside the tinted glass electric doors and I sat on it as the weight of the thought settled in on me, the sliding doors ghosting open then shutting again. My wife had left, deliberately avoiding my presence as she did it, telling me by phone what she was doing. That she needed time away from me. Above all, she pleaded, give me room, give me space. Don't try to find me.

But now I had to. Didn't I? The world wasn't standing still because she needed to break away from me for a while. Things were moving, events were in motion, and they could suck me down and away if I sat and did nothing. And if that happened she'd still be affected, both herself and Roxy.

I stood up and wiped the imagined dust from the seat of my pants. I went upstairs to my desk and began to pull up whatever we had on Ralphie Wandorski. I was going to put in a request for the records of Roy Lee Evans but I stopped short. I hadn't wanted to do this before and I still wasn't sure if it was smart. Moran was sitting at his desk, punching in a phone number, probably to Tampa. It couldn't hurt him, I thought, not in any way that I could see, but I didn't want to ask him. He was still my partner, after all. Maybe I'd do it later myself, if I had to.

Instead I called the phone company. Roxy had contacted me long distance four nights ago and I needed the number she had called from and I couldn't wait for my bill. Despite the over air conditioning common to public buildings in Florida, I was sweating as I wrote down what they told me. It was an Alabama number. Turning to my computer I used a reverse directory to look it up.

It belonged to a Roger and Anne Swenson of Huntsville, Alabama. I'd never heard of them. I was familiar with the name Huntsville but I had no idea where it was. There was an atlas in my desk drawer and I took it out and with sweaty palms found the right page. Northern Alabama, not far from Chattanooga, or even Atlanta, really.

I sat back in my chair and wondered what I should do next. I could dial the phone, hop in the car, or reconsider my options and do nothing. I could just take my chances that things with Pope and Ralphie wouldn't spiral beyond my reach and suck in both Roy Lee Evans and myself.

I was still stuck in indecision when Lieutenant Greene himself appeared at my desk and in a barely contained voice said, "What the fuck do you think you're doing?"

Chapter 13

"Sir?" I said, looking up from the atlas. Behind him I saw Moran hanging up his phone.

"I just got a call from Tampa, from Detective Marquez. She told me that a couple of men had shaken up some pissant who drives for Rudy Pope, that an ambulance was called to one of his restaurants and that two men were seen leaving the Casa Amarilla apparently driving away in a bright ass yellow muscle car that looked like it was some teenaged motor head's wet dream." He turned and looked at Moran. "Why, oh why, were your two names the only ones that came to mind after that phone call?"

Crap, I thought. I pushed myself back from my desk but Moran spoke before I did.

"We were there, Lieutenant. We were following up something we got from Randy Shawcross's computer. We just asked Rudy a few questions. He had one of his guys there, someone serving him lunch."

"What the hell did you do?" said Greene. He turned back to me.

"They were okay when we left," I said. I couldn't believe Ralphie or Rudy Pope would be preferring charges but my neck was already in the noose. "What exactly happened?"

"Well?" he asked Moran and I knew I had been right.

"Pope asked us nicely to leave, and we did." He held his palms out toward the lieutenant. "We didn't touch him."

This seemed to take away some of Greene's momentum. So he didn't really know what had gone on, most likely didn't even have a specific complaint. Someone outside probably saw Ralphie go through the window and called the cops. Ralphie wouldn't have talked, Pope wouldn't have let him. Greene was fishing.

"Do you want us to look into it, Lieutenant?" I asked. "We could compare notes with Tampa, see what we come up with."

Greene looked back and forth from Moran's desk to mine. Finally he said, "Never mind, damn it. But you should have a strong sense, a very strong sense, that someone's watching what you guys do. Both of you." He turned around and headed back down the hall toward the elevators.

"You see that?" I said to Terry after he'd gone. "That car of yours is going to get us into trouble."

He snorted. "You're right. It was all the car. Now I know."

I gave him a wink and went back to my atlas so I could figure out distances and travel times. The decision about what to do next I'd put off a while longer. Too much was happening that wasn't in my control and I wanted to breathe for a while, just breathe, and let a few things come to me for the afternoon. Nothing heavy should fall out of the sky in the next few hours, or at least so I hoped. But Greene's attention was worrying me.

I still couldn't get the rampaging lieutenant out of my mind. There may have been more going on behind the scenes than I had realized. My board hearing hadn't been scheduled yet and I started to worry if that was because the guys that wanted me out, the guys like Greene, were still lifting the mountain to drop on my head. I told Moran I was going to make a phone call and went back outside to call my lawyer.

Leslie Alcaro answered on the first ring. "Jeff?" she said. "How are you?"

On pins and needles, Leslie. "I'm fine. Some things have been happening around here and I thought I should check in with you and see if you've heard anything. About my hearing, I mean."

Sounds of shuffling paper came across the line and after a few seconds she said, "No, nothing I've been made aware of. The police board in Tampa is making sounds about scheduling something in about sixty days."

"Isn't that unusual?"

"To wait this long? A little, I'd say, but it's really up to them. They could have bigger fish to go after, a backlog, who knows? They don't tell us. I could ask if you need me to but we might be better off just letting the thing run its course. Who knows what they could do?"

"Like drop my case?"

She paused a moment, and I could imagine her biting her top lip. "It's possible," she finally said.

"But not likely?"

"I don't think so, but who knows. If I had to guess I'd say they're just letting more time pass to let the the Safrenza trial fade from the public mind."

"Yeah, maybe," I said.

"Is there something going on?"

I told her about the Randy Shawcross case and how it appeared it may have connections with her side of the bay in Tampa. When I told her about Ybor City and Rudy Pope I could hear an intake of breath on the line.

"What's wrong, Leslie?"

"Oh, god," she said. "Rudy Pope. You know my husband?"

That was a surprise. "I didn't even know you were married, Leslie. You never told me."

"Well, I am. We're separated. He's involved with Rudy Pope's group. It's complicated."

"Well, unless you also work for the man, you should be all right. It may not look good for you but innocent is innocent."

She gave a bitter laugh. "Not always, Jeff." Then, "Could we meet? I could come over there, maybe get a bite, talk through a few things."

We'd never met outside her office before. "Yeah, sure, I suppose. When are you thinking?"

"Do you have time tonight?" She was speaking more rapidly now. "I could come out this evening. If that's not too soon, I mean...."

"Leslie, relax. That would be fine." Or would it? I wasn't sure what was going on. I gave her my address and she repeated it as I went, adding in a few directions.

"About six?" she asked.

"See you then."

"Goodbye, Jeff."

We hung up and I wondered what was going on. She'd sounded more worried now than she ever had before when talking about my case. Apparently I'd find out at six.

Moran finally got a call back from Ding Dong and they spoke for a few minutes before hanging up. He was shaking his head as he cradled the handset. "She wanted to know why we was talking to Pope," he said to me.

"What did you tell her?"

"That a website we found on Shawcross's computer might be one of his operations."

"And she said?"

"Nothing. I don't think she's thinking much of our dead body over here. Sounds like she's more wrapped up in Schoenfeld's high profile and all of the people he may have been involved with in his political life."

I thought about that for a moment. "You buy it? She always was as much of a political animal as she was a cop." This could be good news for me. It might get the heat off the Roy Evans thing for a while if it was credible.

"Don't know. Schoenfeld and Shawcross had to be talking about something on their cell phones, though, right? And I don't know about you, but there aren't too many people I'd share my user name and password with, especially for a pornographic website."

"Not even me?" I asked.

"Bite me."

I smiled and agreed with him but I still couldn't think of a solid way to get at the site. We had checked with a guy we both knew in vice and the Little Y, Inc. website was news to him. And unimpressive. He didn't seem to find anything interesting in it whatsoever.

"Hey," I said, suddenly. "You mind if I take a couple of days, make it a long weekend?"

He gave me a look that I didn't understand. "In the middle of this case? You okay?"

"You know what's going on with me. I was going to take some time when Darlene Shawcross called about her home invasion. Thought I might pick it back up. Not sure we can do much about Shawcross without Tampa's help anyway, and you heard Greene. Might be a good idea to lay low for a little bit."

He looked a little puzzled but he said, "You got the time, man, take it. You could use it."

Apparently I'd made my decision without really thinking about it. I went to Greene's office and filled out the form, then waited while his assistant went in to see if he'd sign it.

"You're all set," she said to me when she returned. "Enjoy your time off."

"He didn't say anything?" I asked.

"Nope. Just signed his name." She settled back into her chair and resumed typing on her keyboard.

"See you Monday," I said as I left but she didn't bother to reply. I thought the lieutenant's manners must be rubbing off on her but that was fine with me. I had other things on my mind. I was going to have dinner with Leslie Alcaro and then I was going to find my wife.

I left the building from there. I didn't even tell Moran goodbye. I drove home and threw some clothes and toiletries in a bag and cracked a beer in the kitchen. Shouldn't have agreed to meet Leslie, I thought. I just wanted to hit the road, to finally do something positive about Lori and Roxy. I had no illusions as to the outcome of finding them, assuming I could, but trying was the thing. A large part of it was just getting away from here, the house, the job, everything.

There was some ground beef in the fridge and I pounded out a couple of hamburger patties and fried them in a pan on the stove. I made do with whatever fixings I could find and, along with a fresh beer, took them out to the lanai to eat my late lunch and wait for Leslie.

A gentle shaking caused me to half jump out of my chair. The plate on my lap fell to the floor and an empty beer bottle tipped and rolled in a line away from the house. Leslie Alcaro stepped back, smothering a laugh as I whipped my head around, hands on the arm rests as I started to push myself up.

"Easy, tiger," she said.

"Jesus, Leslie." I lowered myself back down. "Really?"

"You didn't answer your door so I came around back. The screen door was unlocked."

She stood there in a rose colored sundress and open toed shoes, tanned legs showing from the knees down. In one hand was a large purse, like a tote bag. I ran my hand through my hair, pushing it back from my forehead.

"You know cops carry guns, don't you?"

She put her purse down and pulled up the other chair. "Oh, stop. You can't shoot me till after your hearing. You're smarter than that."

"As far as you know." I stood and scooped up my plate and the empty beer bottle. "Can I get you something?" I waggled the empty in front of her. "I think I have a few of these left."

"Um, sure," she said.

"You okay?"

"We'll talk about it."

I took that as a cue to leave her for a minute and I went inside to the kitchen, placing the plate in the sink and grabbling two cold beers out of the fridge. I twisted off the tops and tossed them in the garbage under the sink. When I got back to the lanai, Leslie had moved her chair so she had a better view of the canal. It was also closer to my own.

"This is nice," she said.

I handed her one of the beers. "The boat likes it." Now that I was awake I was conscious of my pending road trip. I checked my watch, took a small pull from my beer, and waited for her to get to it.

"Are you here alone?"

I shouldn't have been as surprised to hear my lawyer bring up my wife but then I reminded myself that Lori had called her looking for me a couple of days ago. Before I could figure out a good answer, she said, "Lori's gone, isn't she?"

My hand brought my beer back to my lips and I took a longer drink than before.

"I—I don't mean to pry or anything. But the other day, when she called me...."

"Forget it," I said.

"You okay?"

"Fine," I said automatically, then spent some time thinking about the question. "It's complicated, you know. Some things kind of went on that she didn't really know about. She didn't like that. So she left."

Leslie looked back toward my boat, the sun rippling off the minute waves in the canal. "Can you fix it?"

Now that was a good question. I wondered if I could I fix it. I really didn't know.

"Maybe," I said. "Maybe not. Mostly I think I just want to know she's okay. I mean really okay. She took our daughter, and I worry. Actually, she's my adopted daughter."

"Have you heard...."

"Roxy called me. She wouldn't say where they were. I think she was actually making sure I was all right." I shook my head.

Leslie reached over and touched the back of my hand. Her fingertips were cool from the beer bottle and I felt an unexpected tingle at her familiarity.

"And are you?" she asked.

"Sure," I said. "I just have to get some things straight in my head." I turned to look at her and she looked back, without moving her hand. "I just need them to be safe. They've both been through a lot." I'd done too much to protect them to let either get hurt now.

Leslie pulled her hand back and I was sorry the contact was broken. "My husband's been gone for a long time now. Eight months."

"How's that going?"

She laughed. "It's not long enough. I don't know. Should never have married him, but we probably all say that when it falls apart, don't we?"

I didn't answer. She was most likely right.

"His name is Carlos." Leslie turned in her chair as she said the name. "Do you know him?"

That caught me by surprise. "Do I know him? How would I do that?"

She reached down into her oversized purse and pulled out a manila folder with two photographs in it and handed it over. I took it and studied the two shots. After a second it dawned on me where I'd seen him before. Leslie saw it on my face.

"So you do?"

This was the man I'd seen at Pope's bar in Ybor City, the one that turned away when Moran and I went to visit his highness and Ralphie Wandorski yesterday.

"Not by name," I said. "I used to see him around when I worked Tampa. And then—"

"What?"

I couldn't see any reason not to tell her, so I told her about seeing Carlos at Pope's bar. She wasn't surprised.

"Carlos has been working for Rudy Pope for a few years now. When I met him I thought he sold cars in Carrollwood."

"He probably does," I said. "Pope has connections with a few dealerships in town. Carlos is probably on the books for legal reasons."

"Because crooks don't get W-2s."

I took a slow sip from my beer. "What do you need from me—"

Leslie turned away so her back was toward me. She didn't turn far enough. I saw the tears glistening on her cheeks.

"I made a mistake," she said, looking out at the canal again. "And now I don't know how to get out."

We sat in silence for a while, quietly letting our thoughts run their courses through our minds. Was Lori my mistake? I loved her but she had baggage when we met, like we all do, but there was something in her, something I saw, that made me think—what? That I could save her? I wish I knew from what. Me, as it's turning out.

Then I thought: maybe she could have saved me....

"I'm going to lose my job," Leslie said quietly.

We turned to face each other. "You can get another."

"Like you?"

She was right. Getting fired as a lawyer probably meant that getting another job—as a lawyer—was as difficult as getting a job as a cop after being fired as a cop. Possible, probably, but definitely not an upward move.

"Can't you divorce him, do something, before it comes to that?"

She shook her head. "He won't let me. He sees me as some sort of protection, a bargaining chip maybe. I don't know."

I hated to say it, but I didn't stop myself: "What can I do to help?"

Leslie reached across and touched my hand again, this time with more than just her fingertips. I felt myself gripping back as she curled her hand over mine. "I don't know," she finally said. "I just wanted to tell you. I've always felt like I could talk to you. I just— I just wanted you to know."

We sat like that for a while, and then, a bit later, she let go of my hand and I thought the moment was broken. Instead she slid her chair closer to mine, took my hand again and laid her head on my shoulder.

"Don't move," she said, and I didn't. "This is for me."

We didn't talk any more. I wondered if this should feel more wrong than it did. I could smell flowers in her hair, feel the softness of the gentle brown curls against my cheek. It was nice. I thought of my upcoming trip to look for Lori and Roxy but this time there was no ache in my stomach as I did so. This meant something, I was sure, but I wasn't smart enough to know just what it was.

Chapter 14

Later that night I hit the road, heading north on 275 for the seven hour trip to Atlanta. I had thought about flying but when I took into account the cost of the walk-up ticket and the need to rent a car, it didn't seem so appealing. In addition, assuming there was a late night flight available I'd probably arrive at about the same time if I drove myself. So it was up to Atlanta in the Jeep, then an hour or so over to Huntsville. Plenty of time to think. Or to leave my mind out of it altogether, which might be better.

The problem with driving north-south through Florida is that the state is so damned long and the highway is flat and devoid of visual appeal. The three and a half hour trip to the Georgia border seems more like three and a half days. There's a rest stop near Gainesville that's built on stones patterned to look like a giant snake which most drivers don't even notice. It's saying something when the scenic highlight of the drive is the layout of stones at a rest stop.

I'd had to slog through the tail end of an accident snarl into and out of Tampa and by the time I hit Atlanta it was almost four o'clock in the morning. There was no interstate to Huntsville so I pulled into some roadside motel off the 285 connector north of the city. I needed sleep and I wanted a shower and a chance to wash the road grime from my body.

When I awoke I was surprised how fast I had dropped off and how rested I felt. The skies were overcast and rain was clearly threatening. I stood at the lone window, overlooking the parking lot, and marveled at how much less tension I felt. And all I'd done was leave town.

And spend time with Leslie. For an instant I thought about calling her but then I let it go. I didn't have anything appropriate to say.

I showered and dressed then dropped my key on the table as I left. It was quicker than actually checking out and I didn't feel like talking to somebody just to get a receipt I'd toss in the garbage.

The only way to get to Huntsville from here was over blue highways and back roads, or by taking the interstate out of the way and heading either back up or down, north or south, depending on which direction I left Atlanta. I decided to go the back road route just because I was tired of looking at freeway. I drove through a McDonald's for some breakfast and headed out, unsure of how long it would actually take to get there. It would be more than the hour I'd guessed when I'd first looked at the atlas at my desk but that was okay. The nearer I got to Lori the longer I seemed to want to take to get there. It was fear, I guess, or something equally as irrational.

When I finally made it to the city it was well past lunch time. The neighborhoods I drove through seemed dingier than what I was used to, and many of the houses were made of wood instead of the omnipresent cement block in Florida. I followed the main drag into town and stopped at a gas station for directions. The Swenson house wasn't far and the neighborhood turned out to be better than the ones I had come through. Most of the houses had front porches of some sort, many of which held people of indeterminate ages sitting in chairs or on stoops watching the occasional cars drive by. What they did in the intervals was anyone's guess.

The rain in Atlanta had held off but the skies had remained overcast with an angry, multi-shaded gray mass looming low overhead. I pulled the Jeep to a stop at the curb in front of Roger and Anne Swenson's house and turned the ignition off. I was shaking, I realized, and grasshoppers were doing a number inside my stomach. For the first time I wondered if this was really a good idea. During the trip up I had never allowed myself to ask that question. I had merely wound myself up and aimed myself up the road.

Lori's white Corolla was parked in the driveway, its Florida plate standing out like a beacon. The sight of it made me break into a sweat.

What do I do now, I asked myself. Part of me realized I hadn't counted on actually being able to find her.

I sat there, staring at my hands on the steering wheel until I realized I hadn't let it go since I'd parked. I forced my fingers to open, turned off the ignition and put my hands in my lap, never looking above the steering column. There was a sudden peal of thunder from somewhere overhead.

And so I sat. For how long, I had no idea. I had slipped into a place where I wasn't consciously thinking, every thought squirming and wriggling away before I could grasp it. I had nothing to react to. The universe became the inside of the Jeep, the horizon extending as far as the junction of the dashboard and windshield. It took half a minute to turn my head once I realized someone was knocking on the passenger window.

I reached over to pull the handle of the door without looking. My seat belt kept me from reaching it and I felt like an idiot as I pressed the release button and tried again. She pulled the handle and leaned her head into the car.

"Hey," she said.

I opened my mouth to say something, god knows what, but instead I choked and I could feel the tears well up in my eyes. My hands found the steering wheel again and I held on to it as hard as I could, an anchor to a reality that felt like it was already melting away.

The tears were what got her in the car. She slid into the seat next to mine and leaned over and put her arms around me, making me realize how stiff my body was. God, she smelled good, and she was warm, and she was holding me.

"Shhh," she said. "You don't have to cry."

Eventually I forced my hands from the wheel and without disturbing her grip around me I blotted my eyes with my sleeves. It took a much longer time for me to feel as though I could open my mouth and make intelligible sounds.

"Sorry about that," I said. "I didn't expect to do that." When Lori didn't answer, I said, "I found you."

My wife sat slowly upright, gently pulling her arms away from me. I forced myself to meet her eyes, not knowing what I would see, and when I did, I didn't recognize it.

"I didn't want you to."

"I know," I told her. "I tried not to. I was waiting for you to call or write or something. I was trying to give you space."

"I wish you had."

I reached over to take one of her hands in mine and she allowed it but it was clearly passive. It made me feel like I was overstepping but I didn't let it go. Part of my mind recognized how different this was than the night before with Leslie Alcaro.

"Something came up on a case," I said. "I needed to ask you about it."

"That is so bullshit." She shook her head as if she didn't believe me. Her hands retreated to her lap. "What could I know about a case?" There was a message in her eyes but so much of what was happening in that car seemed to be careening past me. "Was it a murder?"

"Where's Roxy?" I asked. It was an abrupt change and she blinked before she answered.

"She went shopping with Anne, my friend. I had a headache and stayed home."

This isn't your home, I thought with a flash of anger.

"Oh," I said.

"How did you find me?"

I gave her a half smile. I didn't want to betray Roxy's trust so I said, "I'm a detective, remember?"

Thankfully she let that stand. "Do you want to come in?"

"Should I?"

It was her turn to look lost. "I don't know, Jeff. I wasn't—I'm not ready for this."

My heart was breaking again as I asked, "Do you want me to leave?"

Now it was her turn. Tears started flowing from her tightly closed eyes. She nodded her head up and down. I withdrew further against my door because it felt like the right thing to do as she held her wrists to her eyes. "I'm sorry."

"No, no," I told her. I wanted to take her in my arms more than I had ever wanted to before, I wanted to stop the tears, not see her be sad anymore. I slumped backwards against my door instead.

"It feels like you've been gone for months," I said.

"Don't, Jeff. Please."

That told me she didn't want to talk about our personal issues. But that would be the unspoken rule, wouldn't it? The one that automatically fell in place when I broke the first one, the one that said, "Don't try to find me."

After a few deep breaths I asked her, "Do you know a guy named Ralphie Wandorski?" I wasn't sure what I wanted her to say. It would be simplest if she said no, even if it was a lie.

She looked at me while she wiped at her face with her hands. "I know who he is," she said. "Yes."

So Ralphie had been telling the truth. The thought made me think bad things about fire escapes.

"And Roy knew Ralphie?" I held my breath as I realized what I had just said, hoping she didn't catch the word.

"Yes, I think so. Roy told me about him. He said this person Ralphie was going to give him some money."

"Jesus Christ, Lori," I said, running my hand through my hair. "When did all this happen? How come I never knew about it?"

"To what end, Jeff? For what purpose? What would you have done differently?"

There was nothing I could say to that. Quietly I asked, "Why was Ralphie going to give Roy money?"

"Roy said it was a loan but I don't know if that was the truth or not."

We sat like that for a while, the earlier emotion exhausted. Now we existed in a bubble, a self-contained universe of something gone wrong, a stale place we had never known before in our marriage.

"Come back with me," I told her, knowing already the futility of it.

She shook her head.

"Please," I said.

"Stop, Jeff. I can't do it. Not yet."

"Why, goddamnit? Why not?"

She looked away, then took a deep breath. "I'll tel you," she said, "but you need to believe me. When I'm with you, when I see you, I think of Roxy. When I look at you I think about what you did to my little girl's father."

The implication hung between us. "What did I do, Lori?"

She started to sob softly. "I don't know."

"What do you think I did?"

"I don't know!"

"I saved you."

"You probably did," she said. "But Roxy...."

"She's my daughter now and I love her. You know that. If I save you, I save her, too."

"She loves you so much."

Again my wife dried her face with the sleeves of her sweater. I couldn't think of anything to offer her. When she was finished she asked, "Roy isn't coming back, is he?"

I took my time answering. I wanted to tell her the truth, tell her everything, but I didn't dare. Maybe I was just a coward. "I don't think so, Lori."

She nodded, looking down at her hands as she squeezed them together in her lap. "I need to go. Back inside." She turned and pulled on the handle to open the door.

"Just like that?" I asked.

"Please, Jeff. I need more time."

"How much time?"

"Don't ask me that."

"I love you, Lori."

She hesitated and it made me uncomfortable. "I love you, too." She said it like the next word would be "but…."

And then she was gone. I watched her as she went back into the house, arms wrapped across her chest, holding her pain. When the front door closed I didn't wait and I started the Jeep and drove around the corner. I thought I'd park for a while and sort out what I was feeling but once I'd started driving I didn't want to stop. Motion, I thought yet again. Always keep moving. Like a shark.

I didn't stop until I needed gas near the Valdosta exit in southern Georgia. They sold me a wooden bucket filled with peaches for three dollars.

Chapter 15

And now I had a few days of my own time, including the weekend. The drive back home was numbing. I had found my wife and resolved nothing between us. It hadn't brought the two of us closer together and instead, it seemed as though by leaving things the same the wall that was between us had grown thicker and taller. It hadn't helped either of us that I'd found her, except that I was now more aware of the actual resolve she was feeling.

Then there was Roy Evans, who had been gone for a while now. It was clear Lori wanted me to talk about him but she wouldn't push and I couldn't offer anything that would satisfy her need to know. It had to be that way but still, I kept hearing her voice: *When I look at you I think about what you did to my little girl's father....*

At least she had confirmed what Ralphie Wandorski had said about Evans. At the moment, though, I didn't really care. I was tired and I needed to get out of the Jeep and rest my eyes.

There were no messages on the machine when I got back to my house and for some reason I was relieved. I thought about getting really, really drunk but that wasn't something I ever did and there wouldn't have been a point beyond courting oblivion. I would be chasing an end without the means.

I dropped on to the top of my bed and tried to close my eyes. After so much driving they were used to staring and it took a minute before they'd allow themselves to stay shut with a dry, itchy feeling.

Vaguely I wondered what Leslie was doing. Then I put a pillow over the top half of my face and gave in to some much needed sleep.

I didn't wake up until the next morning, which surprised me. The stress was taking its toll. There was probably some guilt mixed up in there, too. In the kitchen I boiled water and made up some packets of instant oatmeal. My mind wasn't on the food and I found myself still thinking of my trip to Alabama. I had mixed emotions about the whole trip. Part of me had thought that if I could just see Lori again, that we might be able to talk things out. When she clearly showed that wasn't possible for her, at least not now, it made me wonder if it ever would be. It wasn't feeling like it.

Everything that had happened with Roy Evans couldn't un-happen, but she could always stay safe. Maybe I'd performed my function, like a male spider, and now it was time to be eaten by my mate. Lori clearly wasn't allowing Roxy to be factored into it.

It occurred to me that Leslie Alcaro seemed to have the opposite problem with her husband. That got me thinking about Carlos Alcaro and the fact that he worked for Rudy Pope. Doing what, I had no idea.

I blew on a spoonful of glop and waited for it to cool. Lori had indeed made contact with Ralphie Wandorski. Ralphie definitely appeared to have known Roy Evans. This made me uncomfortable, mostly because I didn't know the exact nature of their relationship and that Ralphie seemed to know more about both Lori and Roy than I ever could have guessed.

Maybe it was because I was pissed off after my meeting with Lori. Maybe I was creeping ever closer to that point where I just no longer gave a damn. It could even have been that I was just feeling like that much of a fuck up and no matter what I did, things couldn't get much worse. In any case, I decided to take another run at Ralphie Wandorski.

Isabel Marquez had told my partner that Barry Schoenfeld had received several death threats in the months since he had announced his candidacy for mayor of Tampa. Her investigation of his death was focusing on those leads and I couldn't fault her for that. Somebody says they're going to kill someone, and that person ends up murdered, of course you're going to look at that.

I thought it was a mistake to make that the priority in this case but it was helpful to me. Moran and I could play second banana to Tampa and follow up on the connection between Schoenfeld and Shawcross without obviously defying Lieutenant Greene's decree. And there definitely was a connection, we just weren't sure what it was. It might very well be this Little Y porn site but what a cat burglar like Randy Shawcross might be interested with that was beyond me at this point.

Ralphie Wandorski was connected to Pope who almost certainly owned the site whether he knew anything about what happened there or not. And Ralphie was tied to Roy Lee Evans, my wife's first husband, a convict that had been let out of a Texas prison and made a bee line to Lori and his biological daughter, a beautiful girl who called me "Dad." I had thought the threat Roy posed was over but I may have been wrong. Ralphie may be resurrecting it.

I cleaned up my breakfast, showered, and was in the Jeep and heading across the bridge to Tampa before ten o'clock. I had an address for Ralphie that I had pulled from DMV and all I could do was hope that it was accurate.

The address was for a house in an area that had come to be known as New Tampa. When I first took the job in Lakeland I knew the area as nothing more than a back roads short cut from the town of Zephyrhills into Tampa. Zephyrhills was north and west of Lakeland so sometimes it was a useful route away from the interstate. Once upon a time Florida had been the country's fourth largest producer of cattle but that wasn't true anymore. Subdivisions like Tampa Palms, built on top of former pasture land, had taken over. There weren't many places left for the cattle and sight of them was now mostly a rarity.

Tampa Palms was not only a gated community but it was manned by a security guard. I badged my way past him and hoped that he wouldn't feel the need to log my visit. I told him I might be meeting some Tampa cops inside and that seemed good enough for him. At least I didn't have to mention Ralphie by name.

On the other hand, I had no idea where "Wayfarer Lane" was, either, so I cruised the streets slowly for fifteen minutes before I found it. My watch told me it was nearly ten thirty in the morning and I was hoping that Ralphie, being in the late night business that he was, would still be home. Especially since the poor boy would still be recovering from a broken finger.

I pulled the Jeep into his driveway, an interesting rust colored pattern of concrete pavers, and went to his front door. I kicked the bottom of the door a number of times with the side of my foot as I kept my finger jammed on the doorbell. I wanted to come on strong and assertive, especially since I had no justifiable reason for being there.

A fuzzy outline grew visible through the blurred glass that framed the door and the peep hole went suddenly dark. I heard something that was probably a curse word before I heard the dead bolt slide back. Ralphie opened the door wearing a royal blue bath robe, his right hand bandaged and held to his chest, a single digit pointing upwards toward his unshaven chin.

"The fuck you want?" he said.

"Good morning, Ralphie," I said. I wanted to appear confident and on firm footing. I needed to keep him off balance if I had any chance of getting anything useful out of him.

"I'm not talking to you, motherfucker."

He started to close the door but I stopped it with a hard left hand.

"Not an option, bud." Then we did our little stare down thing, because we had to.

"Look," I said. "I didn't mean to bust your finger like that. You brought up my wife, man. That's some shit, talking about my wife to my face like that. What'd you think I would do?"

"You threw me through the fucking window, you prick. You could have killed me."

"I threw you on to a fire escape, Ralphie," I lied. Sort of. "There's a difference."

I could see Ralphie working that over that in his mind. If he was as smart as he thought he was he'd shut the door and call his lawyer but I was counting on him living up to my low expectations.

"Why are you here?"

"To ask you a few questions. I'm not here to arrest you or get physical with you. No hassles. Seriously. You might be able to help me out, and I might take that as a positive consideration for events that could take place in the future."

Ralphie didn't like this. I think he would have been more comfortable if I'd come at him with my fists or a blackjack, something he understood better than a cop nearly apologizing for almost killing him a few days earlier.

"I want to know why you gave money to Roy Evans."

A slow smile broke across his uneven front teeth. "So that's it," he said.

"What is?" I asked. "And, by the way, I'd appreciate it if you left my wife out of your explanation." I smiled back at him.

"Tell me where Roy is."

"What makes you think I know?"

He shrugged.

"I may need to find him myself," I said. "I'd rather not have to do that. Sometimes he talks about my wife, too." The smile faltered just a bit on

Ralphie's face. "Makes me a little crazy sometimes." I shrugged.

This was a different situation from what happened upstairs at the Casa Amarilla. There we had been trying to get a reaction out of Rudy Pope and Ralphie had stepped in as a distraction. That tended to confirm that the Little Y site wasn't some side venture that Rudy wasn't aware of, although it could just be an operation that kicked something back to the boss. Here at Ralphie Wandorski's front door, though, we had a different dynamic. Right now Ralphie couldn't figure what I was really doing there, and it made him nervous. The rash bravado from the restaurant was upstairs somewhere hiding in one of his knockoff suits.

He looked out at his driveway, saw my Jeep. "Where's your partner?" he asked.

"Oh, he's running down another lead," I said. "I didn't think I'd need him over here."

The thought of having me here by myself made him even more nervous. Neither one of us knew what might have happened if Terry Moran hadn't pulled me out of Pope's apartment at the restaurant in Ybor City.

"Let's start easy," I said. "How exactly how do you know Evans?"

"From Houston. We did some cars together when we were kids, joyriding, that kind of thing. No big deal."

"That where you learned about chop shops, Ralphie? That get you set up out here?" I knew that this was how Ralphie had initially hooked up with Pope. He'd been supplying cars to a garage in Tampa that hadn't been kicking the expected payments upstairs. The story was that Pope walked in one day with some muscle, took the garage owner for a ride, and turned the place over to Ralphie who had been, as far as he was concerned, in the right place at the right time, working for the now previous owner. At least that was one of the rumors that swirled around Pope when I was with Tampa PD. The former proprietor hadn't been seen again and Ralphie slowly crawled upwards along the ladder to success.

"Something like that," Ralphie said. "Maybe."

"Why'd Roy come to Tampa Bay?" I asked. "To follow in your footsteps?"

"He came here because of—" He caught himself. "You know. I already told you. He looked me up for some dough, that's all."

"You put him to work?"

He thought about whether he wanted to answer that. Then he looked at me and we both knew that his hesitation meant that he'd have to, he'd been too slow to deny it. He hadn't been quick enough to get away with deflecting it.

"Mr. Pope wouldn't have him, not yet. He doesn't like people when they come right out of the joint, not when they're new."

"It's different when he knows them?"

"Sometimes, yeah. Like if they'd worked for him before."

"So you were going to grace Roy with the gift of cash for old time's sake?"

"It was just a loan. He'd have paid it back."

"Maybe by funneling some hot cars back to you?"

"Fuck off," he said.

"Yeah, I suppose." I turned away for a second and looked at my Jeep, as if I was thinking about leaving.

"How much?"

"What?"

"How much was he after?"

"A few grand. Whatever he could get."

"When was the last time you saw him?"

Ralphie gave it some thought. "I don't know, a month, six weeks, something like that."

"Tell me about pornography, Ralphie. Tell me about the Little Y site."

His expression changed and this time he was too quick for me as he shut the door before I could stop him. There wasn't much more I could do short of breaking in so I gave the door a few kicks and left. I could only hope that I'd left him with enough doubts to confuse him. At least for a while.

Chapter 16

We knew that Little Y's servers were in the Tampa area based on the IP addresses our tech Kelly got when he analyzed Randy Shawcross's computer. It stood to reason that someone around the local scene would know something about it. So alone, lonely, depressed, I hit the bricks. The perfect state of mind for dealing with bottom feeding shit like this.

Most pornography films and videos were produced in California, at least it was before they passed a law that required performers to wear condoms. That opened the door for migration out to the aptly nicknamed Sin City and even across the continent down to my little home state of Florida. Tampa, with its strip clubs surrounding the airport, including the one that looked like a flying saucer had crashlanded onto a motel, had long been a pioneer of that form of entertainment and vice. Drive by those joints now and they all have websites listed on their outdoor signs. In recent years, as Miami has grown its reputation as a party town, so had its slice of the porn industry.

I drove out along Dale Mabry highway, past the football stadium and the minor league baseball complex, with the airport off to the west. Most of the well known strip clubs were either on this street or very nearby. I pulled into one of them more or less at random and badged my way past the bouncer to get out of paying the cover charge.

The place was called the Mondo Erotica and it had an actual bar instead of just a collection of tables, the way some of them did. Tables had chairs and chairs allowed for the presence of multiple laps. I found a seat as far from the stage and the booming music as I could get.

"What can I get you?" an augmented bottle blonde asked me as she slid a paper napkin in front of me.

"Nothing right now, thanks." I wanted to get a sense of the place before I started asking questions.

"There's a two drink minimum," she said.

"Great," I told her. "I just need a minute to work up my thirst." Not the best way to win her confidence but I didn't want to feel too much like a real customer.

The music was blaring, mostly that hip-hop crap that future deaf people were fond of blasting out of the custom systems in their cars. There were three stages in the place set in a rough horseshoe arrangement. Colored lights slashed and swerved across the tables placed in front of each one and then swept upwards over the bodies of the dancers working there. Each stage had two brass poles set between floor and ceiling, some getting more use than others. A DJ was not only changing the music but exhorting groups of men in front of the various stages to throw their money up on the stage. You want to see more of Ginger, he called. Then show her the money! Ten more dollars and she'll take something else off!

I sat around for a few minutes and thought that I may not be in the right frame of mind for this, not today. I was still worn down from the recent road trip, from seeing Lori and having it turn out the way it did. Part of me just didn't want to think for a while. But here I was, working the case, because I had to do something.

The blonde behind the bar occasionally glanced my way and at some point I caught her doing it. She came over and asked, "You ready for a drink now?"

"Just a coke, please."

If she thought I was odd before, her raised eyebrow confirmed it for me. She put the sweating glass on a napkin in front of me, nine tenths ice and a splash of liquid, and said, "You looking for something in particular, buddy?"

I took a sip from my coke. I had to lift the bottom of the glass beyond the horizontal to get it. There wouldn't be any more until the ice began to melt.

"Sure," I said. "What's your name?"

"Sherry," she said as she began wiping down the counter in front of me. "Like the old song. What's yours?"

"Stop it," I said. "Your name's not Sherry and you don't care about mine." I showed her my badge. "I just want to find someone I can ask a few questions, that's all."

"What's the trouble?"

I shook my head. "No trouble. I'm just looking for general information."

"What, you writing a book?"

It was funny the way she said it and I let out a small laugh. "No," I said. "Just trying to figure something out."

"You want to talk to me?"

"Maybe," I said. "My name's actually Jeff."

"LeeAnne," she said. "Though I'm not supposed to tell." She gave me a wink.

"Fair enough, Sherry. Ever do any dancing here?"

She shook her head. "Nope, I'm just one of the bartenders. I'd have to undergo a few additional surgical improvements if I wanted to work out there."

She was a bit on the short side, maybe five foot three or four, and while she was no longer flat-chested, I knew what she was saying. "So why work at a place like this?"

"You kidding?" she said. "Guys come in here not just to drink but to throw their money away. It's like a Vegas casino, you know? They're not going to win anything but they're sure the hell gonna spend like they will. It's like playing slots for some of them. They feed the machine until the money's gone. Sure, most of it goes to them—" she gestured with her head toward the stage—"but they don't want to look cheap over here, either."

"Tips are good, huh?"

"Great tips. Usually. Especially when they bring in a celebrity, some chick who's made movies."

"*Those* kind of movies?" I asked.

"*Those* kind," she agreed. "And it's safer here than most bars, too. We've got enough ex-football players here we could start our own team. They look after all us girls, doesn't matter if we're dancers or not."

I made a second stab at my coke and was rewarded with only a damp lip and wet nose. "What about the internet stuff? I saw a sign outside that says you've got your own website."

She took my glass away and spritzed another shot of coke over the same ice and set it back on my napkin. "All of the clubs have their own sites now, I think. I see the same signs you do."

"You ever look them up? Curiosity, or anything?"

"I've gone to a few. Can't really get in, though, you know, to see the good stuff, without signing up for some kind of membership. Once you give them your credit card number, they'll keep re-upping you till you make them stop."

"Anybody can sign up?"

"Anyone who can check a box that says they're over 18 and has a valid credit card." She went away and filled another drink order, then worked on an order from a waitress. When she came back she said, "You can sign up with a phone number, too, I think. Then it gets billed along with your phone."

She wasn't telling me anything I didn't already know. "Ever hear of a site where it's not open for everyone to join?"

She shook her head against the backdrop of a new mindless set of bass sounds and tuneless chanting. "What would be the point?"

"Private club, I suppose." I took a card out of my pocket and wrote my cell phone number across the back. "Do me a favor, will you, Sherry?" She smiled because I used her alias. "Can you ask around a bit for me? See if anyone's ever heard of a local site that's private like that?"

"What's it called?"

"I'm not sure," I said. "Might be something like 'Little Y.' That's what the URL says."

"Cool," she said and tucked the card into the back pocket of her shorts. "But you can't go yet. You haven't bought your second drink." She smiled as she filled another glass nearly to the rim with cubes.

"You know a guy named Ralphie Wandorski?" Whether it be age, caution, or taste, I knew Rudy Pope would never be seen at a club he didn't own, so I didn't ask.

"Skinny guy, goofy mustache, blows wads of cash in places like this?"

"That's the guy."

"Never heard of him. Why?"

"He got anything to do with any of this?" I asked as I lifted my eyebrows.

She rubbed her thumb against her first two fingers. "Just helps this stuff keep moving, you know what I mean."

"Yeah," I told her. "I do."

I emptied my coke with another half-hearted swig, then wiped my nose with my hand. Sherry smiled. "Last question."

"Good. People are starting to notice you."

When you spend your time in a strip club with a bartender and not the dancers that raises concerns, and not just about the lack of money flowing toward the stage. "Where do the girls come from?"

"Most of the time they walk in. Sometimes agents bring them," she said. "All that happens upstairs." She gave me another smile. "I've never been up there."

"Sherry, my sweet," I said as I got up from the bar. "You're the best girl in the place. The view's much better down here."

I went through the same routine at five more clubs. They were the ones that seemed to be the biggest and most popular ones and all of them served lousy soft drinks. I could only imagine what the quality of the booze would have been. I stayed with the bartenders rather than try management because I figured they could talk to more people and be more motivated by a little extra money to come up with something for me. A club manager might know about Little Y but they would be less likely to tell me about it, especially if they already knew Rudy Pope had a piece of it.

So I went home to a dark and empty house. And it stayed that way, even after I stripped off my suit and climbed into bed after brushing my teeth in the dark. I wondered if it would ever change, and I thought of cute girls with fake names serving drinks to fake people watching their fantasies dance on a stage. Life marches ever onward.

When the phone rang the next morning I almost didn't answer it. If I hadn't been passing my cards out last night I probably wouldn't have but now I rolled over and picked up the cordless from the table next to the bed.

"Dad!" I heard and sat upright in a hurry, not believing the voice.

"Rox? Is that you?"

"You were here! Mom told me! You didn't wait for me!"

The disappointment in her voice was real and it broke my heart. "I couldn't, honey. Your mother—"

"I know, Dad, she's having a hard time right now. But you were right here! You could have waited!"

I didn't know what to say. "Next time, sweetie. Maybe I can come up there again, if it's okay with your mom, and we can do something together."

"No, you can't. We're leaving."

"Leaving? From the Swenson's? Where are you going?"

"I don't know where we're going, mom won't tell me."

"Does she know you're calling?"

"This time she does. She still doesn't know about before. Well, I guess she might have figured it out."

"Is it because I came up there, honey?"

"I love you, Dad. I just wanted to tell you I miss you."

"I love you, too, sweetheart. Never forget that."

"You either, Dad. You never forget." Her voice grew quiet and I could hear background noises through the receiver. "I've gotta go."

There wasn't anything I could do. "Take care of your mother for me, honey, will you?"

"I'm trying, Dad. It's just she's just so sad all the time." And in a whisper she added, "I'll call you again, okay?"

"I'll be waiting, honey. I love you."

"'Bye, Dad. Love you, too." And she was gone. Again.

I wanted to go back to sleep but I couldn't. I wasn't tired, I just didn't want to face the world again. There was a strange little book I read a few years ago about Libbie Custer, General George A.'s wife. Widow, rather. It was by some guy named Poolman and it was called *A Wounded Thing Must Hide*. That was me, a Wounded Thing. People complain about the heat and humidity during the Florida summers but what about the brilliant, unrelenting sunshine and the lack of anything gloomy? What about losing the ability to wallow in a goddamned earned depression because of the unceasing *light* permeating everything? Where was I supposed to hide?

I threw myself on the living room couch, squinting at the glare coming through the big glass window looking out on the old sycamore in the front lawn. My watch told me it was nearly eight o'clock, later then my usual six o'clock wake up time, but then "usual" didn't mean the same thing as it used to. Last night I didn't get home until almost three and I could smell the stink of stale strip club and cigarettes in my hair and on my skin. I didn't feel like showering mostly because I wanted to do something. Getting up suddenly, I peeled off my tee shirt and went through the house and out the back to the pool and dove in, the water peeling back my boxers. I pulled them back up and then swam the length of the pool and back underwater, barely managing to hold my breath until I broke the water's surface.

Things hadn't gone well with Lori but I couldn't have expected anything different. She told me to stay away, that she didn't want to see me, and I tracked her down anyway. I folded my arms over the edge of the pool and laid my head across my forearms. Even this early I could feel the intensity of the sun. Lori was being honest with me, though, I hoped. She reacted just the way I thought she would. But I still had to go, I had to find out if Ralphie Wandorski had been telling the truth about Roy Evans.

Anyway, that's what I kept telling myself.

The end result was that it just contributed to the pain. That Ralphie knew Lori, that they had talked about Roy. Ralphie knew about Lori leaving which means that whether she had told him about it before or after, the fact was that there was something else going on, some secret communication, that had taken place behind my back.

Oh, hell, I just didn't know what I thought I had. Maybe Lori called Ralphie from her pal's house in Alabama after she left, which maybe meant the rest of it was none of his business, that he didn't know or suspect anything that could come back at me.

Oh, Christ, Lori, what did you do? Maybe I should be asking what I had really done to her. I thought I knew but things weren't exactly working out the way they were supposed to.

I kicked away from the wall and began to do freestyle laps from end to end. The pool wasn't long enough to get into a good rhythm but I pounded the water for short spurts, churning the water to a rough chop. I stopped with my shoulders burning and water up my nose and down my throat but it was the coughing that finally took enough out of me to make me stand still.

Pulling myself onto the edge of the deck I sat, back to the sun, the cheerful happy rays of the sun, and let it burn the water off the skin of my back.

Burn, baby, burn, you bastard.

A sudden noise from the house made me whirl about. Leslie Alcaro was sitting in the same chair on the lanai that she'd been in before. "Good morning," she called.

At first I wasn't sure if I was happy to see her or not. "Doorbell still not working?" I asked.

"Not when you don't answer."

"Feel free to come around back whenever."

She decided I wasn't being as harsh as I sounded, and in a way that made it so. "Thanks," she said. "I will."

"There's a coffee machine in the kitchen," I said.

"Trying to get rid of me already?"

I looked down at myself in the water. "I'm, uh, not really wearing a suit."

"Roger that," she said, standing up. "I'll be inside."

Leslie went to the kitchen and I carefully pulled myself out of the pool. I peeled off my shirt and wrung it out over the deck then dropped it on a dry spot. Keeping my shorts in place, I twisted the material as best I could, soaking my legs with the runoff. I followed Leslie into the house; she was figuring out the coffee maker. From what I could tell, she didn't turn around as I walked behind her and down the hall to the rest of the house.

I came out of the bedroom to the aroma of whatever coffee Lori had bought. I don't drink the stuff. I like the smell but the taste never lives up to it for me. Leslie was seated at the kitchen island, cradling a steaming mug in front of her with both hands. "You want a cup?" she asked.

"No thanks." I hung the towel that I had been using to dry my hair around my neck and stood across the island from her. "This is your second unannounced visit, counselor. To what do I owe the pleasure?"

A frown took hold of her face and she looked down into her mug. "Is that okay? I'm probably overstepping, I know—"

"It's fine."

"It's just that—"

"Leslie." She stopped talking. "It's fine. Really."

She nodded her head without looking at me. She'd made some sort of decision but I could only guess at what it was.

"I wanted to see you," she said. "I wanted to tell you something." Her purse was on the island next to her and she dug something out of it and slid it over to me across the countertop. "This belongs to Carlos."

I picked up the cell phone, turned it over. It wasn't a smart phone or anything expensive. It was a bottom of the line phone available at most convenience stores. Burners, we called them. Phones that were bought with prepaid minutes and not registered with personal information or with any phone company.

"And you have it because…."

She took a small sip of her coffee. "Carlos and I have been apart for a while now. I— I wanted to make things official with a formal separation agreement. Yesterday I called him and he finally agreed to meet with me."

"Where?"

"Ybor," she said. "At a coffee shop on 22nd. He didn't know what I wanted to see him about, and he got a little upset when he found out. The whole time he had this phone in his hand. He began to get—angry." She stopped and drank some more from her mug. "So angry."

"You okay?"

She waved me off. "I'm fine. It's just hard to see him like that. After a half an hour or so, when I'd just asked him to sign the paperwork, another phone rang, one he had in his pocket. He took it out and saw the number, then he told me to stay where I was and he walked outside."

"Was it a phone like this?"

Leslie shook her head. "No, it was something new and fancy. But he'd left this one on the table. I wondered why he had two phones and I picked this one up. When he came back in, I was still holding it. He barely looked at me. He picked up my pen, wrote out a dirty name, said something nasty and stormed out of the place." She looked up at me. "I was scared, Jeff. He scared me."

I reached my hand across to her and she met me half way with one of hers. "It'll be okay, Leslie." Which is always easy to say when you don't know what's going on and aren't the one involved in the situation.

"Maybe," she said. "So I still had this one in my hand. Carlos had gone. I was getting up to go outside and look for him, and then it rang. I thought maybe it was him, calling to see if I had it, so I answered."

"But it wasn't him."

"No. It was a girl's voice, someone who sounded young, anyway. She asked if this was the number to call about the free tickets to Florida."

"Free tickets?"

Leslie nodded. "She said she'd gotten the number from Craigslist and was looking for the details on how to get the plane tickets."

"Airline tickets?"

"For her and a friend."

Something started to take shape in my head. I saw Carlos in Pope's bar the day Moran and I went over to see Pope and Ralphie Wandorski. I remembered Sherry and the other girls I'd talked to at the strip clubs in Tampa and wondered if I'd just gotten closer to an answer.

"What did you tell her?"

"I didn't know what to tell her. I said I was just holding the phone for a friend and that she should try back later."

"And did she?"

"She hasn't yet."

"Why did you keep the phone, Leslie?"

She pulled her hand away. I hadn't noticed I'd still been holding it. "I don't know, Jeff. I was scared of Carlos, of seeing him that way, I guess. And I didn't want to leave it there."

"So you brought it to me."

"Was that wrong?"

"Well, you stole your husband's phone"—I saw her wince when I called him that—"but beyond that, I appreciate your trying to help me."

"What should I do?"

I thought about it for a moment. "You going back to Tampa from here?"

She nodded.

"Then take it back to that coffee shop and leave the phone in the bathroom or somewhere. Let someone else deal with it. Or you could just throw it off my dock out back. Carlos will probably be looking for it, though, so you may not want it coming back at you if you can avoid it."

She pushed her cup away and came to me around the island. I was only a little surprised when she lifted her arms and gave me a quick hug. I could feel her curves against my chest and it felt nice. Too nice. With Lori everything seemed like a giant conflict right now but with Leslie, things were simple and her touch felt good. It was welcome, and even though I liked it part of me knew it could be the biggest complication of all. Still, I held her until she decided to let go.

Chapter 17

I'd brought home the CDs containing the porn stuff from Randy Shawcross's computer and I settled in behind my computer after Leslie had gone. I put in one of the discs at random. It contained only one video and I double clicked on the file name to start it.

The faces were pixelated out, just like in the pictures and the two videos I'd already seen. There was a woman, a redhead apparently, spread out naked across a bed. A man entered the frame, tall; it was difficult to make out his hair color behind the distortion. He was naked, too, and he didn't waste his time getting down to business.

The furniture in the room that was visible seemed in good taste if not luxurious; this wasn't taking place in a cheap motel somewhere. There was a headboard on the bed that may have been mahogany or walnut with a matching night table and an antique-looking lamp perched on a lace doily. A different room than the other videos, but in the same class of quality.

That was the first difference from typical porn. This wasn't a hotel room or a stripped-down rented house. Another, it just hit me, was who was doing what to who on the screen. There is more or less a standard formula to most porn scenes and although I wasn't sure what exactly I was watching, I knew that this video wasn't following the standard.

In this one the man started as dominant and he didn't seem to be following a particular routine. He seemed to be all over the place with what he wanted to do. The more I watched it the more frantic he appeared, mauling the woman's breasts with his hands and mouth, then moving down between her legs, then back up again. He was like a high schooler in the back seat of dad's car with a prom date.

The scene was well lit, the shots kept in focus, the camera work smooth; a professional looking film with amateur performers acting without a script. This was my impression. The action itself wouldn't cut it with a hard core porn freak.

There was a surprise at the very end of the video. With nearly two minutes to go, the pair was joined by another naked figure—a man. Rather than paying attention to the woman on the bed, the new actor climbed onto the mattress, his knees next to the other man's, pixelated head meeting pixelated head. Hands began exploring, bodies turned to face each other, and the woman on the bed seemingly forgotten as the video faded to black.

I thought: Now that was different.

Each of the four videos cached on Randy's computer were within seconds of being the same length. This seemed too odd to be a coincidence.

I watched the other two video CDs and saw the same anomalies each time: the high class settings, professional quality production work, amateur seeming activity. The soundtracks were all dubbed in west coast jazz style music. The women in each video were different but the man, at least the one who started each episode, was the same.

The same man, these videos a part of his oeuvre.

I'd scanned through the photos at the office with Terry and the two of us had watched maybe a minute each of two of the videos. It wasn't something I felt naturally at ease doing, watching people having sex on the screen of my computer at work, my partner looking over my shoulder. Here at home, alone, it was different and it was easier to look at what was happening more carefully. I went through the pictures looking for similarities to the people in the videos, after a while forgetting that what I was looking at was supposed to be erotic. Nothing was adding up here. If the material was supposed to be arousing, I couldn't see how all the effort in production values made up for the lack of particularly stirring content.

I closed the windows on the computer and turned off the monitor and thought about my wife, about the last time we had been together romantically. Before Roy Evans had disappeared. Before Lori decided to leave.

I went into the bedroom and stripped off my clothes. Suddenly I felt like taking a shower. I still smelled like chlorine from being in the pool earlier but that wasn't the reason. The hot water lasted for nearly fifteen minutes but the water that came afterwards wasn't cold enough to drive me out. The fact that it changed did, that I was now living alone and my job had become a form of hell, and that I didn't see a way out of the circumstances I had created for myself. Got to keep moving, I told myself as I shut off the water and toweled myself dry.

Never stop.

Darkness eventually fell around nine o'clock but it was far too late to help my mood. I dressed in some light cotton slacks, put a tie over a button down shirt, and pulled on a blue sport coat. Basic cop uniform but that's what I wanted. Last night I shook down the help and tonight I was going after the talent itself.

It stood to reason that if there was a porn site operating locally they were drawing from girls already in the area. At least that was my first thought; for all I knew they were merely showing films and pictures shot in Timbuktu. There was no way to really tell at this point but I saw Rudy Pope strictly as a homeboy. Keeping to his own patch was how he had stayed around and stayed alive all these years. Unless the films were a buy and resell kind of thing, he was producing the stuff here and that meant someone around would know something, even if it weren't the bartenders and other staffers at the local clubs.

No matter what, I couldn't shake the feeling that something was off, that I wasn't seeing the big picture. Leslie's news from earlier was disquieting, too.

Sunday night wasn't a big party night but what the hell else was I going to do. I'd spent the afternoon in the pool, washed the boat, went for a run, fixed the screen in a garage window. Anything I could find to keep busy, to keep my mind out of the dark places. Thoughts of Ralphie, Roy, Lori and Roxy fought random bouts of depression as I somehow pulled my way through the day. When I took my time off I told the department I wouldn't be back until Tuesday but I was seriously considering going in tomorrow as usual, just so I wouldn't have to go through all this again.

In the meantime, I could at least get some legwork done on the Shawcross case. Or the Schoenfeld case, or even a different one against Rudy Pope, whatever it turned out to be. I wondered if Izzy Marquez was making any headway on their political death threat angle on Schoenfeld. If that worked out, then the connection with the King of Cats could just be coincidental at best, and all of this might not be worth the paper it took to stuff in a file. Tampa's angle did take the focus off Shawcross, though, which was the only reason Greene was staying off our backs on this one. Not that I was on the clock anyway. What Greene didn't know….

It was a little after ten o'clock when I hit the Dale Mabry strip and pulled into the parking lot of the Mondo Erotica. The bouncer recognized me from the night before and waved me through before I could show my badge. This time I went for a table rather than the bar. I wanted to talk to the dancers tonight, singly if I could, and I found a seat three tables away from the center stage.

I checked out the bar to see if Sherry/LeeAnne was working tonight but I didn't see her. A waitress with a gold sequined vest and tiny spandex shorts appeared at my side, placed her hand on my shoulder, and asked, "What'll it be, honey?"

The physical contact was a nice touch. The first hint at promised intimacy for the customer. It got people a lot closer to paying for that first lap dance than they probably realized. "Just a coke," I told her. "Light on the ice, if you can."

"Be right back, sugar," she said.

The music was awful. I grew up in a house of music but the unspoken rule had been that if it wasn't Sinatra or one of his boys, it wasn't music. My parents are gone now but in the last years of their lives they never turned on the radio unless it was to a news talk station. They had begun to obsess with politics. Maybe the same thing was happening to me, only on a different scale.

The waitress glided by and left the coke on the table in front of me. I was still reaching for my wallet when I noticed she wasn't waiting. She either put me on a tab or made me for a cop and was comping me the drink. I took out a ten dollar bill and dropped it on the table anyway. She could pick it up later.

On the stage in front of me was a heavily made up blonde, too skinny for her boob job, wrapping her arms around the bronze fireman pole and swinging to the floor with one long, white nyloned leg extended. There were similar girls doing similar things on the stages to the left and right. Rather than assault the girl's g-string and interrupt her routine, customers were simply placing paper money on the stage and smiling up at her.

I took a twenty from my wallet and made sure she was looking when I went up to the stage and dropped it on top of a loose pile of ones and fives. She smiled at me and I went back to my table just in time to stop the waitress from picking up my untouched coke.

"I thought it was empty," she said.

"They come that way."

She scooped up the tenner and disappeared. The dancer on the stage went through another song, some hip hop or rap abomination that sampled one of the truly innovative funk songs I remembered from high school. If I focused on those parts, I could almost enjoy it. When it was over, White Nylons bent forward to gather her financial booty, augmented breasts retaining their shape as she bent and swayed. She got my twenty, looked up and blew me a kiss. I returned it with a smile and a nod.

It wasn't too much longer before she appeared at my table. That was the game. "Buy me a drink?" she asked. The girls from the other stages had also appeared on the floor, looking for the patrons they pegged as the biggest spenders. New girls had taken the stage, new music blared from the speakers, new exhortations spewed forth from the DJ.

"Sit down," I said and pushed the chair to my left out from under the table.

"I'm Cyndy," she said.

"With an 'S' or a 'C'?" I asked.

She laughed. "With a 'C'," she said. "But with two y's and no other vowels. It might be better the other way, though. Starting it with an 'S.'" A sly and practiced wink. "What's your name?" She leaned in close, arms folded across her chest which was now covered with a sheer gauzy shirt that opened down the middle.

"Call me Jeff," I said. Without saying anything the waitress deposited a napkin and a glass with something that may have been champagne in front of Cyndy. She wouldn't be comping me drinks for the girls so I must be running a tab. And these drinks were expensive, I knew, at least double if not triple what they'd be in a normal bar.

"How'd you like my show, Jeff?"

"You were the best one up there," I told her.

She smiled and picked up her drink, her eyes never leaving mine.

"Listen, Cyndy," I said. "I'd like to ask you something."

"Really?"

I showed her my badge. "I need some help on a case."

She laughed and took my badge from my hand. "I've heard that one before." She studied my ID, both badge and picture. "How come this says St. Petersburg?"

"That's where my case is. Tampa's where the help is."

She pursed her lips, reached for her champagne. "What is it you think

I can do?"

I reclaimed my ID and put it back in my pocket. "First of all, keep drinking. I don't want to jam you up with anybody."

"I will. Thank you."

"Secondly, I want you to know that all I'm looking for is information. Anonymous information. I'm not vice or anything like that. I'm just trying to figure something out and nothing you tell me can get you in trouble with anyone. I won't write it down, I won't remember your name, nobody else will show up and hassle you."

"What do I get for doing that?"

"First, do you believe me?"

"Sure. I guess."

I took my wallet out and put it on the table. "You get a healthy tip without having to do a lap dance."

"I don't mind the dancing." Cyndy took a sip from her champagne glass and winked. Couldn't stop herself. "What do you want to know?"

"If I was looking to put up a website, like the one for this place here, and I wanted some girls for pictures, what would I do?"

"What kind of pictures?"

"Does it matter?"

"Sure it matters. You want girls for straight sex, solo modeling gigs, girl on girl stuff, orgy scenes—"

"Okay, okay," I said. "I get it." I took a turn at my coke and noticed she was watching my eyes again. "Straight sex shots, mostly. Maybe with video, sometimes with multiple partners."

"Ooh, now you're getting interesting." She drained her glass and set it back on the table with a plop. "Girls know people, you know? Like you, coming in here, talking to me. You could get me interested in something, and maybe I have a friend or two I can bring along. It happens like that sometimes."

"Management doesn't mind?"

She held up her empty glass. Within five seconds the waitress had replaced it with a new one. "Not as long as you keep buyin'."

"There's no conflict of interest with their own sites?"

"Hell, no, honey, not in this business. We have to pay the boss just to be able to dance here. The girls go with whoever will pay them. Everybody knows that. Most go back to their regular gigs, or else they find new ones. That's just the way it is. There are always clubs, and there are always girls."

"You ever hear of a site or a company called something like 'Little Y'?"

She giggled. "Nope. Sounds like a new kink."

Cyndy seemed to know the game, but it wasn't helping. "Any idea why you'd blur out the faces of the girls in the pictures? And the men?"

"The faces?" she asked, shaking her head. "Haven't seen that before. I've seen where they'll blur pussies and cocks and shit, but not the faces. That's kind of funny. Who cares about the faces?"

She was saying something that had been bothering me. You wouldn't hide the faces for any kind of censorship; there was only one reason that came to mind. I threw down a couple of twenties and thanked her for her time. I felt like hitting myself in the head with a brick as I wound my way through the tables and out of the club. Outside the warm humidity wrapped me like a blanket and I could feel a hint of condensation forming on my skin.

You would hide the faces in a porn movie for the same reason you'd hide a face anywhere else: you wouldn't want them recognized. It wasn't anything about the acts that was secret, it wasn't about the pornography itself, it was who was about the people who were doing it.

I sat in my car with the engine turned on and the air conditioning blasting while I tried to figure out if I had actually stumbled on a revelation that made sense. Or even one that was helpful.

Other websites don't blank out the faces and identifying characteristics of their performers, nor do any porn flicks or magazines I'd ever heard of. The performers retain their anonymity, assuming they want to, by being faces in the crowd, ones among the many. Background noise. And it isn't their faces that anyone is looking at. Usually.

I knew some performers didn't try to hide. There were some who had crossed over into production, retaining ownership of the products they made, putting more of the profits into their own pockets. These people promoted themselves and their names like advertising brands. But the performers that didn't want to be recognized, the ones that didn't want their mothers, fathers, sons, daughters and clergy to know what they did for money, were protected by flimsy stage names or just plain chance. Their identities weren't threatened by the people who view their product. Again, usually.

If the talent working in the rest of the industry didn't care about having their identities obscured, if they didn't mind the possibility of recognition, remote or otherwise, then why would it matter to Little Y?

Little Y is private, and because it's private, the administrators of the site control who sees what's in it. So what if it was possible for the clientele to recognize the performers. If you didn't want them to, then it would be natural to obscure the faces and leave the other parts, but the question was still why.

Something was finally making some sense. Now I just had to figure out what it had to do with Randy Shawcross and Barry Schoenfeld.

For the hell of it, I made the rounds of the same clubs I had been to the night before but nobody I talked to said they'd ever heard of an operation called Little Y or any website that was local and running as a private site. It seemed the girls that worked the clubs were mostly drawn by the lure of the clubs themselves. Websites were a separate thing. Porn stars could make good money working the clubs once they'd established names for themselves, but I was now convinced that Little Y wasn't putting out sequences with professionals. I didn't believe Little Y's "performers" wanted to be known.

This begged the question, where did the participants come from?

I thought about this a lot, and about Leslie's showing me her husband's phone, and the information about free flights to Florida. It may be nothing, but Carlos Alcaro's connection with Rudy Pope couldn't be overlooked.

I spent almost three hundred bucks that I couldn't expense to the department but it kept my mind off everything else for a while.

I still had one more official day off so I called Terry Moran the next morning. I figured I could work on my own time if I wanted and this way I wouldn't have to expose myself to the station. He sounded happy to hear my voice and I appreciated it.

I told him what I'd been doing the past few nights and he lowered his voice as he said, "Man, you crazy. You did the job in Tampa behind Greene's back?"

"I was on my own time."

"With your own badge, dude."

"What's your point?"

"Just don't get caught, is all. Find anything out?"

I tried to tell him about my insights into the world of pornography and hidden identities but he didn't seem impressed. Maybe I didn't explain it well.

"What now?"

"Have you heard anything from Izzy Marquez?"

"Nothing. I have a call in to her now, just to keep our hand in."

"Can either you or Kelly from Tech Services get Tampa to burn CDs of the cached Little Y stuff on Schoenfeld's computer?"

"I can ask Ding Dong but it might get back to Greene."

"Go through Kelly first. Talk to him in person. Appeal to his inner nerd. If he can make it happen tech-to-tech there might be fewer ripples."

"I'll get it done. What're your plans today?"

"I'm going to Disneyworld, what else. But you can get me on my cell."

Chapter 18

My phone rang when I was on the Howard Frankland bridge crossing into Tampa. It was Leslie.

"Hey, girl," I said.

"Hey, Jeff." She sounded concerned. "Where are you?"

"Actually, I'm headed your way. What's up?"

She told me about bringing Carlos' phone back to that coffee shop. "I went to the counter and asked for change for a twenty, and when I was going to hand over the phone, say I found it on the floor under a table, it started to ring. The owner just looked at me across the counter."

"Did you answer?"

"No, but the owner looked at me strangely. What if he recognized me?"

"As having been there with Carlos?" I changed lanes to avoid one of the inexplicable random lane slowdowns common in Tampa. It would release in a few minutes, again for no apparent reason. "He'd have to recognize Carlos' phone, too, for it to come back on you. What happened?"

"I just put the phone on the counter and told him where I'd found it. He didn't say anything. I took my change and got out of there."

"Listen, Leslie, you've got to relax. You no longer have the phone. If Carlos hasn't been back to the coffee shop he will, he'll get his phone, and everything will be okay."

She took a deep breath. "I hope so."

"You're not scared, are you?"

She hesitated before she said, "No, of course not. It's just Carlos."

"How's he taking the separation?"

"Well, he didn't sign the papers but that may have been him just being a jerk as opposed to him wanting to fight it." I heard her sigh. "Doesn't matter, anyway. It's been over a long time. Right now I'm trying not to get caught up in his bullshit or my job becomes at risk."

"Your job was at my risk when you took my case."

"Not my fault, it was assigned. As long as I get you kicked out on your ass, everyone will love me."

"Sadly, that's probably true."

She told me that Tampa PD had reached out to her with a tentative hearing date in another six months.

"Six months?" I tried to imagine waiting it out for that amount of time. Ouch. "Why so long?"

"Like I said before, the longer it takes, the more time the publicity has to dissipate. Also, I think they look at you as St. Pete's problem now, and if you self-destruct there—"

"Then Tampa isn't the bad guy. Not a bad deal all around. Except for me."

"Well—"

"No, Leslie, I made my bed. Doesn't matter. I may just give them what they want anyway. It's too damn hard trying to make it work like this. I'm not sure I can see it through."

"Why not?" She sounded cross. "No, forget that. I don't know what you're going through. What are you doing in Tampa?"

"Still trying to figure things out. It's this Shawcross case. It has a Tampa connection and I need to nail it down."

"No matter what?"

"Young lady, I think you're starting to get to know me."

I didn't go anywhere but back to the Dale Mabry strip. Most of the upper scale clubs were open for lunch and they did a surprisingly brisk business. Or maybe it wasn't so surprising. I tended to use my lunch break to get away from the job and maybe for some guys the best way to do the same thing is to watch naked women slide on a pole.

The parking lot in the Mondo Erotica had been nearly full but there were still a few tables open. Some of the parties must have come in multiple cars. There were even a few women in there, which surprised me; they were all sitting at tables with men.

I had just sat down and ordered a coke while I picked up the menu, wondering what was safe to eat. For some reason the place didn't strike me as a natural venue for food service.

"Hi," said a voice as a blonde bundle wearing a red and white striped shirt burst onto the chair to my left. "Remember me?"

It took me a second. I was thrown off by the apparent enthusiasm and actual clothing. "Sherry?" I said at last. "Wait. LeeAnne. Excuse me."

"You do remember!" she said and reached out and brushed my triceps with a light slap of her fingers.

"I always remember the ones who keep their clothes on. You were tending bar, right over there," I pointed over her shoulder. "A couple of nights ago."

She let the first remark pass. "You're becoming quite the regular, aren't you? Too many dollar bills weighing you down?"

"I can't find enough places to get rid of them."

"Say no more," she said, mock serious. "You have come to the perfect spot."

The waitress dropped a coke in front of me and didn't stop to see if I was ready to order. This was part of the game, I knew. Slower service to keep the customers drinking, spending and tipping. "Did you want something?" I asked Sherry/LeeAnne.

"Oh, no thanks. I was just in to pick up my paycheck and lo and behold, there you were. Mr. Saturday Night. Find out about your websites?"

I shook my head. "Not really, no. Why? Did you think of anything new for me?"

"Well, actually," she said, leaning closer. "I may be able to help after all. I was going to call you when I got home."

"What's up?"

"I have a friend, she used to work here. She quit three or four months ago, not just this place, she says, but the whole dancing thing."

"She retired?"

"Now she calls herself an actress."

"How does that help me?"

"An actress? In Tampa?" She shook her shoulder length hair. "Ain't no Broadway around here. How's she' going to make a living being an 'actress' in this town?"

"You think she's fronting."

"I ran into her at the makeup counter at the mall by the airport. Her name's Stacey. She was buying two kinds of foundation, cream and powder. And a lot of the cream."

I shook my head and tried not to laugh. "You've lost me."

Sherry/LeeAnne gave me a pout. "I asked her why she needed both kinds. She said she uses them for work. The powder for her face so it doesn't clog her pores. She uses the cream because she has chicken pox scars on her neck and along the tops of her shoulders and down into her chest, up here." She fluttered her hands around her sternum.

Maybe it was the gender gap or a lack of knowledge concerning women's makeup but I still wasn't seeing it.

"What kind of acting work makes a woman care more about what her body looks like, instead of her face?"

I raised my eyebrows. "You think she's making dirty movies."

She sat back and smiled at me, happy to have made her point. "Well, if you met her, you wouldn't think she was qualified for much else." In a whisper she added, "Not many of these girls are."

"The smart ones all tend bar." The waitress passed by another time without stopping. "I'd like to meet her. How can I reach her?"

"I have her number. Anything in it for me?"

Now I was glad I hadn't ordered a meal; this was getting expensive. "I can float you a little something," I said. If this Stacey had anything useful to say, I might be able to get reimbursed from the snitch fund. But that would depend on Lieutenant Greene and I wasn't sure I could go there.

"Great," she said. "I could use the help. I'll call you as soon as I get a hold of her."

She took some money from my hand and I got her to tell me the girl's full name before she left. I threw a couple of those pesky dollar bills on the table and left before the waitress had another chance to avoid taking my order.

The bright sunshine hurt my eyes and they were still adjusting when I stopped in a sandwich shop and got an entire meal for what I would have spent at the Mondo Erotica for a soda or two. No tip necessary but I dropped another dollar bill into a jar on the counter. When the server handed over the food, I took it out to my car and ate it with the front door open, dripping sauce onto the pavement in front of me.

I called Moran at his desk but he didn't answer. My watch told me it was a little past one; he may still be at lunch.

As soon as I took my thumb off of the cancel button, the phone rang in my hand. I checked the display: Terry Moran.

"Speak of the devil," I said when I answered. "I just tried your desk."

"Where are you?" he asked.

"Tampa. Where are you?"

"I'm at Roy Lee Evans' house. You want to come down here?"

Oh hell no. "I'm on my way." I hung up without saying goodbye. Shit, I thought. Shit, shit, shit.

Chapter 19

The canary yellow Monte Carlo was pulled up in front of an overgrown lawn belonging to a peeling cinderblock house, a whole nest of city code violations. The yard was mostly dirt with knee high weeds, maybe a splotch of crab grass hear and there. Sand spurs. I parked across the street and got out of the car. Moran was nowhere to be seen.

He may have been inside, or somewhere in the back. I started across the street and then I saw him coming down the sidewalk, half a block away and I moved to meet him.

"What's up, partner?" he called.

"I was enjoying my day off. What's going on?"

"Don't know," he said. "I've been up and down the street talking to the neighbors. This isn't the kind of neighborhood where the residents all hang out together but I thought I'd check it out."

"And?"

"Nobody's seen our boy Roy Lee for a while."

"How long?"

"Months, it seems."

"Hmm," I said, carefully neutral. I was thankful I was wearing sunglasses. "What brought you out here?"

"You pissed?"

"No, I'm just asking."

We started walking back toward Evans' house. "Ralphie Wandorski said he was going to give Evans some money, right? We don't know what for. So I thought, what if Evans was doing something for Pope through Ralphie? The money could have been payment for services rendered. If those services had something to do with the Little Y pornography site, we might have another lead to work here. Follow?"

"I follow, but it seems thin."

"I thought I'd look the man up anyway."

"I thought we said we weren't going to do that."

"*We* didn't, I did. I thought I would save you the aggravation." He was looking at my face. "That okay with you?"

I didn't say anything, just nodded.

"Man, it didn't work, did it?" he said. "I'm sorry, partner, I wasn't trying to go around your back, it's just been bothering me, letting it lie, it just seemed like it could be a loose end worth checking out."

How do you argue with somebody who thinks they're looking out for you?

"There's something you ought to know," I told him. We stopped walking on the street one house down from Evans'. "I went over to Ralphie's house the other day. In Tampa Palms."

"What? Are you flippin' crazy? He invite you in for tea, you talk football for a while? Jesus Christ."

"I had the same thoughts you did. I thought he might be willing to talk to me."

"You mean you thought he would still be afraid of you." He looked at the sidewalk, his hands on his hips. "The day I figure out what goes on in that head of yours...."

"Bastard had his hand in a cast, index finger pointing straight up. He told me Pope didn't hire cons straight out of the joint, not if he didn't know them. Ralphie said the money he was going to give Evans was a straight loan."

"You believe him?"

I shrugged. "Who can tell when you deal with these assholes. But that's what he said." We started walking again. "Makes sense, anyway."

Moran kept watching his feet as we went along. "You know, if Greene had the balls to really keep an eye on you—"

"I know," I said. "Good thing he's got you."

We walked up Evans' driveway and over to the front door. There was a mail slot set in the door with no box behind it. By lifting the metal flap we could see a pile of uncollected mail, an assortment of junk, magazines, catalogs and a few envelopes.

"Looks like the neighbors were right," I said. "Did you check the garage?"

"Empty," said Terry. We walked over there anyway, stepping over and through the weeds. It was an attached one-car, with windows in the corroding aluminum door and a windowed door along the side wall. Wiping the grime from the glass we could see inside a little better but it didn't matter as it was truly empty aside from a few trash bags stacked near the door leading to the inside of the house.

"Bet those smell ripe," said Moran.

We walked around out back. If anything the condition of the yard there was worse. In a better neighborhood the other residents would have been complaining to the city. "You run down the landlord?" I asked.

Moran checked his watch. "Should be here any minute. That's why I called you. Thought you might want to go inside with me."

I cocked my head and knew I should shut up if I could. "Why?"

"I don't know," he said, and walked ahead to peer inside the next set of windows.

Someone was bound to come here to check the house eventually. I never imagined it would be me.

I went around to the front of the house and picked the sand spurs off my lower pant legs and socks. A rusting Chevy Blazer pulled into the driveway and made an abrupt stop. Out popped a short Latino man, Mexican or Cuban, wearing a floral print shirt, board shorts, and a pair of leather flip flops. He looked at the condition of the yard and swore in Spanish.

"Are you the police?" he asked me.

"Yes, sir. You are…?"

"Florio Alvarez. This is my house. You're not the one who called me?"

"That would be me," said Moran as he came around the corner of the house. "I'm Detective Moran. This is Detective Prentiss."

Terry started asking him questions about Evans and I walked back up the driveway and looked through the windows again, wondering if I'd missed anything. After a few minutes Moran and Alvarez came up behind me.

"Ready to go inside?" Moran asked.

"After you," I said.

Both of us stood aside for Alvarez who worked his way through a large ring of keys and found one for the front door. Inside I bent down and sorted the mail, looking for anything unusual. Moran and Alvarez went past me down the short hallway as I made one pile out of the magazines and catalogs and another of the envelopes. Purple ink caught my eye and I plucked the envelope out of the pile.

Lori's handwriting. I looked up but the other two were around the corner, in the kitchen. I folded the envelope and slid it into my back pocket. I took a closer look at the rest of the mail but they were just bills addressed to Evans and more junk.

I brought the two piles into the kitchen and dropped them on the counter. Moran was looking into the refrigerator. "Beer, milk gone sour, there's a chicken in here gone green." There was a garbage can on the floor that smelled just as awful. Mouse droppings littered the floor around it. I nudged the plastic container with my foot and a pair of roaches scurried over the side and disappeared under the cabinet baseboards. Alvarez was keeping a running commentary about the unreliability of his renters and Moran and I ignored him.

In the bedroom, the bed wasn't made but the sheets looked flat and smooth, as though they hadn't been slept in for a while. There was one pillow, dented, and it looked to me as though it didn't belong with those sheets. It's the light, I thought. I thought of the last time I was there: you don't see these differences in the dark of night.

Moran opened the closet. Hanging rod about half full, piles on the floor. "No suitcases or bags," he said.

I went to the bureau and pulled open the drawers. A few things were in each, not much. "No underwear or socks."

"You think he packed up and left?"

"No suitcase, no undies. There a toothbrush in the bathroom?"

Terry went around the bed and into the attached bath. "Nope. Medicine cabinet's cleaned out."

I turned toward Alvarez who looked as though life were kicking him deep in the cajones. "You know anything about this?"

"I know the son of a bitch is two months behind in his rent. I've been in Miami for a few weeks so I haven't made it over here to talk to him. He wasn't answering his phone when I called. Beyond that—" He shrugged.

We filed out into the living room. Nineteen inch TV on a pressboard screw it together stand in the corner, DVD player on a shelf below. Orange covered couch, frayed fabric at each corner. The same low pile carpeting as in the rest of the house, soiled and gray in the traffic paths. The only other room was a second bedroom that looked completely unused.

"What do you think?" Moran asked me. He walked over to the stacks of mail I had placed on the kitchen counter, scanned through the envelopes first, then the magazines.

I followed just behind. "Same thing you do. Evans scrammed."

"Surprised?"

What did he want me to say? "I'm not disappointed," I answered, which was the truth.

Alvarez started making sounds about what he was supposed to do and I held my hand up to stop him. "I think I'd start legal eviction proceedings if I were you."

"What do I do with his stuff?"

"Same thing you do with all your skips," I said. Whatever that was. I didn't care. I just wanted to leave the house and rip open Lori's letter.

Moran thanked Alvarez for coming out and showing us the house, then the two of us left him in there, still cursing or whatever he was doing in Spanish. We stopped in the street, in front of the Monte's driver side door. "You're not surprised to see him gone, are you?" Terry asked.

I shrugged.

He looked into my face. Some time passed. "You have anything to do with it?"

Again I was conscious of the sunglasses covering my eyes. "You mean did I ask him to leave?"

He shrugged. "Or otherwise compel him to do so."

And here we were, right in the place I hoped never to be. I had to tell him something. "Terry, he was a punk and a bad man. He was capable of hurting my wife and my daughter, even though Roxy is biologically his. I don't know why he left but if he's gone I don't see how that can be a bad thing."

A lie. A lie of omission.

"It's a relief to me, to be honest."

Terry nodded his head slowly, digesting my answer. "I'm going to ask you something, and I don't want you to go through the roof about it, okay?"

He's not buying it, I thought. "Go ahead."

"You think there's any possibility he's out looking for Lori?"

Relief. "No," I said. "She and Roxy are alone."

Genuine surprise. "You talked to her? You know where she is?"

"Yes, I talked to her. And she asked me about Roy. She wouldn't have done that if he'd found her."

"Does that mean you guys are getting things back on track?"

"Nope," I said, feeling the weight of the letter in my back pocket.

"She's moved on again. And I don't know where she went."

We stood like that for a minute, as though each of us were considering the Roy Evans problem when actually only one of us was. "Evans took his toiletries and his underwear so it definitely looks as if he took off for somewhere. But you don't think he had a line on Lori and Roxy. Was he running scared? Is he coming back?"

"How the hell should I know?"

Moran didn't answer. "It keeps going back to Ralphie Wandorski, doesn't it? If Ralphie's telling the truth, it wouldn't make sense for Evans to leave without his money. Unless he got spooked for some reason and jack-rabbited away from whatever deal they were working."

I said nothing, wishing I could think of a way to make him let it go. Hell, maybe Ralphie and Evans had really been working something. Until the other day I hadn't even been aware the two men had known each other.

I did know that Evans sure the hell wasn't part of Little Y or anything else to do with Rudy Pope. That was a fact. Ralphie was still the unknown, but what had we expected? For Ralphie to tell us the truth?

Moran and I went our own ways after that, Terry back to the station, myself aimlessly driving. I didn't know what Moran had expected to find in Evans' house, and I was grateful that he'd thought I might want or need to be there when he checked it out. I had already known that it wouldn't shed any light on the Shawcross/Schoenfeld case but what I didn't know was what Moran was thinking. Would he let his questions about Evans die, or did his apparent disappearance pique Terry's curiosity? I didn't know if there was anything I could do about it one way or the other without calling attention to myself. I wouldn't want to make Greene and his bosses that happy.

Now that I was alone I found myself afraid to open Lori's letter. I thought of several things it might say but the biggest issue was why exactly she'd felt compelled to write it in the first place. And I wondered if I had betrayed her when I'd taken the letter. A voice in my head said I was just protecting myself. Still, I wondered what she'd say if she knew.

I drove across the peninsula on First Avenue North and crossed over onto the barrier island known as St. Pete Beach. I drove south on Gulf Boulevard and into the town of Passe-a-Grille, then turned west for a block or two to get to the beach. Being down at the southern tip of the county, the beaches here were relatively uncrowded, the hordes from the north turning off at the beaches nearer to them. I pulled into a metered spot and turned off the Jeep.

I held the letter in my hand, staring at the purple ink, envelope addressed to "Roy Evans," no return address in the corner. The postmark from St. Petersburg was dated the day she'd left home. More evidence of planning, I thought. I opened the envelope along its top edge, carefully. Inside was a single sheet of paper, again in Lori's trademark purple ink. .

"Roy," the letter said. "I don't think you'll ever get this but I needed to send it anyway. If you do though, please know that I'm sorry for everything that has happened to you since you've been out of prison. You shouldn't have come to Florida. I didn't want to see you and Roxy didn't want to see you. But what we wanted was never what mattered to you, was it? It was always about you and what you wanted. Only you. I don't know where you are now but I hope that you are well and can finally find peace. Without us. Goodbye."

The letter was unsigned but Evans would have had no doubt who had written it. Lori had told me she didn't want to have contact with Roy but she never mentioned the letter. She shouldn't have sent it; it was exactly the kind of attention that fed his need to keep pursuing her. I read the letter a few more times before something hit me. Almost the entire thing was written in the past tense.

I stared at the laughing gulls hovering in the air above the beach, black heads bobbing with the beating of their wings, then dropping suddenly to the sand, fighting each other for a scrap of hot dog bun or popcorn kernel. I wondered idly about what happens with all the sand they inevitably swallowed.

This letter was Lori's goodbye to her ex-husband and the father of her daughter. She'd written that she didn't think he'd ever read it but if she'd really believed that, why send it in the first place? Would she have left me if she'd known he might see it? I wondered how long she'd known his address.

Hundreds of gulls took off en masse and flapped away down the beach. Maybe one day I'd get a letter from Lori written in purple ink and without a return address. I didn't have to wonder what it would say; I could probably write the damn thing myself.

I destroyed the letter and envelope in a fit of self pity and took the fragments to a public waste bin near the parking pay station. It was much darker in my car when I returned.

Chapter 20

I don't know how long I sat there but the temperature quickly climbed into three digits. Sweat poured from my body and completely saturated my clothes. When I finally opened the door and tried to get out, my pants were stuck to my thighs and I had to manually lift the fabric off my skin so that I could move my legs enough to swing them out and stand.

Unfastening an extra button on my shirt I walked down the sidewalk toward the snack bar/gift shop building. There was a man made dune peppered with wild sea oats between me and the beach so I couldn't see where the waves met the shore but I could hear the steady cadence of the breaks. Closer to the horizon I could see a barge or a tanker running the channel into the bay.

My mind was coasting on auto pilot; no thoughts of Lori, of murder investigations, failed careers, capital crimes. I wanted a coke, a cold one. When I reached the snack bar I thought about crossing the street and entering the cool air conditioning inside the Hurricane restaurant but the necessary interaction with hosts and waiters or waitresses seemed too much. I went beachside to the snack bar counter and ordered a large drink. Mechanically I took a straw from the holder, handed over some cash, then took my drink and stepped back into the shade of the over-hanging roof.

Coconut suntan oil, laughing children, sunburnt tourists. More laughing gulls. Brown pelicans dive bombing the waves between the swimmers. Kestrels. The dirty salt smell of the ocean and the unceasing sounds of the waves washing onto the sand.

Letters from my wife to her abusive ex-husband, a man who was released from a Texas state prison and immediately relocated to Florida so he could stalk and threaten her and his biological daughter in an effort to bring them back under his self-serving influence. But they had become my family and I'd had to do what I could to protect them.

I finished the last of the liquid in my cup and tipped some of the smaller ice cubes into my mouth. I pushed them over into one cheek with my tongue until they'd melt into small enough pieces for me to chew. No part of the drink would go unused.

Roy Lee Evans was gone. If he hadn't disappeared, he would have killed my wife and daughter. I really believed that. I reminded myself how many times I'd seen stalking cases turn to rage and murder. I told myself this each and every morning when I awoke. I'd seen too many cases, and the ones with escalating behaviors, like this one, were the ones that didn't end well for the chosen victim. Especially when the victim was a woman who had found a new man.

The cell phone attached to my belt rang and I dropped my wax covered paper cup into the nearest garbage can. If this is Terry Moran, I thought, I'm not going to answer. I'd had too much for the day.

But the display said otherwise, showing a number I didn't recognize and I pushed the Talk button and said hello. It was Sherry/LeeAnne from the Mondo Erotica. She had contacted her friend Stacey the actress from the makeup counter. Stacey was willing to talk to me but it would have to wait until tonight.

"Is she working?" I asked.

"She didn't say. I've got to be behind the bar tonight but I can introduce you two and let you have at it."

I smiled at her language. "That's fine. I'd like to ask you something else."

Wariness in her tone. "What now?"

"Can I call you LeeAnne?"

She laughed. "Sure you can, sugar. Just keep it to yourself when you see me in the bar."

"Deal," I told her, and hung up, feeling a bit lighter.

The club was something less than half full but was still very, very loud, with the blaring music making up for the lack of customers. I sat at the bar while LeeAnne slipped me soft drinks along the damp countertop and I waited for her friend.

She didn't show until nearly eight thirty. I'd been watching LeeAnne work the bar in her Sherry persona, pouring and joking and raking in the tips with both hands. She seemed to have a following almost as big as the dancers'. I could see why she enjoyed her job. Where the customers were concerned, all she had to touch was their money.

Stacey walked in and sat next to me, catching LeeAnne's eye. "This the guy?"

"He's the man," LeeAnne said with a wink.

Stacey took a cigarette from a pack in her small gold purse and fumbled with her lighter. When she got it working, she lit the cigarette, inhaled deeply then studied my face as though committing it to memory. Her eyes dropped to check out the rest of me then bounced back up. "You're a cop, right?"

"LeeAnne didn't tell you?" I wasn't sure which name to use but she knew who I was talking about.

"No, she did." Stacey took another deep drag from her cigarette and I could hear the burning paper and tobacco crackle through a rare pause in the music and DJ chatter. "You don't look right, though."

"You want to see my badge?" I said, reaching for my pocket.

"No, honey, you save it. I'm just saying. Let's go somewhere."

"What's wrong with here?"

She looked around the place again. "No, I'm not comfortable in this joint, if you don't mind. The wrong people come in here. You can buy me dinner some place else."

I dropped some bills on the counter for LeeAnne and noted that she hadn't offered to get Stacey a drink. I wanted to say goodbye but she was talking up an older man in a Hawaiian shirt. I let Stacey lead me out the door and to the parking lot where she stopped, waiting for me to step alongside.

"Which one is yours?" she asked.

"Don't you have a car?"

"I got dropped off. You have to drive."

I pointed at the Jeep and we walked over and I opened the passenger door for her as she climbed in. We went south on Dale Mabry mostly so I didn't have to wait to turn against the non-stop traffic. There was a Tex/Mex joint on the other side of the highway overpass and a franchise steak house further down on this side of the street. I suggested the latter because it would be a quieter and easier place to hold a conversation. Stacey shrugged and stared out the window, playing with her purse. Thankfully she didn't try to smoke in the Jeep.

It took a little over a minute to reach the steak house. A car rode my bumper into the parking lot and I slowed down more than I needed to so he would pay attention. I didn't want to get rear ended. As I pulled into a parking space he took off around the corner of the building.

I got out of the Jeep and walked around to the passenger door. Stacey leaned forward and bent down to do something with her shoe. It took her a while. In the light of the parking lot I couldn't see the scars on her long neck LeeAnne had mentioned but that could have been the makeup. She looked around as if she hadn't paid attention to where we'd been going then gave me a smile and finally stepped out of the car. There came the sound of footsteps behind me.

I started to turn and someone pushed me hard between the shoulder blades, knocking me forward into Stacey and against the front seat of the Jeep. "Hand over your wallet, motherfucker. Turn around and I'll cap your ass."

Stacey's face was inches from mine and she pushed against my shoulder as I straightened up. Her face was a mask of fear as I reached into my pocket for my badge and held it open over my shoulder. "This what you're looking for?"

I thought whoever it was would take off running. The one who spoke didn't sound hopped up enough to be stupid enough to take down a cop. Instead a hand slapped the holder from my hand and it flew into the car parked next to mine.

"Take out your piece and kick it under the car, man. Do it now!"

I felt the pressure of something hard jammed into my lower back. I slipped my weapon from the holster on my left hip and put it on the ground in front of me.

"Kick it!"

I did, propelling it behind the Jeep's right front wheel.

"Now your wallet, asshole. Give me the money."

"It's in my back pocket," I said.

"Get it!"

I reached around with my right arm, twisting my body slightly until I felt the pressure ease from my back. I kept moving my arm back and whirled around, pushing the gun barrel so that it was no longer pointed right at me. I could see the two of them. With the gunman's body between mine and his friend, I grabbed the wrist holding the gun and twisted hard while I brought my left leg up as fast as I could, crushing his balls with my shin.

The gun came loose in my hand as he drove his folded body forward into my stomach, shoving me into the side of the Jeep. My back hit the door frame and made me twist toward his partner. Instinctively I pulled away, ducked and threw myself into a backward roll. The second man was now in front of me, one hand held low in front of his groin for protection. Apparently they'd only brought the one gun. The one I'd hit was still on his knees by the rear wheel.

I stepped on his hand as he began to reach for the dropped gun, and stooped and picked it up myself. The other one didn't say anything, and he didn't run; he took little steps away from me as I moved closer. I could feel real anger coming on, the kind that comes from having my own issues and frustrations unlocked by the adrenaline spike brought on by a personal attack. I was looking forward to getting my hands on this punk.

Around the front of the restaurant came a squealing of tires. I didn't look but the downed man by the wheel pushed himself up and made a dash for the car, falling forward as much as running. The rear door closest to him popped open as he got there and he dove inside. The man I was facing spit once on the asphalt between us and took off, too. I didn't chase him. Reason got the better of me and I knew that whoever was in the car could be—probably was—armed and I didn't want to be outnumbered again.

The car peeled off and bulled its way into the traffic heading north, too fast and at the wrong angle for me to get the plate number. All I saw was a brown Mustang or Chrysler pseudo-muscle car; at some point they all lost their style and blended together to me.

"Are you okay?" I asked Stacey, who was now standing next to the Jeep tearing at another cigarette, her hands shaking. She nodded as she thumbed her lighter.

I asked her to step aside while I went down on my knees next to the front wheel and retrieved my gun. I brushed it against my pants leg and put it back in its holster. The other gun was a piece of crap, a pawn shop reject with white adhesive tape wrapped around its grip. I picked it up by the end of its barrel and dropped it into my jacket pocket. My left shin was bruised where I had kicked its previous owner. There was a small satisfaction in that.

"I don't think I'm hungry anymore," Stacey said.

"Let's go in for a drink. It'll calm you down."

She shook her head as she blew smoke from her nostrils. "I don't want to go in there. I want to get out of here right now."

I gave her a long look then pointed at her cigarette. "Drop that thing and get in the car."

She looked sullen and pale but did what I told her.

"Where to?" I asked when we were both inside.

"I don't know, just drive. Jesus, I'm shaking all over here."

I pulled out into the flow of traffic and followed her directions, taking her home to a townhouse in south Tampa not far off Westshore Boulevard.

"God, who were those guys?" she asked on the way.

"Don't know. Some dopers looking for some quick cash or something." I looked over to see her clutching the dashboard handle mounted above the glove box. "Don't worry about it. It's over." I had taken off my jacket and wrapped it around the pocket with the assailant's gun in it, then jammed it on the floor under the seat. I'd have it processed tomorrow when I was back at work.

We didn't speak again until we arrived at her home. I had the post adrenaline jitters bad and I held the wheel hard to keep from letting her see my hands shake. As the rush faded I was left with the memory of the nearly self destructive rage that had threatened to take over back at the parking lot. I didn't necessarily want to die but it was a sign of just how messed up my life was right now that it didn't feel much like I cared a whole hell of a lot. Probably just a normal reaction to all my stress. I wondered what Lori would think if I was suddenly gone. Sorrow? Relief? A mixture of both?

Once inside Stacey's townhouse she made herself a screwdriver while I sipped a glass of tap water at her kitchen table and tried to sit far enough back to be out of the clouds of her cigarette smoke. Eventually we both calmed down enough for her to begin talking.

She told me that her real name was Linda, no last name, and she came from a small town in southern Georgia. She had tried dancing as a living but she wasn't good enough at it to work in the kinds of places that paid the big money.

"Some people just don't have the rhythm, you know? Or the stage presence. Something."

I nodded. So far Stacey didn't project the kind of intriguing excitement that even someone like LeeAnne put out while tending bar. "I couldn't do it. What'd you do next?"

She hemmed and hawed about some bullshit and I told her that I wasn't looking to make any trouble for her. For anyone. I just wanted information that could help me on a case. If she wanted to screw up her life with booze, drugs and the underbelly of society that was her business.

She gave me a weak smile and told me about how she started "going" with men. We both knew what she meant. She said she was better, much better, at things other than dancing.

"Tell me about your acting gig," I said. I didn't need to hear about the rest of it.

She was working on her fourth drink by this time and had thankfully run out of cigarettes. "Well that's a special deal, you know."

"No, I don't," I said. "How so?"

Then she started talking about hooking instead, how she fell into it while dancing in a club up in Ocala and worked her way down south. She got with a pimp she met in a dive on Nebraska Avenue and started dancing after he was popped and sent to prison in Hillsborough County.

I studied her face while she talked; she was obviously avoiding my question about her acting career. Stacey was a tall woman, nearly six feet in her low heels, with a flaming auburn mane of hair that she'd already told me was her real color. Her cheekbones were high around a long, straight nose and although she may not have been a good pole dancer at a club, her body was toned and shapely. Her posture was erect and that added an air of poise to her presence that she may not have otherwise effected. She noticed me looking and stopped talking. Absently she scratched at her neck, then stopped when she realized she was leaving tracks in her makeup.

"Tell me about your scars," I said.

"Bane of my life," she said. "When I was a girl and got chicken pox, my mom wasn't around too much and I was mostly raised by my grandmother. She had a hearing problem so a lot of the time my brother and I did whatever we wanted and she never had a clue. Anyway, my brother Charlie told me that I had to scratch the scabs off or else they'd grow and grow and never stop. I'd scratch them off then do it again when they came back. Eventually they quit coming but by then it was too late. I never touched my face, though. Thank God."

We sat silent for a few minutes while she nursed her drink some more until I gently reminded her about the movies she made.

"Nothing really weird, you know. It's not like they're bringing in animals or hooking us up to cattle prods or anything."

"Where do you shoot?"

She fluttered a hand into the air. "There's a warehouse in Brandon made to look like a nice house inside. It's got different rooms, furniture. They send a car for me so I don't think I could tell you exactly where it is."

"You don't look out the window?"

"It's not that kind of car. This one's got booze and all sorts of stuff in it."

"I see."

"Listen," she said, standing up. "I need a minute or two here. That shit in the parking lot just isn't going away. I'm going to change clothes, do you mind?"

"Do you know Ralphie Wandorski?" I asked.

"Of course I know Ralphie. All the girls know Ralphie." She started to move out of the kitchen. "Some wish they didn't."

On a hunch, I asked, "How about Carlos Alcaro?"

That stopped her. "The agent? He's the one that brings them in, honey."

"The girls?"

"Who else?" She pushed her hair away from her face. "Just give me a minute, okay?"

I gave her ten. Then I stood up slowly and made my way to the second floor of the townhouse. Stacey was lying on top of a queen sized bed in the room to the left of the stairs. She saw me come up and said, "Come here, sweetie. I just had to lie down."

She had changed into a man's oxford shirt, her long auburn hair spilling over the collar and across a pillow; on the bottom she was wearing a pair of baggy gym shorts. The outline of her breasts showed through the fabric and she may not have had dancer-style moves but she was a beautiful woman. I walked around to the side of the bed away from her and sat down on the edge of the mattress.

"I'll tell you what you want," she said. "Can you just lie down here and be close for a second? You don't have to touch me or anything. I just want to feel safe for a little while."

I thought it may have been a line but the truth was the day had been long and I was emotionally and physically exhausted myself. I kicked off my shoes and lay down with my head on the pillow next to hers. We didn't touch.

She started telling me more about making pornographic movies, general stuff, and she didn't bring up Ralphie Wandorski's name. Or that of Rudy Pope or the Little Y website. I thought I'd let her talk for a while and then ask her specific questions when she was more at ease.

I grew comfortable, perhaps because for a change I wasn't the one keeping all the secrets. Why I closed my eyes I'll never know. I knew when I did I wouldn't want to open them for a while. At some point she stopped talking and I felt a warm closeness settle against my left side. A little later I slid gently into a sleep without dreams for the first time in weeks.

When the sun rose in the morning she was still next to me only her shorts were somewhere on the floor and her shirt was unbuttoned from the top to the bottom. Her body was as beautiful as it had looked last night and I wondered why the hell I was seeing it now. My own clothes were rumpled from the sleep but still safely on though I already knew nothing had happened.

I thought about waking her but given her line of work, these were probably her prime sleeping hours. I slid carefully off the bed, picked up my shoes and walked softly down to the kitchen. I'd have to hustle to get home, changed and showered before going in to work. After scrawling a note on the back of one of my cards, I left it on the table and let myself out of the townhouse. The sun was burning bright orange and low on the horizon and I felt better rested than I had since Lori had left. I almost felt guilty for feeling so relaxed but inside, I knew it wouldn't last.

Chapter 21

I called Leslie after I'd finished up at my house and was about to head into the department.

"How are you doing, Jeff?"

I really hated questions like that. I wanted to say, "How the hell should I know?" but I knew that wouldn't be fair. Leslie was turning out to be more than my lawyer, that seemed to be coming clear. She seemed to actually care. I wondered briefly how I felt about her but then decided it wasn't time to think about it yet.

"Doing okay," I said. "Hey, listen, I have a quick question for you."

"Oh, yeah? What's that?"

"Does your husband—"

"Please don't call him that."

Whoops. "Sorry. I mean, does Carlos drive a brown Mustang or Dodge, something like that?"

"Oh, geeze," she said. "Let me think. He's always driving new things." I remembered his connection to Pope's car lot. "I'm pretty sure I've seen him with something brown, but I couldn't tell you what model it was. You'll have to settle for a definite maybe."

"Fair enough," I said. "Do you happen to know where he was last night?"

"Separated, remember?" Her voice got quieter. "Why are you asking about Carlos? Did you see him?"

"I saw some guys get into a car. It got me wondering, that's all."

"But you had to put them with Carlos somehow."

"Are you being my lawyer or a separated whatever you are?"

"I'm not sure if I should be insulted right now, though I don't exactly know why."

Shit. "Leslie, I'm sorry. I'm just... blunt sometimes. Too much so."

"First step is admitting it."

"I'm sorry, okay?"

"Buy me lunch and I'll forget all about it. You around today?"

"I don't know yet," I stalled. "I haven't been in the office for a few days and I'll have to see what blows up when I walk in the door."

"Fine," she said, sounding like a lawyer. "Let me know when you figure it out."

"Ding Dong Marquez called yesterday," Moran told me when I finally made it to my desk.

"Oh, yeah? What's up?"

"They ran down one of these guys who was sending threats to the deceased Mr. Schoenfeld. Guy named Marvin Bleeker. Guess what he had in a box in his garage?"

"A Red Ryder BB gun with a compass in the stock?"

"You could shoot your eye out with a thing like that. Try a 12 gauge side by side double barreled shotgun."

"Can they match it to Schoenfeld?"

Moran shook his head. "No spent shells at the scene."

"They think he's it?"

"Don't know. But they're holding a press conference after lunch."

He handed me a sheaf of faxes with the Tampa PD header on them and I skimmed through what they had on their suspect. "Looks more like a wing nut to me."

"Could be," said Moran. "Sometimes it's not just sane and normal people that cut prominent figures in half with shotguns."

"Can we tie him to Shawcross?"

"That's next."

I gave him back the papers and watched him slide them into a file on his desk.

"So what've you been up to?" he asked. "Or do I not want to know?"

I told him about my interviews on the Tampa strip and what happened in the steak house parking lot. I'd brought the punk's handgun up in a plastic bag, still wrapped inside my jacket. Then I told him about meeting Stacey although I left out the part about where I spent the night. And what she looked like barely covered as she lay next to me, still asleep in the morning. It made me realize how much I missed not sleeping alone.

"Learn anything?"

"Maybe a film location, a warehouse complex somewhere in Brandon."

"Pope involved?"

"The girl knows Ralphie but she was cagey. Couldn't pin her down. I hope I can see her again, get her to open up some more." I didn't mention Carlos Alcaro yet.

He gave me a look that I didn't answer. Instead I took my plastic bag down to the forensics lab and asked them to dust the gun inside for prints. They asked if I was in a rush and I said no. The truth was unless it came back with something I could pass on to someone else I'd probably have to forget about it.

I went back to my desk and started back at Shawcross's phone records, looking to see if this guy Bleeker had called Randy, or vice versa, in the past six months. There was nothing there with the number Terry had gotten from Marquez.

"We have Bleeker's records?" I asked Moran.

"Nope. But I gave Ding Dong Shawcross's numbers so they could check."

That would work, too. I picked up the phone to call Darlene Shawcross, see if she'd ever heard of the guy. While I was listening to the ringing on the other end, I saw Lieutenant Greene come around the corner and look at me and Moran. I didn't meet his eyes; instead I picked up my pen and started making pretend notes on the pad in front of me. I felt like a naughty child. He went over and said something in Moran's ear just as Darlene finally picked up.

"Hello?"

"Hey, Darlene, it's Jeff Prentiss. I'm glad I caught you before you left town."

"Oh, hi." A bit out of breath. "I was cleaning up some things in the garage. What's going on?"

I told her about Bleeker and how Tampa was looking at him for the Schoenfeld killing. She said she'd never heard of him.

"Do me a favor, will you? There's going to be some kind of news conference after lunch. If you're around can you see if you can catch it on TV and tell me what you think? They'll probably have this guy's picture and some more background info. It might jog something."

She told me she'd do it and asked if there was anything new, other than what was coming out of Tampa, on Randy's case. "Not yet," I told her. "But we're still working it."

We hung up and I looked at Terry.

"Let's go," he said.

"Fun in the sun."

It was just myself, Terry and Greene in the lieutenant's office. He seemed subdued, if anything, going out of his way to be professional in his manner. He wanted an update and we brought him up to speed on where we were with Shawcross and stopped after we told him about our phone check and my call with Darlene.

"I hoped for more," he said, then looked at me. "But you've had a few days on your own, haven't you?"

I didn't say anything. He knew damn well about my time off.

"At least the heat from the press went away when the probable next mayor of Tampa got blown away." He sat back in his chair. "What's your opinion? Are the cases connected or is this just coincidence?"

"Schoenfeld and Shawcross? We still don't know. We think there may be something on the website angle but we haven't cracked it yet." This from my partner, who was trying to carry the conversation for both of us. I was following the old "speak when spoken to" rule. Greene didn't seem to mind.

He sat back in his chair. "We need to clear this thing. Tampa's going to arraign this Bleeker guy for writing letters but the most that'll buy them is some time before the media ramps back up. A day or two, probably, maybe a week. It would be good if you guys made some serious progress by then."

"Yes, sir," said Moran.

"Make sure you know whether this guy had anything to do with the King of Cats. If this turns into another feeding frenzy for the media I want it to stay on that side of the bridge. Just keep your own faces away from the cameras. I mean it."

We stood up to leave. I turned away without saying anything but Moran told Greene, "We'll get on it," and followed me to the door.

"Just stay the hell out of trouble," Greene added as we left the office.

"Too late," Moran said, grinning at me and whispering.

"Fuck you," I said in the same tone. If he only knew.

Back at our desks, Moran said, "You didn't tell him about your interviews in those Tampa clubs."

"My lawyer wasn't present," I said.

"But you were dong police work, dude. You were working the job."

"You didn't tell him, either."

"Good point. All he really cares about is two things," Moran said, checking to make sure he wouldn't be overheard. "Clearing cases, and not getting shown up by you."

"You make it sound like I'm after his desk."

"Nope, it's the other way around, and you know it." He picked up some papers from his blotter. "You want to see if they'll give us access to Bleeker?"

"Definitely. You make the call, will you?"

"What are you going to do?"

"We need to figure out how to find a warehouse made into a movie studio over in Brandon."

"You're not much on territorial jurisdiction, are you?"

I didn't answer. Moran was right, and there was protocol that needed to be followed. We had technically crossed the line when we had gone to see Pope, not to mention what I'd been doing around Tampa while showing my badge. Moran was strongly giving me the hint to be more cautious.

Marquez would let us talk to Bleeker but not until late in the afternoon, after her press conference. In the meantime we tried to brainstorm ways to find a pornographic movie set hidden in a suburban warehouse just east of Tampa.

"They'd need movie equipment like lights and microphones and tripods, stuff like that, right?" asked Moran.

"We could hit the phone book, interview a/v equipment suppliers. What do you think about furniture?"

"Think they'd buy it, or rent it?"

"It's a bad idea," I said. "Either way, we'd never be able to track it. Way too many sources."

We broke out the phone books and divvied up the audio/visual suppliers and went back to make our calls. It was a long shot, I knew. The suppliers wouldn't be anxious to talk to us and we couldn't make them talk without a warrant, whether they delivered anything to a Brandon address or not.

At this point what we could really use was an informant. If someone didn't come forward who knew something about what Randy was doing, or what his relationship to Barry Schoenfeld had really been, we may not be able to solve the case.

My cell phone rang as I was hanging up from my second cold call. It was Darlene Shawcross.

"I found something in the garage," she said. "It was in a box on a shelf and I've never seen it before."

"Is that unusual?"

"It would be if it was in the house. Randy took care of the garage, though."

"What is it, Darlene?"

"I'm not sure. I think it's some kind of camera."

"We'll be right there," I said.

Chapter 22

There were boxes, mostly empty, of wireless video camera equipment tucked back against the garage wall on the upper shelf of a free standing set of shelves. What Darlene had found was the receiving unit, the piece that would be attached to a VCR in order to record the wireless signal coming from the camera.

"Ever work with these things before?" Moran asked me.

"Nope, just seen them on TV. You said you never heard Randy mention anything like this?" I asked Darlene, who shook her head.

To Moran I said, "This could mean that this stuff had something to do with what he was up to."

"We really didn't talk about that part of his life," Darlene said. "He kept me out of it as much as he could, and I really didn't want to know about it anyway."

I'd lost track of how often she'd told us that. Yet she'd spent his money, lived in his house, drove his cars for who knows how many years, I thought. Whatever the real truth, I was sure it couldn't have been easy for her.

Moran dragged a step ladder over and I climbed up and handed down all of the cartons from the shelf and then we took them into the living room. In addition to a receiver there was a portable video camera tucked away in its original box, a single video tape locked inside.

I set it down and organized the boxes in a line on the floor. There was one for a small pinhole camera, one for a transceiver that would take the signal from the camera and send it out, and another for a receiving unit that could be attached to a VCR for recording.

Moran was paging through a manual for the transceiver. "This thing ain't legal," he said. "Not in this country."

"What do you mean?" I asked.

"Seven mile range, line of sight. Broadcasts too far for the FTC's rules. Says the unit is either for export or licensed amateur radio users only."

"Randy have any kind of license like that?" I asked Darlene.

"No, nothing. Not that I know of, anyway."

"Our boy may have been doing something illegal after all," Moran said, pulling over the box for the pinhole camera.

I picked up the portable camera and found the on switch. I turned it to its "VCR" setting and pushed the small green play button while holding the viewfinder to my eye.

The images had to have come from the pinhole camera. It was apparently motion activated and mounted a foot or a foot and a half off the floor. As I watched a chair was jerked into motion and moved out of frame. A pair of tasseled loafers shuffled into view and the camera automatically changed focus. A bookshelf that must have been on casters was pushed aside to reveal a small safe set into the wall.

"You got anything?" asked Terry.

"Give me a minute."

The back of a man became visible, kneeling in front of the safe. He blocked a portion of the door but left the dial visible. As he worked the combination, it may have been possible to pick out at least one of the numbers on the dial—I couldn't tell from watching through the tiny viewfinder—but that would be all you'd need to work out the other ones from the video. When the door opened, a slightly shaking hand, fully sleeved in a light colored sweater, inserted a small stack of manila folders onto the top shelf, disappeared, and then reappeared briefly to toss what looked like a small leather-covered journal on top of them. Then the door shut, the hand spun the dial, and the bookcase was slid back into place. The chair legs did not come back, and after a few seconds the picture jerked into another shot, this time with the chair rolling into view, followed by the same loafered feet. I lowered the camera and pressed the "stop" button.

"Can we take this?" I asked Darlene.

She looked like she wanted to ask what I'd seen but then thought better of it. If she hadn't been involved with that part of her late husband's life she certainly wanted to keep it that way. "Take it," she said. "Take all of it. Please."

Moran raised his eyebrows at me but didn't say anything as I started to gather the components into their boxes. Outside he opened the trunk of the Monte Carlo and asked, "You weren't watching any naked hoohas on that thing, were you?"

"Nope," I said. "But I think we now know what Randy was working on."

"We do?"

"He was taking down a safe."

"What kind of stash?"

"Not that kind of safe," I said. "This one had papers and notebooks."

"I thought he only liked diamonds and pearls. Doesn't sound like his M.O." He gently lowered then pushed the lid of the trunk down until it latched and we walked around to the driver and passenger doors.

"No," I agreed. "But neither does messing with a man like Rudy Pope."

We stopped off for a sandwich on the way back. I was feeling relaxed, more so than I had in weeks, and a vague sense of guilt began creeping in on me. I hadn't tried to find Lori again, and I didn't know if I should. I wondered if that would help drive her away. It didn't give me the feeling it would make her want to come back. Then I thought about Leslie and the lunch we could be having together right now. I missed talking to a woman, I realized. I'd have to call her so she wouldn't wait.

I swallowed the last bite of my Reuben. If I didn't stop thinking like this I'd lapse into a full blown depression.

"You sure that was Pope's office?" Moran asked, washing down a mouthful of cheeseburger with a cherry cola.

"Ninety nine percent," I said. "With that sweater and those shoes...."

"That's no proof of who was wearing them."

"That's the missing one percent. But the only threads we can find in this thing keep pointing back to Rudy. I don't see anyone running a game on *us*, do you?"

"You mean like if someone left that tape for us to find? To move us off track?" He shook his head. "Doesn't make sense."

I agreed. "To me, either." I checked my watch. "Let's get back. We should check out Ding Dong's press conference in the break room."

We were only a few minutes away from the station. Moran drove the Monte Carlo into the lot across the street and we walked over, Moran with a box of video equipment tucked under each arm. As we were passing through the small tiled reception area, somebody called me from behind the glassed in partition as we passed. An officer, Martha Reave, was flapping something in the air at me. I stopped and went over to her window and she slid a nine by twelve envelope through the slot.

"I was about to put this in your slot," she said.

"What is it?"

"It was just messengered over five minutes ago."

My name was written in black felt tip across the front. The back was taped shut. "Thanks, Martha."

Terry had waited by the security door leading down the hallway into the office area, propping it open with his foot. "What'd you get?"

"Don't know." I worked a corner of the flap above the tape until I could get a fingertip inside, then tore the envelope open across the top. Inside was a single eight by ten photograph. I pulled it halfway out of the envelope and stopped dead.

The picture was of me, lying in bed last night with a mostly naked hooker/porn actress snuggled against my side, her bare ass exposed to the camera.

What?

Then I saw the other things: the handcuffs lying on the pillow next to Stacey/Linda No-Last-Name, the foot long red beaded wand-like object, something polished and chrome and bullet shaped, and a small black mask with an elastic strap.

Terry turned and walked back to me. "What's up, man?"

I slid the picture back into the envelope. The last thing I saw was a mirror set flat on the nightstand, a small pile of white powder covering the surface.

"I gotta go," I said and turned, backtracking outside through the electric doors and into the sunlight like a drowning man seeking air. Only it didn't come. My collar felt tight, my stomach knotted into a ball, and I felt a distinct chill despite the blazing sun and instant perspiration.

I moved left along the sidewalk because it was the quickest way out of view of the station and I walked as fast as I could away from there. Behind me I may have heard my partner's voice but I neither slowed nor looked back.

A few more blocks and a few more turns and I realized that while my mind was racing white hot no real thoughts had formed. I stopped in an alley leading that led to a parking lot behind an old white stone building that had been converted to an assisted living facility. The envelope was wet with the sweat that had dripped down my wrist onto my hand and had been absorbed by the paper. I had an urge to ball the thing up or rip it to pieces and drop it into the nearest dumpster. *Not yet*, I thought as I pulled the picture out, all the way this time, and studied it more closely.

It was exactly what I thought it was at the station. I'd been set up, and it looked bad. I was a cop with a controversial past working for a bureaucracy that would like nothing more than to see me thrown out of the department in disgrace. Without embarrassment to themselves, of course, which was the tricky part.

This would be exactly what they'd need.

I hadn't been drugged or incapacitated, I was just tired, especially after the action in the restaurant parking lot, and I had let my guard down. I'd let myself relax in the company of a woman I did not know, one with a more than questionable background, and had allowed myself to fall asleep in her company. She, apparently, had had other things to do.

The picture wasn't a fake as far as I could tell but it didn't really matter. At the very least, if it got to Greene I'd have to explain why I was with this woman, what I'd been doing in Tampa on my supposed time off, and the contacts I'd been making in the Dale Mabry strip joints. There'd be an investigation and it wouldn't stop there. I'd be lucky if they didn't keep looking into everything else I'd touched, too.

I rubbed my eyes with the thumb and forefinger of my left hand and swore as I abraded them with street grit and stinging perspiration. Was there a closet across from Stacey's bed? I tried to remember but I couldn't be sure. There had to be, though. And someone must have been inside and as the girl had unbuttoned her shirt and worked off her gym shorts, and laid out the paraphernalia and mirror and blow or whatever it was on the table. Then of course they took the picture.

Jesus Christ, I thought. If this came out, I didn't want to think what Lori would think. Or Roxy, for god's sake.

So this was what it was like on the tightrope when the rope starts swaying and the net gets yanked away. There was no way I could see to jump clear. I could imagine a sick falling feeling as I leaned against the stone wall.

I jammed the photo back into the envelope, folded it twice and shoved it into my back pocket. I had another urge to destroy it but I thought better of it. It took me a minute to get my bearings and realize where I had walked to and where my Jeep was parked. It would be pointless, I knew, but I had to get to Tampa.

Chapter 23

I burned into the Mondo Erotica and used my badge to make my way into the day manager's office, a man named Dwight something. When I asked about my friend LeeAnne aka Sherry, he tried to dummy up but when I walked around his desk and started pulling out the drawers of his metal file cabinet, he blurted out, "She's gone, okay? She quit this weekend. No notice."

He got up and stood next to the cabinet, trying to crowd me away. I slammed shut the drawer I had in my hand and told him to have a nice goddamn day, and then I left. Next stop was the townhouse Stacey had taken me to but again, I knew what I was going to find. I was right. The front door was locked and there was no answer when I rang the bell and pounded on the windows. I looked in the usual places for a spare key and didn't find one.

The thought of doing something rash, like kicking in the door or breaking a front window, came to me but didn't stay long. Really, I knew what I was looking at. An empty townhouse. A bedroom with a closet facing the wall where Stacey had placed her bed. Furniture that may or may not still be in there. Nothing to see.

I'd allowed myself to be set up. The obvious suspect was Grandpa Mafioso himself, Rudy Pope, but I'd have to spend some time working out the why. No arrests were imminent in the Randy Shawcross murder and all we really had was a sketchy tie to a murdered pol in Tampa and a pornographic website that featured movies with actors that had blurry spots for faces.

Pope wouldn't necessarily know that, though. He couldn't be sure what we had or didn't have and this could be his way of throwing a wrench into the works. But why decide to pick on me? I may have been an easy target but my influence was decidedly limited. He'd have to assume that anything I knew would be in a file somewhere, or shared with my partner.

I climbed back into the Jeep and thought about what to do next. The dashboard clock told me it was almost three o'clock. The question that kept coming to mind was who else was going to get a copy of that picture.

My cell phone rang suddenly, jarring me out of my thoughts. I checked the display before I answered: Terry Moran.

"Hello."

"You okay?"

I had no idea what to say. "Peachy. And yourself?"

"Knock it off," he said. "You were conspicuously absent in the break room during Ding Dong's press conference."

"What do you mean?"

"People were looking at me and asking about you. Greene stuck his head in once and then went back to his office."

"He say anything?"

"Looked like he wanted to but not in front of a dozen or so guys. Maybe he thought you were taking an extended bathroom break. Where are you now?"

"Tampa."

"You ready for our meeting?"

Oh, Christ, I thought. We were supposed to interview Marquez's suspect, Bleeker, this afternoon. "Yeah, of course. I'll meet you there. Where've they got him?"

"Downtown. Franklin and Madison. I'll be there in forty five minutes."

"I'll see you there."

He hesitated and I didn't leap to fill the void. Then, "Dude, what was in that envelope?"

"Just a piece of crap, Terry."

"Is Lori okay? Roxy?"

How the hell should I know? "It's not about them. I'll see you in a few," I said and hung up.

I started the Jeep and started rolling slowly through the parking lot. That picture could show up anywhere at any time, like a bomb that only I could see. The sandwich I'd had for lunch sat like a stone in my stomach but my mouth was dry and sandy, as though I'd just walked out of a desert sand storm.

"Shit!" I shouted and pounded the steering wheel with my palm. How long could I keep screwing things up?

If Greene or his bosses get to see that picture, I thought, I'll have my answer.

I arrived at the TPD district headquarters about five minutes before Moran and when he walked in I immediately looked away. I couldn't tell why, it was just something I did. He walked up and hit me on the shoulder. "You cool, man?"

Now I could look at him. "Five by five," I said.

He studied my face. "Your color is off. You look white as hell but you're sweating like a donkey."

"They hide it better than me. We going in?"

Moran used his cell to call Izzy Marquez and she appeared just a few minutes later. We cleared security and took an elevator to the fifth floor. She and Moran made small talk while I stood in the corner, my mind on anything but Carl Bleeker.

Marquez led the way to an interview room and both Terry and I took seats at the metal table while she stood on the opposite side. "You guys making any progress on your end?"

Moran looked at me, then began talking. "We don't have any suspects at this point. We're trying to run down what the King of Cats was working on, hoping that might take us somewhere."

She raised her eyebrows. "So he was looking at a score? Where?"

"We don't know yet," Moran said. "But it may have something to do with Rudy Pope."

"Pope?" she said, pulling out the lone chair on that side of the table and sitting down across from Moran. "That old fool hasn't been relevant for the last hundred years or so. And even back then he was just a hanger on."

I had a different opinion but I didn't offer it. She wants to shun the pariah, that was fine with me. Moran said, "Like I told you, we're not sure, but we're looking at it."

She wanted to know exactly what we had and Moran was playing it coy, which was probably the right move. Our own ties to the investigation were tenuous based on my involvement and Greene's instructions. Marquez was a shark and if she smelled a bigger bust she'd go right around Moran and all over me to make it. I realized I didn't want someone like her harassing Darlene Shawcross.

Moran told Marquez that we think Shawcross had been surveilling Pope and may have been interested in an office safe somewhere. That seemed to dampen her aggressiveness. Rudy Pope's business papers were a far cry from the Koh-i-Noor.

She glanced at me, went back to Moran. "What about Carl Bleeker? You guys find anything on him?"

"Not a thing. That's why we're here."

"Of course that's why you're here," she said, a bit testy. "But he told us he's never heard of Randy Shawcross or the King of Cats. I was hoping y'all had some kind of lever on him."

Terry shrugged. "We just came to see what we could see."

Marquez stood, her interest nearly completely gone. "Good luck then. I'll have him brought in."

As she left the room, the movement of air from the opening and closing of the door added vital fresh air to the small, nearly claustrophobic interview room. I could feel my heart pounding in my chest and there was perspiration dripping non-stop off the back of my hairline onto my shirt collar. Moran was looking at me but didn't say anything.

A uniformed officer brought in a prisoner wearing yellow overalls and leg chains. His hands were cuffed in front of him. He was about five six, thin, with a careless hair cut that gave a crooked look to his head, and poorly complected skin. There was a small gap between his bottom two teeth and he kept his lips apart as he was guided to the chair across from us.

"Your name's Carl Bleeker?" Moran asked after the uniform had left the room.

The man swallowed once and nodded.

My attention wandered already. Over my right shoulder was a two-way mirror and I knew that if Izzy Marquez hadn't completely dismissed Schoenfeld's connection to Shawcross she'd be on the other side of it now, standing in a closet-sized room critiquing everything we did.

With a shock I realized the folded envelope with my picture in it was still tucked inside my back pocket. The hard chairs pressed the folded paper corners into my skin and the longer I sat there, the more I could feel its presence. Another bead of sweat dripped off the end of my nose and fell into my lap. I turned and looked at the mirror. Was anybody back there?

There was a camera in the opposite corner, focused downward onto the table. That would be running, I knew. I swiped at my forehead with my jacket sleeve. Somebody would watch it sometime. It suddenly felt as though they'd focus on me and not Carl Bleeker. I imagined what I looked like to the trained cops who might be watching this scene play out. Bleeker was mostly calm and composed, a bit anxious maybe, but his skin was dry and he was at least sitting still in his chair.

My chest was heaving and I suddenly felt that I had to get out of there. I was imagining the paper of the manila envelope dissolving in the perspiration soaking through my clothing, sloughing off, revealing jigsaw puzzle pieces of the folded print within.

"What's the matter with him?" Bleeker asked Moran, who turned his head to look at me.

I had to leave. I couldn't sit there any more, not with that burning packet in my back pocket, my heart racing, my body overheating, my mind unfocused.

"He's not feeling well," Moran said. He looked at me again. "He's on his way out, anyway." Then to me: "You've got to be back in St. Pete in half an hour, remember. You should take off."

It took a second before I realized what he was doing. Without a word I got up and exited the room, feeling like I had been the one in prison and that someone just thrown open the gates. As I walked down the hallway to the elevator I heard the door to the observation room open and not close. I waited for Marquez or somebody to call out but they didn't. I wasn't about to look back. Thankfully the elevator opened as I got there and I didn't have to wait. I pushed the button for the lobby and then had to force myself when it reached the lobby to keep from running out the front door.

I had been expecting a phone call and when it hadn't come before the end of the business day, I had actually started to relax to some degree. But then a car pulled into my driveway and when I looked out the window, I saw that damned bright yellow Monte Carlo parked behind my Jeep. I went to the front door and there was my partner, a confused and stressed look on his face.

I stepped back from the threshold and he came in, noting the beer I was holding in my right hand. "Got another one of those?" he asked.

He followed me into the kitchen and I pulled a cold one out of the refrigerator and handed it over. He twisted off the top and threw it at me. I caught it instinctively and walked over to the trash can and dropped it in. Then I turned around and faced him across the tiny room.

"How'd it go?" I asked.

"I didn't get anything from him. If he knew Shawcross I couldn't tell. And I'm not sure why he'd lie about it, either. According to his jacket he's got no ties to Pope, gambling, or pornographic websites. After talking to this dude, I'd be shocked if he knew how to spell 'Ybor City.'" He took a pull from his beer. "Could have used you, though. A lot of the time you see things that I don't."

I managed a heavy shrug.

"I got to tell you, man, you looked guiltier than he did. You shot out of there and Ding Dong came in looking for the cannon that launched you."

"She came in on the interview?"

"Uh huh. She was more interested in what was going on with you than with whatever I was getting out of Bleeker."

Shit.

We stood there, drinking our beers in silence. I had changed my clothes into a t-shirt and a pair of shorts. I was drier now, and much calmer, if that's the word for it, than I had been in Tampa. It helped that I had finally burned the envelope and its contents in the charcoal grill I kept poolside. Somehow that made me feel better though I knew that what that picture represented was far from being dealt with.

"So are you going to tell me about it, or what?" my partner asked.

That was a good question. I didn't have an answer for it.

He mistook my hesitation and said, "Look, man, don't you know you can trust me? Greene wanted me to look after you, but you know that. And you also know I'm not his toady. You're my friend, dude, but something's going on with you and whatever it is isn't doing either one of us any good."

My windpipe seemed to narrow and I didn't try to speak.

"I get that you're going through some hard times now. Lori's gone, but she'll come back, man, she has to. The job's tough but you keep going long enough all that stuff in the past will fade away. It just takes time. That's got to be the reason they don't rush your hearing date." He killed the rest of his beer and put the empty on the counter. "But you're burning up, man. You take time off and you do work when you should be getting your head together. You're acting like a nut job at work and people are starting to notice. You don't find joy in anything around you. You're the most righteous dude I've ever met, always doing the 'right thing.' So where's it going to take you? You're the only who *cares* about that stuff, man. Shouldn't that tell you something?"

I still didn't speak.

"Come back to our side, man. It's got to be lonely out there by yourself."

My voice croaked as I started speaking. I stopped and took a swallow of my beer. "You're a good friend, Terry."

He looked hard at me. "What was in that envelope?"

I couldn't tell him everything. I couldn't tell anyone everything. But I led him out to the lanai and we sat on the outdoor furniture with the brown water in the canal winking shards at us from the evening sun. Then I told him about Stacey and the picture.

Chapter 24

"But you didn't touch her? You never saw the sex toys or that other shit?"

"I didn't know anything about any of it, Terry." I sat back in my chair and closed my eyes.

"You were set up, man." He thought for a minute. "No law against those things anyway. No reason you shouldn't be seen with this Stacey, is there?"

"Not that I know of. I'm sure that's not her real name, though."

"Would you pass a drug test?"

I looked at him. "Jeeze, man, of course."

"Might be something to think about, maybe get ahead of this thing."

I shook my head. "First, someone would find out. Secondly, if I needed to use the results, it would already be too late. Lastly, all Stacey or her bosses would need to say is that I was doing the offering, not the partaking. Still screwed all around."

Moran was shaking his head. "You've been set up, man."

"You keep saying that."

He leaned back into his chair, too, and stared at the still water on my swimming pool, blue and inviting but for another time. Another life. After a minute he said, "Got any ideas?"

"Just one."

"I told you you shouldn't go around breaking digits and throwing bodies through windows."

I shook my head. "Ahh," I said. "I never listen."

"This really sucks, man. If the brass gets that picture, you're screwed." He raised his arms above his head, hooked his fingers together, then brought them down and cracked his knuckles. "So what do we do?"

"I don't know. Both girls are gone but even if they marched up and confessed it wouldn't make any difference."

"That's bull. We'd bust their asses and you'd walk away."

"Nope," I said. "They'd get me for being out on my own in Tampa without notifying TPD. They'd get me for being in strip joints and consorting with hookers on my time off. Oh, wait. I was working then, wasn't I?"

"So what? There's nothing there."

"For you, maybe. For me, there's no such thing as 'benefit of the doubt.'" Something new occurred to me. "Oh, shit," I said.

"What?"

I told Terry about the attempted robbery in the steak house parking lot that led to me taking Stacey home in the first place.

"And you never reported it?"

I told him the gun was downtown with forensics but I hadn't heard from them or followed up on it.

"But still, man, they may slap you on the wrist for being sloppy, or maybe careless, but they can't take that to your fitness for duty—"

"Terry, stop it. They can do anything they want to and you know what that means in my case. I've given them a crack and all they need to do now is blow on it and it'll open up and swallow my ass. I'll be through." And I might even end up in jail. Or worse.

"This just isn't right." He stood up and started pacing along the pool's edge. "We need to get to Ralphie. We can get him jammed up with these murders and get him to spill what he did to you. We just have to do it quick, before he does something with that picture."

"Hey, I'm serious. Stop it," I said. "In the first place, he may already feel jammed up and that's why he set me up with Stacey. He gets me busted and the circus moves back to St. Pete. He can hold up his cast and show his stitches and probably draw a pass from our guys on the Shaw-cross thing. Unless Izzy Marquez can tie Ralphie to Schoenfeld, Tampa will leave him alone, too."

"So what are you saying?"

I didn't know. I could chuck it all right now, throw in the badge, but I couldn't be sure even that would stop it. And if Ralphie brings Roy Evans into this, and I couldn't think of a good reason why he wouldn't, it could get a whole lot worse.

"Time for another beer," I said. I stood, walked through the sliding glass doors and around into the kitchen. When I went back with two cold ones we sat back and watched the sun play on the water in the pool and across the gentle ripples of the canal. Every few seconds a fish would fly out of the water, gaining a foot or so of altitude and landing three or four feet ahead with a slap, disappearing back into the water.

"What was that, a mullet?" Terry Moran asked.

"Beats the hell out of me," I said. But I knew it was. I just hadn't looked.

My partner finished his beer, gave me a long look, then stood up and put his free hand in his pocket, his back turned to me. "Why do I get the feeling there's more to this story?"

I didn't look at him. "Because there always is."

Moran left when his wife called and wanted to know if he was on his way home for dinner. I pushed him out the door and went back to the lanai. My mind was full of white noise, a picture of static; so many things needed to be thought about, decided on, dealt with. I couldn't get traction on anything, I had nothing to hold on to, no place to start. So I sat, feeling the heat and the humidity on my skin and listening to the sound of a lawn mower somewhere down the canal, my mind gone numb. Every time I tried to wrestle with an idea, Lori's face would pop into my mind and I'd ask myself over and over, what the hell would she think about what was happening?

Would she even care? She had her own problems, I supposed.

And what about Leslie? I remembered our missed lunch date and felt a growing pressure to call her, to let her know what was happening. For legal reasons? Yeah, sure.

I was growing morose. Lori was working through things—or not—but she was doing it on her own. If things were different we could have been working on them together but clearly she felt she couldn't do that, at least not now.

At some point my cell phone rang and I froze for a second, a sudden shock freezing my system. There wasn't any news that was apt to be good news. I pulled my phone out of my pocket, half expecting to see Lieutenant Greene's office number on the display but it was something else. No name, just a number from an unfamiliar area code.

"Hello?" I said, my nerves jangling.

"It's me," came the familiar voice. "Roxy."

"Sweetheart!" I called, much too loudly.

"Calm down, Dad! I'm at a pay phone and I only have a minute."

"Where's your mother?"

"Inside the grocery store. I don't want her to see me."

So she's still avoiding me, I thought.

"How are you?"

"We're both fine, but we keep moving. I need to ask you something."

I had stood when I answered the phone but now I sat back down on my chair. "Go ahead, sweetie."

"Were you here?"

I felt confused. Lori had told her about my visit and we'd talked about it. Then why was she asking now? "Yes, honey. I came up to see your mother. You and Anne were out shopping or something."

"Mrs. Swenson?" she said. "That was when we were in Alabama. I meant yesterday."

I didn't know what she was talking about. "Honey, I don't even know where you are. Yesterday or today. What's going on?"

She sounded confused. "Mom went out last night. She said it was about you."

"About me?"

"Well, I think so."

"What do you mean, honey? What happened?"

"Nothing happened," she said. "I asked her where she was going and she wouldn't tell me. She said that it was about my dad and I didn't know if you were here. I didn't want her to not let me see you again."

There was a sudden hitch in my breathing and I felt a moisture in my eyes. "No, honey, it's not that. Your mother just needs to work some things out, you know that. If I was there I would just complicate things for her."

"That's so full of crap, Dad!" There were tears in her voice, too. "It is!"

"No one's going to keep us apart, kiddo. We just need some more time to work through this."

"How much more?" she yelled. "God, I hate this!"

I didn't know what to say to that. "So do I, Rox."

"Well, where did mom go last night then?" As if she wasn't sure she believed that it wasn't to see me.

"I don't know—"

"Oh, she's looking for me now. I've got to go. Really."

I didn't want to let her go. "Roxy…" I said.

"What, Dad? I've got to hang up!"

"Don't fall off any horses, kid."

"Love you!"

She hung up before I could say it back. I hit the "end" button on the phone and slouched down in the chair. So I learned that they were out of Alabama, and Lori went to see someone about Roxy's dad. Shit, I thought, which dad would that be? I didn't know if she meant me, or Roy Evans. Just who the hell did Lori go see?

I didn't have any more beers in the refrigerator. My stomach felt constricted, uncomfortable, and although I felt hungry, I didn't want to eat. I would have drunk more beer just to be doing something with my hands but I didn't think I *needed* it. I've met people I thought were probably alcoholics only they wouldn't stop drinking long enough to find out.

So I wasn't using alcohol to fill the night's void and I was too physically exhausted to get into the motion thing, be it running, swimming or even walking. I just sat in my vinyl padded chair beneath the mesh covering of the lanai and watched the day shrink away. Part of me wanted to get up but I had nowhere to go and not enough energy to fake something.

Alcohol wasn't my curse and neither was dope of any kind. Twice in high school I'd been handed a pipe with marijuana in it and I took hits both times. The first time nothing happened. The second time I actually inhaled into my lungs, the way I'd seen cigarette smokers do, and then it was different. It left me woozy, feeling disconnected from my body, and it killed my time in the mile that I had to run in gym class later that same day.

That experience had been enough for me. It wasn't that the actual high was so bad, but I couldn't understand why people wanted to give parts of themselves up to a drug, become not able to enjoy a social situation or relax without smoking or ingesting something. It was a weakness, I had thought, and I told myself I would always be stronger than that.

And look at me now, I thought. If I could check into an opium den for a month or two....

It turns out my weakness was something different, not something chemical or illegal, but something inside me. It would sound noble to call it "honesty." I think I'd call it a character flaw because that's how so many other people seemed to treat it.

When I went off in court during the Safrenza case it never occurred to me that I was painting a bullseye on my chest. I didn't think then and I didn't think now that it was appropriate to let a known killer, a truly vicious man, skate on a capital beef just because an error occurred in police procedure. The search warrant hadn't been violated on purpose, it was just one of those things. It happened all the time, really. If a wrong had been done, whether on purpose or not, then damn it, prosecute that wrongdoer, even if he is a cop. His actions didn't change the fact that Raoul Safrenza participated in the killings of an entire family with his own hands wrapped around the grips of an aluminum baseball bat.

While the thought may be laudable, or it may not, it's a topic for lawmakers and politicians to debate. Not for a lowly cop calling out the judicial system on the witness stand in open view of the public. But even that wasn't my biggest mistake. The real problem was that I had allowed myself to give a damn, to decide what I thought was right and wrong, and give myself permission to try and make others see it, too. I understood the point and the value of the legal issues at hand. What I didn't think was right was that there was no mechanism for looking past, a zero tolerance policy that ignored evidence that was so clearly overwhelming.

Somewhere during my testimony it occurred to me that the lawyers were the only people conducting the trial who aren't sworn to tell the truth, the whole truth, and nothing but. The judge is sworn to be impartial and maybe that's another flaw of the system. Maybe the judge should be more involved with judging the lawyers, the ones who—

Oh, crap, I thought. I'm doing it again. Why don't I just learn to let it the hell go? Nobody else cares. Safrenza walked, my career was mortally wounded, at least in Tampa, and were it not for the union I'd have been cleaning and refueling boats at a marina somewhere.

Ultimately I had no idea if it was it worth it, the suicide of one's career over a moral high ground. Certainly no one in authority could afford to believe what I thought I did. I didn't know. It sure as hell wasn't productive of anything and here I was, still hanging on to a shard of my career, still trying to do right, still trying to be the honest cop.

Only I wasn't, not really. The past few months, whenever I felt a twinge of self-righteousness or self pity, a moment of umbrage when I thought, why me? I only had to think about Roy Lee Evans to feel as though every bad thing that ever happened to me was somehow justified. If we make our own happiness we should also be responsible for our own hells.

Part of the time we must be. But we don't plan to win the lottery and we don't plan to meet our ends as the result of a violent and ultimately unexplainable act. Sometimes shit just happens. Or, as my father used to say, accidents don't happen, they're caused. There are implications to that statement that most people will never realize.

I thought when I had found Lori and Roxy and we became a family that a miracle happened, that I'd achieved something that I'd had no right to ever expect. Yes, there was baggage from her past but part of what I could bring to her life was an awareness that it was over and that her history didn't need to have a negative effect on the rest of her life. And being with Roxy, watching her grow and demanding that I spend time with her, hearing her call me "her dad" when she spoke with her friends, all of that....

And then Evans gets out of a Texas prison and wants something that I was never able to fully determine. Did he want Lori and Roxy back because he wanted to be a family with them? Was he after a second chance, an opportunity to do something better than he had in his pre-prison term life?

I didn't think so. I thought he was a borderline psychotic motivated by something dark and not understandable by people who lived most of their lives above ground and in the light. If he loved Lori and Roxy it was a different sort of emotion than any I ever knew. I believe it was a selfish, twisted motivation that led him to find us half a country away. I believe he wanted to punish Lori and Roxy for daring to leave him, for presuming that they could change the nature of their relationship with him without his permission. I believe his own warped ego was demanding a price be paid for his embarrassment at their transgressions. I believe that he was willing to do them violent and permanent harm if they didn't give him what he wanted.

When he began stalking Lori at work, exhibiting the classic passive-aggressive behaviors of leaving small presents in her car and at her desk, sending notes and cards through the mail, watching Roxy across the street from her school, the pattern was all too clear.

Or so I thought. Again and again I wondered what right had I to make such judgments, as if I could divine the thoughts taking place in another man's mind.

And yet if I did nothing and harm came to my family at the hands of this man, given what I believed about his state of mind, knowing what I know about the damage such men can and do cause, what would that have made me? A moral coward? An incompetent with his head buried neck deep in the sand? How about an accomplice?

Restraining orders and the like do nothing for people like Roy Lee Evans and in fact often spur them on and encourages them to greater and greater transgressions. All the legal paperwork does is make the situation known to the police. That can be a problem for the eventual victims or their survivors depending on how things finally ended. And they always did end, one way or another.

This time it was me. I ended this situation. So far it's cost me the family I was trying to protect and made me even more vulnerable in my job with consequences that could ultimately affect not just my employment but my freedom, possibly my life.

I thought about the picture of Stacey lying next to me in her bed, sexual paraphernalia strewn about, her magnificent mostly naked form fitting next to me, and I didn't feel anger. I realized I'd adjusted to my new reality and in some way that didn't make obvious sense to me I felt grateful that I had been able to relax for those few hours, despite its upcoming and inevitable cost. It didn't seem to matter that it was all phony.

Something was out in the open now, or almost so: nobody had set me up just to send me a keepsake photograph. There was often a relief when something suppressed breaks surface. For good or for ill it must then be dealt with and no matter the consequences, at least the gnawing of your insides will finally be over.

The stars had finally broken through the memory of the orange and purple sunset and I closed my eyes. I was exhausted but I didn't know if I could sleep. I was wondering how my guts would feel in the morning when I reached for my phone and dialed Leslie Alcaro.

Chapter 25

Moran was already at his desk when I walked in the next morning. He shook his head in response to my raised eyebrows and I sat in my chair already a little out of sorts. I had half expected to be walking into a firestorm. That photograph was going to land somewhere.

I called forensics and asked about the gun I'd brought back from the Tampa mugging. The tech there told me they'd found some partial prints, enough to do at least a probable match, only they didn't score a hit in the system.

That was probably okay, I thought, after thanking them and hanging up. I'd had to create a case number when I'd turned in the gun, otherwise they couldn't look at it, and I started typing up the paperwork now. I'd told them I'd found the gun in a parking lot, all by itself, and that's what how it stayed in the report. The "mugging" had to be part of the set up, the mechanism that got me to take Stacey back to her town house. It wasn't a surprise that we couldn't match the prints. Knowing what they were about to do to me, they probably felt pretty good about not being pursued. They thought they had me on a leash.

And they sure as hell did, at least for now. My immediate concern was still for Lori as I still didn't know who she had gone to see about Roxy's "dad." The only name I could come up with gave me chills, but I couldn't be sure.

Aside from the gun, the other loose end I wanted to take care of was the video tape we had recovered from Randy Shawcross's garage. As yet another excuse to get away from my desk, I got the tape from Terry Moran and walked it down to our Technical Services office. I waited there while they made two copies for me. Since I was in rule violation mode today I walked out and put one of the copies in the glove compartment of my Jeep before returning to my desk.

Moran had been spending time on the phone with Izzy Marquez and he was just hanging up when I got back. I put the original video tape along with the copy on his desk so that he'd have everything in one place.

He said, "You don't write, you don't call...."

"And I don't miss you that much, either. What's up with Ding Dong?"

His smile turned into a wrinkled nose expression, as if he was too polite to articulate his thoughts but had a convenient way to show them anyway. "She's still pushing Bleeker but all she's got is this circumstantial crap. She thinks he probably did it but she's starting to think she can't prove it. She wanted to go for a polygraph to try for a confession but the man's PD won't let him."

The polygraph can be a breakthrough tool if used the right way on somebody who's actually guilty. I'd seen an FBI guy once walk a murder suspect through a series of questions that weren't in dispute. The suspect had answered them all correctly and the agent turned off the machine and calmly showed the suspect what his correct answers looked like on the paper. They'd had quite a conversation about it, how the process worked, and both the suspect and myself learned a lot.

Then he turned the machine back on and asked the suspect a different set of questions, things that had nothing to do with the case, and instructed him to purposely lie and try to fool the machine. When they were finished, the agent again turned off the machine and showed the results to the suspect, accompanied by detailed explanations of everything they were seeing. The suspect was almost enjoying himself, learning the difference between truthful answers and dishonest ones.

For the third phase, the agent restarted the polygraph and asked questions directly related to the case. Very quickly the agent turned off the machine again and showed the results to the suspect. "We've got a problem here," he'd told him. "We know what truthful responses look like—" He held up the paper from the first set of questions. "And we know what deceitful responses look like." This time he showed the paper from the second set. "What do you think we have here?" The suspect examined the paper from the questions related to the crime he was charged with. He'd been led to this point logically and scientifically and had been skillfully backed into a corner. The agent got his confession and the case ended with a conviction.

But something like that wouldn't work with Bleeker if the man's lawyer wouldn't let him participate. That could mean he thought he was guilty or that Bleeker's questionable state of mind might prompt him to volunteer information that might not be in his best interests. People confessed to crimes they didn't commit almost every time a major case hit the newspapers.

"So I'm not sure where that leaves us with Shawcross," Moran said, leaning back in his chair.

"We know that Shawcross and Schoenfeld were linked by both phone records and the Little Y porn site. Little Y may be one of Rudy Pope's enterprises, and we have a tape that Randy apparently made of Pope opening a safe in one of his offices. I'm not seeing much of a role for a borderline nut job like Carl Bleeker."

"Unless he was working for Pope."

I snorted. "Not likely. Rudy likes people who are criminals but look good in suits. I don't think Pope would touch this guy with a ten foot pole."

"Maybe a contract thing? Pope gets Bleeker to take out Schoenfeld then backs away, no connection for him to the crime."

"Maybe. Then who took out Shawcross? Do you see Bleeker as being physical enough to beat up a fit man like Randy Shawcross, then tie him up and drag him behind a boat through the water until he drowned?"

Moran shook his head. "That sounds like more than a one man job."

"And it sounds more like Pope. He's got guys that can do that. You talk about this with Marquez?"

"Ding Dong isn't impressed by the phone records, says a guy like Schoenfeld knew literally thousands of people, political and otherwise. The fact that he shared a porn site password with one of his buddies doesn't phase her, either. She said she wouldn't be surprised if dozens of them shared the same credentials. Schoenfeld's credit card records do confirm he was paying Little Y nearly fifteen hundred bucks a month, though, so they apparently belonged to him."

"Fifteen hundred? That seems awfully high." I thought about that. "So how does she explain the two murders?"

"Her guy was a public figure who received death threats, followed by a shotgun blast. They find a guy who sent death threats who owns a shotgun and has no alibi and little ability to defend himself. The King of Cats thing doesn't get much play with her. If he was doing a job he probably earned what he got. I think she's got a workable case and doesn't want to dirty it up. Or she's doing the political thing, looking out for the mayor's office above her."

"Hell, maybe she's right."

"Bullshit. You don't think so any more than I do."

"Why don't you put in a records request for our boy Ralphie, see if he has a registration for a boat?"

"I'll try for a license on a boat trailer, too."

"Good idea," I said, "though Ralphie likes the good life and would probably keep whatever he'd have at a high and dry marina. We might try taking a look at those."

"What are you going to do?"

"I need to check on a number."

"Whose?"

"It's not part of this."

Moran nodded, then looked down at his desk. "I get the feeling sometimes that you're not telling me everything that's going on. In fact, you and I both know you're not. Sometimes I spend time wondering why that is."

"Because you don't have enough to worry about?" I tried to sound light and casual but that wasn't enough to get me a pass from my friend.

"Go on, then," he said, whisking me away with his hand. "I've got real police work to do."

I ran the number that Roxy had called from and I got the address of a supermarket up in Gainesville. So, Lori had left Alabama and come closer to home, although I didn't know exactly where. I had to decide if it was more important to find her and risk further damage to our relationship or let it go and trust that whoever she was talking to was not a threat to her.

But the image of Ralphie Wandorski kept creeping back into my mind. He'd had contact with Lori and he knew Roy Evans. Those two facts were enough to make me very nervous. I'd always thought of Ralphie as a punk, a car thief who worked at a chop shop at the right time and was lucky enough to get himself noticed by Pope.

Since he had clearly worked his way up the ladder and gotten closer to his boss, he'd obviously become more valuable in ways beyond knowing how to boost and dismantle other people's automobiles. Based on the set up with Stacey, I'd say he wasn't a bad hand at extortion and blackmail.

Unless someone else was behind all that—but who?

My mind kept going back to the impossible thought that Ralphie had been in contact with Lori. I couldn't get myself right with that, couldn't accept that while she'd run away from me, while she'd *hide* from me, she would still communicate with a hood like Ralphie Wandorski. Too many things kept circling back to Roy Lee Evans and there didn't seem to be anything I could do to get away from the man. All I really wanted was to forget about him, relegate all thoughts of him to something past, expunge him from history. Protect my family. But it was his memory that had become the wall between Lori and me, and what separated the two of us was the exact thing that connected her to Ralphie Wandorski.

What I knew for sure was that Ralphie could not help Lori with Evans or with anything else. All he could do was hurt her, emotionally if not physically, either to get to me or to get at me. Either way it didn't matter. Wherever Lori and Roxy were, I wasn't going to give up protecting them. I'd done too much already, and gone too far.

Roxy's call told me what city they had moved to after leaving Alabama. I started the internet browser on my computer and searched for horseback riding facilities in Gainesville. There were about half a dozen results that came back. I read through some of the descriptions and picked up the phone. I'd call what seemed like the largest one first.

As I was dialing I saw Moran poke his head around the dividing wall between our desks. I didn't turn to look at him and a moment later he disappeared. I knew he could hear my end of the conversation if he wanted to; I hoped he didn't.

When the phone was answered by a woman's voice, I identified myself as a police officer. I told her that I needed to find a woman and her daughter that may have ridden there within the past few days. She laid the phone down and went to get the owner.

When he came on the line, I repeated what I'd told the person who had answered and asked that he look through their waiver file for Roxy's name. Riding horses was not without risk and before riding anywhere, participants had to sign a waiver indemnifying the facility against lawsuits should you get hurt on their premises or with their animals. The owner sounded a bit puzzled but told me to hold. Once again I heard the phone hit what sounded like a wooden desk or counter.

It didn't take him long. When he came back he confirmed that Roxy Prentiss had ridden there two days ago. I asked him if the waiver had been signed by Lori Prentiss and after a brief hesitation, he said that it had.

"Listen to me," I told him. "My name is Jeff Prentiss. I'm a homicide detective with the St. Petersburg Police Department. Lori Prentiss is my wife and Roxy Prentiss is my daughter. I need to know the address my wife wrote on that waiver."

The man was clearly flustered. "We don't usually—I mean, I can't just tell you—"

"Sir," I said, cutting him off. "Not only am I a police officer, I am Roxy Prentiss's father, her legal guardian. There is a potential situation that could cause my wife and daughter harm and I need to know where they are. Right now."

"I don't see why you just can't call your wife directly, um, Detective." The man clearly wanted to get off the phone.

"There are reasons," I said. "Do you have a pen?"

"What? Yes. I do."

"Write down this number." I gave him the number for the department switchboard. "We're going to hang up now, and I want you to call that number. Ask for me, Detective Jeff Prentiss. You'll know I am who I say." Then I hung up, ending the chance for further debate.

Ninety seconds later my phone rang. I snatched it up quickly and said, "This is Detective Prentiss."

It was the owner of the riding stable. I asked him if he was satisfied I was who I claimed.

"Well, yes, I suppose so. But I still don't know—"

I cut him off. I told him I could be there in person in less than three hours. I told him I could bring the Gainesville police with me. I told him I could get a subpoena if I had to. I told him all sorts of things until he finally surrendered and gave me the address. I wrote it down in my notebook, telling myself that I had it now "just in case."

"But I'm going to have to tell your wife that you called, the next time I see her."

"If you have to," I said. "But I wish you wouldn't. It won't help how she feels." I thanked him then, and told him he'd done a good thing, and I apologized for the unusual situation. When we said our goodbyes I had the definite feeling that he was wishing he'd never come to the phone. Or owned a riding stable.

"Really," I told him. "Thank you for your help." He stammered a meaningless response and hung up.

I cradled my phone and looked toward Moran's desk. I didn't see or hear him. I didn't know what that meant.

Lori's address was in my notebook. I'd found her again. Guilty feelings washed over me but that was fine, I'd earned them. I'd handle it somehow, the same way I was getting on since Lori had left. In other words, not very well.

I put the notebook in my pocket, feeling better just knowing where Lori and Roxy were, and at the same time aware that it was another tear in the fabric of our relationship. If the stable owner did tell Lori I had called, I could only hope it wouldn't cause her to run again. At least not yet.

Next I put in a call to the Hillsborough County Sheriff's office and spoke to a woman who, once I'd identified myself as a St. Pete detective, put me through to the sheriff. I'd met him once or twice but discounting my negative press clippings, I didn't know if he'd remember who I was.

But of course he did. Never underestimate an elected official's capacity for placing names and faces.

"What can I do for you?" he asked, a hint of cracker accent coloring his voice. Sheriff Burwell had come from a family of orange growers but when his parents sold off their groves to real estate developers he'd eventually taken his inheritance and turned political, running for sheriff on the strength of his family name and the ability to finance much of his own campaign.

I told him we were interested in finding out about any limousine traffic to odd buildings in Brandon, specifically warehouse or commercial buildings big enough for manufacturing operations. He asked why, of course, and I told him there was a possibility somebody was using such a location to make movies of a pornographic nature.

There is still an element of southern Baptist holy rolling hiding in pockets across the deep south, not quite swallowed by the influence of the infusion of drug dealers and out of state relocaters. I could hear the indignation in his voice as he told me he'd make a personal point of having his deputies keep an eye out.

He hadn't thought to ask me why a homicide detective was looking into a vice matter and I was thankful I didn't have to fudge an answer. If I'd been forced to tell him the truth, I'd have risked him going public with something as high profile as either our murders or the involvement of

Rudy Pope. It would be a natural platform point for his next reelection campaign. I thanked Burwell and hung up. Maybe he'd come up with something, maybe not. While it's not illegal to have a stretch limo pull up in front of a steel-walled warehouse facility, it's an odd enough thing to be noticed by a cop, either in the daytime hours or, especially, after dark. And I was having more suspicions about when it was likely to be.

Almost as soon as I'd sat back in my chair my cell phone rang and I pulled it off my belt. Darlene Shawcross. For a moment I hoped that maybe she'd found something else of Randy's but that thought ended as I heard the tears in her voice after I said hello.

"They came back, Jeff, they came back—"

"Calm down, Darlene. Who came back? Are you okay?"

"Those two men who were looking for Randy's laptop after he died. They were here again. They just left—"

"Lock your doors, Darlene. I'll be right there. Keep that phone in your hand and you call me if you see them coming back, okay? I'm on my way right now."

We hung up but I was already moving down the hall. Terry fell in behind me.

"What's up?" he said.

"Darlene Shawcross. Her visitors came back." We sailed past the elevators and went right to the stairs.

"The same guys that were there before?"

"That's what she says."

"Aw, shit," he said. Those were the last words either of us spoke as we burst outside into the bright sunlight and sprinted across the street to the gleaming yellow Monte. It was closer than my Jeep. We got in and Terry propped the flasher on his dash and hit the siren he'd had installed.

We got there in about seventeen minutes taking full advantage of the light and siren although in Florida those things no longer meant that traffic pulled over to the shoulder. In a state where very few people paid attention to traffic laws of any sort, this was never a surprise. During the trip I kept wondering if we had endangered Darlene by overlooking something in our investigation because we were still trying to figure out what the whole thing was all about.

She opened the front door as we pulled to the curb in front of her house but she didn't come out. I took the front steps in two bounds and before

I realized it I had her in my arms. She squeezed me tightly and I could feel her body shake as she sobbed quietly. Moran came up and we stepped inside away from the door as he shut it behind us. I put my hands on her shoulders and backed her up. Her left cheek was a mottled blue and purple and my heart sank as I realized they had hit her. Hard.

I left her with Terry and went into the kitchen where I dumped ice from the freezer bin into a dish towel hanging from the oven door and wrapped it into a bundle. Terry had led her to the couch in the living room where she was breathing deeply instead of crying and I handed him the ice pack and sat on the chair across from the two of them. She didn't need both of us physically crowding her.

"What happened, Darlene?" I asked as gently as I could.

"It was those same men, Jeff, in the black SUV. I heard car doors and I looked out the window but they were already coming up the steps and then—"

Terry rubbed her back. "Take it easy, take it easy. We got time." He was as affected as I was.

"I hadn't locked the front door after I'd picked up the paper this morning. They pushed their way in and I couldn't stop them. I couldn't stop them...."

"What did they want?" I asked.

She looked at me, the purple on her cheek bright from the cold coming off the ice pack. "They wanted the video tape."

"The one we took from your garage?"

She nodded, her mousey blonde hair falling across the bruise. "I told them that it had been in the garage but that it was gone. They made me take them out there and show them where it had been. They wanted to know what was on it."

That was interesting, I thought. "What did you tell them?"

"I told them I gave it all to you. That I never saw it."

My stomach turned over as I thought of the photograph. "Gave it to me, personally?" I asked. "Or gave it to the police?"

"The–the police. Why?"

"Is that when they hit you?"

She nodded again, sniffling. There was still a tissue box on the end table and I nodded my head at it to Moran who pulled it over and placed it in her lap.

"What happened next?" I asked.

"They brought me back in here, threw me down on the couch. They didn't seem as though they knew what to do next. The shorter one, the one who hit me, pointed a finger at me and told me not to call you guys again. That if they had to come back, things would be a lot worse."

"I am so sorry, Darlene...."

"*We* are so sorry, Darlene," Moran added.

She gave us a crooked smile. "I know you are," she said. "I shouldn't have stayed around so long, I should have gone to San Diego by now."

That broke the tension I was feeling and I smiled, too. "That would probably be a good thing for you."

She looked over her shoulder at Terry and then back at me. "Do you think—are these the guys that killed Randy?"

She was looking me in the eyes and I knew I couldn't bullshit her but the fact was that we just didn't know. "They may be, Darlene. We really can't be sure. In any case there's a very good chance they could work for the man who wanted it done but it's too soon to tell right now."

It was a lame answer despite its accuracy and she looked down at her lap and pulled another tissue from the box. I asked her if they'd taken anything else or looked anywhere else and she said they'd gone into the other rooms of the house but didn't stay very long. I was thinking about getting a forensics unit out here to dust for prints when she brought up the fact that they had been wearing gloves. "Like the ones doctors wear," she said.

"That's okay," I replied. "It probably doesn't matter anyway."

We stayed with her while she packed two suitcases and Moran and I loaded them into the trunk of her car. She gave us each a hug before she drove away, the fresh tears tracking down her discolored face like punctuation marks. They exclaimed the same futility I was feeling.

Terry clapped me on the shoulder and we started walking toward the Monte Carlo. "I did not need that," I said.

"Tell me about it. What do you think about putting her in front of some mug shots? Could get lucky."

I shook my head. "I don't think we need to," I said, thinking of the three men who'd accosted me in the parking lot of the Tampa steak house. "I think I've seen these guys before. And if we don't have their prints we won't have their pictures."

He stopped walking. "You planning on getting more specific?"

"Yes," I said. "Just let me think about it for a little while."

Moran shook his head. "End of the day," he said. "I want you spilling your guts by the end of the day, even if it's not for the report."

I nodded. We got into the car and I took the flasher off the dash and Moran pulled slowly away from the curb.

"There's something else I'm not getting," he said.

"What's that?"

"If Pope thinks Shawcross got tape of the combination to his safe, why not just change it? Can't be that hard to do. If he couldn't do it himself he could call somebody and have it done for him in a heartbeat."

"That," I said, "is a very good question."

"So what do you think?"

"Beats the hell out of me."

Chapter 26

We rode back to the office without saying much more. The timing of the assault bothered me more and more as well as the fact that the two men had physically struck Darlene. They hadn't needed to do that, especially after she had just told them the truth.

There were notes on both of our desks to see Greene when we got in. The familiar sinking feeling reasserted itself in my stomach but I thought if this was about the photo, there'd be no reason to bring Moran into it. Unless they were going to smear Terry, too....

"Take a seat," Greene told us after we'd been admitted to his office. Moran looked at me once as he lowered himself into one of the two chairs in front of the desk. He knew what was going through my mind.

"I've been going over your dailies," Greene said. "Where are you guys at with the Shawcross case? As of right now." Greene was direct, an efficient administrator who managed by gruffness and intimidation. He got results from people because they feared him, not because he was a nurturing or inspiring leader. You could ask him to go out for a beer with the rest of the guys off shift but you knew he wouldn't accept, and that was fine with everyone. He wasn't the kind of boss who mixed with the rank and file inside or outside of the office.

I had been trying to keep my head down as much as possible since I'd transferred to St. Pete so his management style was fine with me. He was rigid, thorough, and political; he only looked upward. Anyone beneath him in the chain of command was just that, beneath him. As far as he was concerned he only needed to impress his bosses and he did that with black and white results, including a decent clearance rate for homicides.

Moran started filling him in on where we had been that morning and what we thought it meant in the context of the entire case. Throughout his presentation Greene kept silent and took some notes on a yellow legal pad on his desk. Occasionally he flicked a glance my way but didn't linger. I couldn't keep myself from scanning his desk for the kind of manila envelope that had held my copy of the Stacey picture.

After Moran's presentation, Greene tapped his legal pad several times with the eraser end of his number two pencil.

"What's Tampa going to do with Bleeker?" I asked, mostly as a way to show minimal participation.

He pursed his lips and laid the pencil down on his pad. "Izzy Marquez is going after indictments for making death threats to Barry Schoenfeld. She still likes him for the murder but is holding off for now. Since you guys don't have anything new on that, I'm inclined to think she may be right."

In my peripheral vision I could see Moran turn his head and look at me as if to say, You going to challenge that? But I didn't. I had to start learning how to keep my head down.

It struck me that maybe this was why I had been set up with that picture, to force me to sit on anything that showed actual progress on the investigation. That would explain why I'd received the only copy. At least for right now.

The picture probably couldn't get me arrested but it would certainly push me out of the force, regardless of my pending hearing over the Safrenza case. On the other hand, whoever had arranged this thing may not be through. They could be setting me up to look like a dealer, a pimp, anything that would make a smell.

Moran turned back to Greene and again I was thankful for my friend, a man who deserved better than to be stuck with a pariah like me as his partner.

"If you guys can prove that Shawcross stuck a camera in Pope's office with an eye to taking off his safe, you've got motive. You should stay on that and let Tampa deal with the Schoenfeld thing. That's where the attention is, that's where the media is, and you might be able to clear this thing without attracting any more attention our way."

"Until the arrest, you mean," Moran said.

Greene gave him a look. "Of course. Anything else?"

They both turned to look at me and I just shook my head. I was feeling lost on my own investigation, a puppet with no strings.

"That's all then, gentlemen," Greene said, dismissing us.

Out in the hall, on the way back to our desks, Moran asked, "What do you think?"

I told him the truth. "I don't know what to think. If he had the picture, I wouldn't still be here."

Moran nodded. "Too true."

"And there's another thing," I said.

"What's that?"

"He wants us to clear the case without messing up Tampa's against Bleeker."

"You don't think Bleeker had anything to do with it, do you?"

"Unless he's more than he looks like, and he'd have to be the biggest patsy of all time. I think Lee Harvey Oswald would have something to say about that."

We made it back to our cubicles and as I sat I could feel a slight relaxing in my abdomen. I looked at my desktop, wondering selfishly just what the hell was going to happen to me next. I wondered if antacid tablets would make the ache in my stomach feel better.

From behind me, Moran said, "So what's our next move?"

I could think of two but both of them meant doing my job as though there weren't an executioner's axe hanging over my neck. I didn't want to say the words. The future was too far out of my reach and control. I didn't know what would happen with Lori or the Stacey picture or with Roy Evans. I didn't know how much of what I'd done was going to catch up to me. I didn't know anything other than that for the moment I was still a cop and that I was still collecting a paycheck.

"Fuck it," I said softly.

"What's that?"

"Let's go see Pope," I said.

"Sure," said Moran. "Since that worked so well the last time."

We walked into the Casa Amarilla in Ybor City. This time they seemed to know who we were. Two well-suited bouncers stepped up and asked us what we wanted. Like they didn't know.

"Ralphie around?" I asked.

"No, sir," said the one that was doing the talking for the pair. "Haven't seen him."

I didn't like his tone or his attitude. "How's Ralphie's hand doing?"

Moran stepped forward, adjusting the vinyl case slung over his shoulder. "How about Mr. Pope? If he's available, we'd appreciate just a minute or two of his time."

The man looked from me to Moran and then at his partner. "Wait here," he said, and walked past the host stand and around a corner.

I put my hands in my pockets and studied the murals painted on the walls. The colors were faded now but once they had been bright blues, reds and especially vibrant yellows. The scenes were of peasant countrysides, Spanish or Italian, I supposed. Maybe Cuban. Mostly the scenes were of farming life and livestock grazing and various sorts of festivals, complicated pictures of simple lives. Decades of tobacco smoke had dulled their finish with a coating of nicotine. I couldn't stop fidgeting.

The bouncer appeared around the corner and jerked his head at us. His partner fell in behind as he led us through the kitchen and up the same stairs that had taken us to Pope and Ralphie Wandorski a week ago. He opened the door without knocking and we filed in behind him.

I couldn't help but look for Ralphie but Pope was alone, seated behind a table with a newspaper and a cup of tea steaming in front of him. He was wearing another cardigan sweater. Because of the table I couldn't see if his shoes were a match for what was on the tape from Shawcross's garage.

He looked up at us with that same semi-vacant stare and sat back in his chair, folding his hands together in his lap. He seemed neither curious nor bothered that we were there and part of me wondered if he in fact even remembered our previous visit. I looked to my right at the window over the couch and saw that it had been repaired. The bouncers had stayed in the room on either side of the steel door.

Suddenly I wasn't sure how to begin. For all I knew Pope would toss a copy of the Stacey picture on the table, give a big smile, and say, "What can I do for you gentlemen?"

Moran ended the silence by identifying us as though it were our first ever meeting.

A flicker of annoyance crossed the wrinkles and age spots that dotted his face. "Do you think I don't remember you? Why do you keep wasting my time? What do you want here?"

"We're still looking into the murders of two men, Randy Shawcross in St. Petersburg, and Barry Schoenfeld of Tampa."

"Bah," he said and waved the back of one of his hands at us, smacking his lips in distaste. "I know nothing of these men."

"They seem to know you, Mr. Pope," I said. "In fact, one of them may know you better than you suspect."

I nodded to Terry who stepped forward and took the bag off his shoulder and set it on the corner of Pope's table. "We'd like to show you something, see if you can tell us what it is we're looking at."

He wrinkled more of his features but he didn't say anything else. While Terry removed the video camera and set up a copy of the tape from Shawcross's garage, his gaze seemed to gloss over again and he looked for all the world like an old man sitting on a park bench somewhere, thinking of nothing but being warmed by the sun.

When the camera was ready Terry pushed play and turned the unit around to face Pope, flipping out the small color screen so he could see the picture.

At first only his eyes moved, and then as his face contracted into a squint, a spindly brown spotted hand came out of his lap and adjusted the angle of the screen. He clearly knew what he was looking at. The tape lasted about thirty seconds and by the end of it Pope was visibly quivering in tight lipped anger.

"Recognize anything in there, Mr. Pope?" Moran asked.

His face was darkening as he looked up at us with a pinched, ugly expression contracting his features. "You know I do or you wouldn't be here," he hissed. "Again I ask, what is it you want?"

I stepped forward and leaned on the table with the fists of both hands. "Leave Darlene Shawcross out of this," I said, matching his emotion.

"I don't know who that is," he hissed.

"Where's Ralphie?" I asked.

"I don't know that either. What do you want with him?"

I felt pressure from Moran's hand on my arm. I ignored it.

"How about one of your girls named Stacey? Or a bartender named LeeAnne?" I could feel the color rise in my own face and my voice sounded like a far away thing surrounded by an echo.

Pope's composure returned as I felt mine slipping away. I wanted to grab the old man about his scrawny neck and make him tell us what happened with Shawcross and what the connection was to Schoenfeld. I felt an urge to do violence and other than the prior incident with Ralphie, that had never been how I'd done my job.

I pushed myself backwards from the table, bumping into the two bouncers who had stepped up behind me. As I turned to face them Pope called out, "Leave them be! Do not touch them!"

I looked back at Pope whose face was a mask, slowly resuming its shape as an image of indifference or vacancy. He had taken charge of the room and defused my own anger without precipitating the kind of physical discharge that I had given in to with Ralphie Wandorski.

He waved the camera away and Moran quickly gathered it up and zipped it back into its bag. "There is no evidence of a crime there," he said. "And if there is, it is none of your concern."

"That depends," I said.

"On me," he replied. "I would have to prefer charges against the person responsible for making that film."

"Maybe you already have," said Moran.

Pope's face was as unlined and relaxed now as it was when we had first arrived. He sipped his tea then cradled the cup with his left hand as if to warm it. "So now you tell me I have motive for a killing," he said.

"It could look that way," I told him.

"If we speak more it will be with my legal counsel present."

"Thank you for your time, Mr. Pope. We'll be leaving now," said Moran. He slung the video bag over his shoulder and took a step toward the door before he realized I hadn't moved.

"Don't forget what I said about Darlene Shawcross." I waited until he had refocused his eyes on mine and I said, "A lousy picture won't stop me from coming back."

Again the wrinkled features and darkening age spots. I couldn't tell if he was confused, intermittently senile, or really pissed off. Maybe parts of all three.

As we reached the door, flanked by his bodyguards, he croaked out, "I don't want you two to come here again."

I gave him a wave over my shoulder and kept walking. "Like that matters," I said.

Back in the car we sat for a minute, Moran behind the wheel and unwilling to start the car.

I didn't look at him. "What?" I asked.

"You're losing it, man. I thought you might go off in there again."

All I could say was, "But I didn't."

After another minute I said, "Start this thing, will you? We're starting to roast in here."

Moran turned the key, dropped the car into gear and started driving away. "Where to next?"

"You think he killed Shawcross?"

"Pope? I think he had a damned good reason. I don't see why anyone else would care about his safe."

I wiped the sweat off my forehead with my sleeve. "But how would Shawcross know what was in the safe? Whether there was anything in there he'd want?"

"You mean like jewelry, stuff he always took?"

"Yup. Pope's not exactly Zsa Zsa Gabor. Why would the King of Cats go after an old bastard like Rudy Pope?"

Moran thought about it for a while. "You think someone put him up to it?"

"It fits. And Pope killed him for it, too."

"Tampa has no record of Schoenfeld being in bed with Pope."

"What if Schoenfeld was in bed with somebody else?"

"What does that mean?"

"We need to nail down this Little Y porn site thing. If Schoenfeld put Shawcross onto Rudy Pope's safe, that's one connection. The other is the porn site."

"How do we do it? According to the site we can't even join the thing without being recommended by another member."

An idea was forming in my mind and I didn't say anything.

"Now what are you thinking?" Moran asked.

"You don't want to know."

He shook his head. "Those are the words of a man who sounds like he's about to do something profoundly stupid."

"It's about all I've got left," I said.

"You're serious, aren't you?"

I shrugged.

"You can be a real dumbass son of a bitch sometimes, you know that?"

He pulled onto interstate 275 heading west toward the Howard Frankland bridge. "Seriously. You're too smart for this. We'll get Pope and Rudy and whoever set up that picture. We get them on a murder beef and we'll find someone, maybe the girl, to give up the blackmail shit."

You don't get it, I wanted to say. I'm still screwed. I was still *there* with the girl, I was still doing things that could get me suspended, and that would hurt me at my hearing. And depending on what else comes out I could also get investigated and that could lead to who knows what.

"Aren't you smarter than that?" he asked. "Please tell me you're smarter than that."

"It's not that, Terry," I told him.

"Then what?"

How do you say it? "I'm just not sure I give a damn anymore."

"Yeah, well," he said, changing lanes to the left. "The rest of us still do."

Chapter 27

I was in a funk. I didn't know if I had just kicked out the last support and was now waiting to be buried alive in the cave-in. Rudy Pope had looked more offended or surprised than guilty but how could you really tell with an odd old man like him? He reminded me of that mobster in New York that evaded prosecution for years because he walked around his neighborhood in a bath robe. The cops thought he was nuts until they busted him on a wiretap sounding sane enough when he issued orders to have another mob boss clipped. In any case, if he was counting on me to lay off because of the blackmail picture, I had at least poked him in his rheumy old eye. Now I had to decide if I hoped he thought I was bluffing or not.

When we got back to the station in St. Pete, I told Moran I'd be back in a while and I went over to my Jeep without going inside first. I knew as I was leaving that Moran was still in the lot, watching me drive away, but he never called out and I never looked back. I made my way back to the freeway and all the way into Tampa again, this time over the Gandy bridge. A lot of people didn't like the thing but since it was old, the first bridge to connect Tampa and St. Petersburg across the bay, the rails along the side had spaces that went all the way to the concrete. You used to be able to see rolling water when you looked down at the roadside while you drove. It gave me vertigo when I did it, and I only looked for a second here and there whenever I had driven over it, but I always felt something was lost when they renovated the structure a few years ago, replacing the old style rails.

As I drove I explored the emotional flatness that I was feeling. I'd been tense for so long, every day not knowing if something from my past would surface, having to tiptoe around everyone at my job, and then having my wife and daughter move out of our house. But now I was flat, bottomed out, almost beyond caring what happened next. I knew this wasn't rational thinking and I knew I cared about what would happen next, but the weight of my various problems was pinning me down so that I didn't feel like there was much I could do about it.

Lacking any obvious course through my personal mine field, I could at least take a shot at closing this case. I could maybe do some good for Darlene Shawcross and take Rudy Pope off the board along with his pet rat, Ralphie Wandorski. And if that took a little heat off of me in the end, I wouldn't complain. Right now, though, it seemed more likely that I was closer to contributing to my own downfall. Emotional stress leads to poor judgment and it doesn't matter how much of you sees that, it never seems to be enough to stop it. Part of the brain becomes impaired.

I was supposed to meet Leslie this afternoon. After I'd called her last night she suggested we get together to make up for our lost lunch and it felt good to know that I was going to see a friendly face.

She was waiting for me when I got to an Italian restaurant that sat beneath a hotel on Westshore. She stood up when I got there and threw her arms around me and squeezed me hard. I hesitated at first, then returned her hug. It was quick—we were in the middle of a restaurant—but it let me know how she felt about what was happening to me. For a second I thought how personal it was. I wondered if that was really a good thing, or if I was screwing something up without realizing it.

We sat down next to each other at a table for four. "How are you?" she asked.

I took a sip of water from a glass that had been poured before we'd been seated. "I don't know," I told her. "I'm feeling a bit—out of control."

She reached out and patted my hand. "We'll fix this," she said. Then she grabbed my fingers and held on. Damn it, it felt nice. I squeezed her fingers back.

"Tell me everything," she said.

"It's too embarrassing."

"Not if you didn't do anything wrong. Tell me."

So I told her everything about what had happened in Tampa on my days off and over the weekend. I told her about LeeAnne, Stacey, the hold-up in the steak house parking lot, and the aftermath at Stacey's fake townhouse apartment.

"Tell me again about the car," she said.

I described it to her again, the best I could: brown muscle car thing, either one of those recent non-descript Mustangs or possibly one of the new Chrysler retro-style muscle cars. As I finished I noticed we weren't holding hands anymore.

A waiter had come and taken our orders. We barely paid him attention and both of us ordered salads because it was easy. Eating didn't seem to be a big priority at the moment.

There was an expression on Leslie's face and her focus turned to her lap. "I told you about my ex, Carlos," she said.

"And that he may have ties to Rudy Pope. What about him?"

"After you called me last night, I drove out to his apartment. I knew the address from our separation papers. Do you know what I saw parked out front?"

I could guess. "A brown car like the one I described?"

"How about a Dodge Charger?"

That could fit. I sat back in my chair and told her to tell me exactly what it was she thought Carlos did for Rudy Pope. She told me again about the bolita games and then went on, saying that about a year and a half ago, Carlos started bringing in more cash. He'd started carrying around a second cell phone and spending more nights at a house in Carrollwood.

"How do you know that?"

"Carlos isn't shy about—bragging. He wasn't alone at that house."

"I'm sorry, Leslie."

She shrugged. "Don't be. I married young, too quickly, and much too stupidly. By the time I finished law school, we were already finished."

"Why didn't you get out then?"

"It's not so easy, is it?" She looked at my eyes as she said it but I turned away.

The waiter delivered our salads and I made a point of cutting off his waiter-speak. It was a pet peeve of mine that a waiter couldn't just take my order, deliver my food, then back off. The "how are you doing today" and talk about the weather and the specials and the bogus attempts to bond with me in order to land a larger tip made me take a lot more of my business to fast food restaurants than I otherwise would. What really ticked me off was when they came up and asked, "How is everything?" while you were involved in a conversation. And I tended to face rudeness with rudeness. Over the years my food was probably enhanced with a variety of different saliva.

Leslie noticed my attitude around the waiter. "You're still uptight."

"I don't remember how not to be."

"Do you think Carlos could have set you up?"

"Somebody did," I told her. "The first thought was Ralphie Wandorski, but that might have been too obvious. He'd have to know I'd come looking for him. But Carlos...."

Leslie took a notebook from her purse and tore out a page. "Here's the address for his apartment, and this"—she pointed—"is the one for the house in Carrollwood. What are you going to do?"

"I'm not sure yet." I was still over a barrel with that picture out there. "Be honest with me, how does this affect my case?"

She sat up straighter, and sounded more like a lawyer again. "To be blunt, it isn't good. Our stance has always been that you may have been a bit headstrong but it springs from a strong moral position. With this picture, though, anyone can make you out to seem like anything they want."

I nodded. "About what I thought."

We had finished picking at our food. I threw some cash on the table so I didn't have to look for the waiter again. He wouldn't like me but he'd like his tip. Leslie and I stood and I took her by the elbow and led her out of the restaurant area and into the hotel lobby.

"Walk me to my car?" she asked.

"Of course."

We went across the street and she walked with me to a late model Toyota in the open lot. She turned around at the door and said, "Come here."

I did. I didn't think about it, I just did what she told me. Her hands went up around my neck and she pulled my face close to hers. I held the sides of her ribs as she kissed me slowly and tenderly. After a moment I responded. She pulled back slightly then did it again before letting me go.

I stepped back. "Leslie—"

"Don't, Jeff," she said. "That was for me. You don't have to say a thing."

"But—"

"Really. It was just for me." Then she turned, unlocked her door, got into the car and started it up without looking at me. I stepped back and gave her room as she backed up and drove away.

Just for her. Well, what about me?

I walked down to the river past the new museum and down to the seawall at the water's edge. A group of sculling boats was working its way past my perch and I listened to the cadence of their rowing. I thought about Lori and her not wanting to be with me. I thought about Leslie kissing me. I thought about me kissing Leslie back.

I had no idea what any of this meant. If Lori came back, she and Roxy would be my family again. Roxy would be my daughter no matter what, but Lori was going to dictate the terms of our future relationship one way or the other. Roy Evans may be too big a chasm for us to cross. I'd always known it could turn out that way, but I also knew I'd had to do what I'd done, I'd had to keep them both safe.

Leslie was fresh, she was new, she was beautiful, and for whatever reason, she seemed to actually care about me. I'd been so wrapped up in my own problems for as long as I'd known her—those problems were the reason why I knew her—that I hadn't seen her the way she'd apparently come to see me. Looking back, I could see the hints, and from both sides.

I liked her. I think I'd always known that. What that meant I had no idea, at least not right now.

I pushed thoughts of both women out of my mind and took out my notebook as I walked back toward where I'd left the Jeep. A distraction would be good, doing work would be better. And as I was already more than halfway screwed, I looked up the address of Barry Schoenfeld's home off of Bayshore Boulevard.

Going there would clearly be encroaching on Izzy Marquez's turf. It would also be a political risk and I wouldn't want to tell Moran about it unless I had to, but if we were going to truly solve this thing and not simply put away some mental deficient with a letter writing kink and a shotgun in the closet, we had to find out about the connection between Schoenfeld and Randy Shawcross one way or the other. We needed more.

I pulled to the curb in front of the house. There was no press, which was what I expected. The case had been flat for the past few days and the vultures had at least temporarily moved on. I had some of the color print-outs we'd made from the cached video clips on Randy Shawcross's computer. They showed the three men and the one woman from the videos and although their faces were obscured, I was hoping that the widow Schoenfeld would look at them and be able to recognize her husband.

I held my badge to the security camera mounted above and to the right of the front door as I rang the bell. I held it there for over a minute before I heard the dead bolt slide back and a chain rattle against the heavy oak door.

The woman who answered was Rachel Schoenfeld, the late Barry's widow; I recognized her from the newspapers I'd seen. There were substantial bags beneath her eyes yet she was composed and when she spoke, her voice was strong and clear.

"My name is Jeff Prentiss. I'm a detective with the St. Petersburg police department. I'd really appreciate it if you could take a moment to speak with me."

She looked confused as she stood back and held the door open for me.

"Thank you," I said, stepping past her.

"I don't understand," she said. "You're from the St. Pete police? About Barry's case?" She shut the door, then led me down the marble tiled hallway to a sitting room in the back of the house adjacent to the kitchen. The home looked as though it could have fallen out of a spread from *Architectural Digest*; no mess, no clutter, no real warmth. But Rachel Schoenfeld looked entirely at home as she gestured toward a fancy carved chair while seating herself on a white fabric covered sofa.

I hated what I was about to do to her but I knew that Izzy Marquez would never consider it and to even ask would be to cement a line in place that would quickly become insurmountable. I told her about Randy Shawcross's murder and asked if the name was familiar to her.

"I read about it in the papers, of course. And your Detective Marquez asked me if I was aware of a relationship between he and my husband, but I told her I knew of no such thing."

I squirmed a bit in my chair. "Did Detective Marquez mention that your husband's cell phone records indicate that the two of them did in fact know each other, and that they communicated frequently over the past two months?"

"N-no," she said, frowning. "She did not." She straightened herself on the sofa before she asked, "Is all of this supposed to mean something to me? What exactly are you telling me?"

Now for the awkward part. "Mrs. Schoenfeld, are you aware of the use of any pornographic websites by your husband?"

She visibly started and her face reddened as she processed my question. The answer was clear before she articulated it. "Absolutely not, Detective. Again, just what is it you are trying to tell me?"

Carefully, I said, "Your husband and Randy Shawcross shared more than just phone calls. They both logged on to the same website using the same credentials."

"Credentials?"

"I'm sorry," I said. "They both used the same login name and password to gain access to a particular website."

"I see," she said, although I wasn't sure that she did. "As far as I know, my husband had no need to partake in activities of that sort. I'm not a computer person myself and all I know is that Barry spent time on the internet when he was in his office but I can't imagine why he would… log in to something like that. He simply wasn't the type." She shook her head. "No. That's just not Barry."

We sat in silence for a moment before she unexpectedly brightened. "Maybe for work?" she said. "Perhaps he was doing research on something for the campaign. That could be reasonable, couldn't it?"

The hope in her voice was painful to hear. It was clear she had loved her husband. Part of that would be not wanting to see scandal attached to his name or reputation. But all I said was, "Could be," as I took out the envelope containing the folded printouts.

Her eyes were riveted to my hands as if she already knew what I was going to show her. I extracted the sheets and unfolded them in my lap. "I have some pictures from some of the video clips that were on that website. They came from Randy Shawcross's computer. I don't want to be insensitive, Mrs. Schoenfeld. You don't have to look at them."

She swallowed as she held her slightly quivering hand out to me. She took the pictures and looked at them quickly, one by one, then went back to the one on top. "Why are their faces like that?"

"I don't know. That's how they appeared in the videos."

She studied each of the three pages, carefully, one at a time. Her expression and posture had hardened and I couldn't read the emotions that I thought were likely going through her mind. After a minute and a half she refolded them and held the pages out to me. "Put them away, if you please." Her voice was quieter than before.

I slipped them inside their envelope and then tucked it away inside my jacket pocket. "Are either of those men your husband, Mrs. Schoenfeld?"

She sat up straighter and she shut her eyes as she said in a strong, clear voice: "Leave this house now. If I ever see anything like that again I will do all I can in my power to sue you and your department and anyone else involved with smearing my late husband's good name. I will see you destroyed in what you do. Now please go."

She wasn't answering my question and I had to know for sure; I may not have another chance with her. I was following her back to the front door as I asked, "So one of those men was your husband?"

The bright sunlight made me squint as she pulled the door open in front of me. "You bastard. If you didn't know it you wouldn't have come here. Get out. And do not let me see those pictures again. Or yourself, either."

There wasn't anything else to say after what I'd just done. I nodded my head once and left with a long, rapid stride. I agreed with her; the sooner I got out of there the better.

Another piece of the Little Y puzzle had fallen into place. I was starting to see why a wealthy Tampa politician could forge a relationship with a convicted celebrity burglar and conspire to break the law. And all it had cost me was a bit more of my self respect and a punch in the guts to an undeserving woman. With all that I'd bet Terry Moran would still be pissed off for not telling him what I was up to.

As I drove, I flipped open my notebook to the address of the house Leslie had given me in Carrollwood. I hoped my second reconnaissance mission would go better than the first, and yield at least as much information.

It took about twenty minutes to find it. There was no brown Charger in the driveway or anywhere I could see on the street. The front door was open, though, with only a steel security screen in place. I parked two doors down and walked back to the house, double checking the address painted on the curb.

A television was on in the living room. I knocked on the steel screen and a feminine voice called out, "Hello?" A young blonde woman wearing workout clothes and a pony tail poked her head out from around a corner.

"Police, miss," I said, holding up my badge. "I wonder if you could answer a few questions for me."

She looked uncertain. "Just me?" she asked. "Or all of us?"

All of them? "How many of you are there?"

"There's four of us, including me. Melanie's not here right now, but Mimi and Carol are—"

"Who is it?" Two more girls came into view, one wearing a bikini, the other a halter top and a pair of tight white shorts.

"This is a policeman," said the first girl. "He wants to ask us questions."

The girl with the halter said, "Let him in, Jules. He's a cop."

I stepped back as the first girl, Jules, turned the security screen's dead bolt and pushed the door outward toward me. "Thank you," I said as I stepped inside. It was warm, with fans in the windows blowing outward, but it wasn't too bad.

Jules introduced herself as well as the other two girls. They led me into the living room and sat together on the couch. I grabbed a chair from the adjoining kitchen and set it in front of them.

"We're not in trouble, are we?" the one in the bikini said.

I sat down and said, "Not that I know of. Your name is…?"

I wrote their names in my notebook. Then I asked where they were from and I got three different answers.

"And how did you end up here?"

"You mean in this house?" asked Carol. "It belongs to Carlos."

"You mean Carlos Alcaro."

"That's him."

"And what are you doing here? What brings you together?" I asked.

The three girls looked at each other. The expressions on their faces were halfway between guilt and something different. I couldn't place it.

"We're all actresses," Mimi said. "Well, we're trying to be."

"Let me guess," I said. "Adult films?"

Jules laughed out loud. "We just call it porn."

A half hour later I walked out of there not knowing what to think of the three young ladies—four, if you count the one I hadn't met—that were staying at Carlos Alcaro's house. They were all of age, all there of their own free will, and were not being abused by Alcaro or anyone else. Unless they wanted to be, I thought, as I climbed into my Jeep. I shook my head. Sad. I couldn't help but think of Roxy.

On the other hand, I'd learned a lot.

As I headed west toward the bridge to St. Petersburg I thought about Rachel Schoenfeld again and wondered at my capacity to injure people without the intent to do so. I wondered where it had come from and how many more people I would hurt before I could find a way to stop it.

Chapter 28

My cell phone rang just as I was pulling into the station lot. It was Sheriff Burwell from Hillsborough County. I thumbed the talk button as I shut off the Jeep and said hello. After he identified himself I thanked him for getting back to me.

"Yeah, well," he said, "a couple of my deputies have seen a few limos pull into a steel warehouse building that's set up as a warehouse facility for light manufacturing. They thought it was strange but never thought anything of it until I asked them. Question is now, what do we do about it."

I couldn't tell a sheriff what to do in his own jurisdiction but I hoped he'd give me a little maneuvering room. "As far as I know, Sheriff, they're not doing anything illegal."

He sounded pissed when he said, "Then what the hell you doing looking for something way out here?"

"If they're making movies there and posting them on their website, the warehouse may be an important link between two murders," I said carefully.

"What murders? There in St. Pete, or in Hillsborough County?"

He wanted to make sure he wasn't getting stepped on. "One murder was here, the other in Tampa."

"The Tampa cops got that one?"

"Yes, sir." I didn't want him to press it and force me to give up Barry Schoenfeld's name. Solving his murder, especially when the city cops had a suspect in custody that hadn't actually done the crime, would be the kind of publicity coup an elected sheriff could never pass up.

He didn't ask for the victim but he did ask something else, which might actually come out worse for me. "Who's got this thing in Tampa?"

"Detective Marquez."

"Hmm," he said. "Okay."

I didn't know what that meant. I wanted to ask if he knew her but I held it back. He most likely did. "I'd like to go out there and knock on their door."

"I'll keep you company," he said. "I can probably meet you out there later in the day, if you like."

"Uh," I said, as though I was considering his request. "I'd rather just pop over there for a quick look, see if I can confirm what it is they're actually doing over there."

"Good," he said firmly. "I'll meet you at the warehouse at, what, three o'clock work for you?"

There wasn't anything I could do. I checked my watch and said, "Perfect. Where are we going?"

I wrote the address down in my notebook, thanked him for reaching out, and hung up. I had about an hour to make it back over the bay yet again, my third trip over today; I had just enough time. I wanted to check in with Moran and catch him up but now that would have to wait; I didn't want to do it over the phone with me on my way to do something else behind his back. Starting the car I tried to think of the nearest burger joint drive-through I could hit on the way back to the freeway. My stomach had been rumbling for hours and the feeling had finally turned into an aching hunger.

Things were moving now and it helped keep the rest of the garbage in my life from overpowering my thoughts. Pulling on the few loose threads we had was finally producing some tangible leads, the only problem now being Sheriff Burwell was involving himself. Ordinarily that would be fine but I was tracking further off protocol with every new step I made. I needed to find out what was so special about the Little Y porn site and I needed to do it soon, before I got too close and Pope or Ralphie did a special delivery of their little frame-up picture to Lieutenant Greene or the press. Despite my partner's professed optimism, there was no doubt it would finish me in the department, not least because my will to fight it was nearly non-existent.

Again I wondered what the hell had happened to me. That was a question I didn't really want to answer. I knew all too well everything I'd done.

There was a McDonald's north on Fourth Street that was near an on-ramp so I headed that way. I sat in the drive-through lane and tried not to think. Nothing in my life seemed capable of simplification, everything I tried, every move I made, was like dropping a cement block into a small puddle. The only reason there weren't more ripples was because I'd destroyed the pond.

When I pulled up to the microphone, the standard greeting and "May

I take your order?" query came through the speaker and something in the girl's voice, her tone or accent maybe, reminded me of my wife. I stammered through my request and pulled ahead, thinking of Lori.

I still didn't know who she had been talking to about Roxy's "dad." The subject was either me or Roy Evans. The only name I could come up with was Ralphie Wandorski but that didn't make any sense. At least that was what I kept telling myself. It hadn't made sense to me that Lori would call the son of a bitch about Roy but she had confirmed that fact to my face when I saw her in Alabama. Carlos Alcaro?

It struck me that I had no real control over anything important in my life and I picked up my order and got back on the road.

Heading toward the interstate, I tried not to think of Lori and Ralphie and what kind of relationship they could possibly have. She wanted her space from me and she took it. If she wanted to talk to Ralphie Wandorski or write letters to her ex-husband, there wasn't a whole lot I could do about it.

We'd fired up Pope and now a cement block was liable to fall on my own little puddle any minute. But in the meantime, I'd check out the Brandon warehouse with Sheriff Burwell, another complication I'd created but couldn't control.

I pulled my cell phone off my belt and started dialing Terry Moran's number but then I stopped and put the phone down on the seat. It wasn't clear what I should tell him. That I'd stepped into Izzy Marquez's investigation and royally pissed off the wife of the slain politician that had taken the media spotlight from the Randy Shawcross/King of Cats murder? And now I was on my way to yet another jurisdiction to poke a new stick into Rudy Pope's eye? He'd probably meet me there and shoot me for my own good. He'd get no argument from me.

The problem was that it felt that what I was doing was wrong but at the same time I couldn't think of anything else to do. I didn't want to sit back and wait for the shit storm to start when I could march ahead and at least try to get to the truth before it hit. They could get me booted out of the department, god knows I set the table for them, and if they did enough work they could do a lot more, but I couldn't just sit still and wait for it. I had to keep moving, and I had to keep doing what I thought was right. The consequences of that would just have to take care of themselves.

I thought of Stacey and my "friend," LeeAnne. Had they been forced to screw me over or was it part of how they chose to lead their lives? Maybe one day I'd find out. If I did, hopefully it would be soon.

I found the address that Burwell had given me and did a drive by past the building. It was a two story steel structure about a hundred feet long by fifty feet deep, with faded yellow paint on the walls and a dirty white roof, stained with downward pointing arrows of rust. It was big enough for a warehouse or even a light manufacturing operation, just like the sheriff had said. The front door was set in the middle of the front wall and there were small, shuttered windows to either side. The parking area in the front of the building was empty. I took this to mean that Burwell was running a bit late.

Driving down the street I could see one side of the building and could get a partial view of the structure's back before a stand of Australian pines cut off my view. The road I was on began to curve away from the facility at that point so I pulled over onto the shoulder and shut off the Jeep. Stepping out of the car, I walked back along the road, crossed a small ditch and made my way through the scrub up to the trees. After taking out a couple of spider webs with my face I picked up a fallen branch and held it in front of me as I walked, collecting insects and sticky things on the burnt orange needles.

When I made it through the trees and had clear sight of the back of the building I could see two rental trucks backed up to the twin loading dock doors. There was no movement outside but dull sounds were making their way through the humid afternoon air and while I couldn't be sure, I thought they were coming from inside the truck beds.

With my stick in front of me clearing the way, I made it back out to the road and stopped to pick a half dozen sand spurs out of my cuffs and off my socks. A car was coming down the road behind me and I turned to see a Hillsborough County cruiser just passing my car. I held up my hand and it pulled to a stop next to me, the electric window sliding down to reveal a man in a sheriff's uniform squinting up at me.

"You must be Prentiss," he said, looking down at my socks. "Been out walking, have ya?"

He looked like he sounded on the phone, middle aged southern boy, unexpectedly wealthy and not ready to retire. Why not run for sheriff, he'd ask. How hard could it be?

I was probably selling him short but I wasn't in the mood for politicking. "Sheriff," I said by way of greeting. I held out my hand and he looked at it before he made the effort to pull his right arm all the way across his body and stick it out the window to shake. "The parking lot's empty but there are two moving trucks out back at the loading docks. You can hear them working in there."

He pursed his lips and turned to look at the building. "That may just suit me," he said. "If they're doing what you say they are, I don't want them in my county."

I flicked the last of the sand spurs onto the road and ground it into the asphalt with the sole of my shoe. "I'd still like to take a look. If that's all right with you."

He looked up at my face again. I got the feeling he was trying to decide how much trouble I was liable to cause him. "Okay," he said at last. "Let's go see. That your vehicle?" He pronounced every syllable of the last word.

"Yes, sir."

"Follow me then." I could hear the whir of his window sliding up as I walked back to the Jeep. We could knock on the door but if they didn't want to let us in I didn't know what else we could really do. Sheriff Burwell would likely thank me for wasting his time and then sit around and possibly escort the two trucks out of his jurisdiction. If this was where they were making the movies for the Little Y porn site, though, it was possible they could be shutting down operations and the chances for getting at Pope could diminish greatly.

There was no point in bringing that up to Burwell. As long as his territory was clean he'd remain a happy man. Pope hadn't been his problem and until a bigger fish came along and made it so, Burwell wouldn't have to deal with it. Greene could put on some pressure, if he had a mind to, but not me.

We pulled into the warehouse parking lot and the sheriff at least had the good sense to not park in front of the door or windows. By pulling in forty feet down his car couldn't be seen by someone looking straight out the glass. I parked on the side of his cruiser furthest away.

Burwell stepped out of the vehicle and straightened his shirt before pulling his wide-brimmed hat off the seat and setting it on his head, adjusting it just so. When he was ready he walked toward the door. He didn't look at me until we got there.

"You set?" he asked.

I nodded.

From inside we could hear the sounds of a radio playing but nothing else. Burwell tried the door—it was locked. "Bit strange for a commercial building in the daytime," he said.

There was a button mounted on the door frame and he pushed it. From inside we could hear a bell ring and when he took his finger away we heard the radio stop. Burwell kicked at the bottom of the door with the side of his foot as though he didn't want to get his hands dirty from pounding on the weathered paint. "Sheriff's department," he shouted. "Open up."

There was silence for a minute as Burwell examined the white paint residue that had transferred to his shoe and then came the sound of a dead bolt sliding back. The door opened outward and a man stood just inside, still holding the know, rings of sweat outlining the neck and underarm areas of his dark maroon t-shirt. "Can I help you?"

Before Burwell could answer, the man's eyes flicked over to me then flew open as he seemed to recognize me. Damn it, I thought, as he pulled the door shut with a slam and took off running into the building.

"I'm going out back!" I shouted to Burwell as I started sprinting. This was the only door in the front of the building and the only other ones I'd seen had been in back. I couldn't remember if there was one on the side but in any case I'd have to go past it to get to the back. That left only one side of the building completely exposed but it was furthest from both the trucks and the driveway into the parking lot.

I'd recognized the man at the door, too, but not soon enough. The last time I'd seen him I'd just kicked him in the balls with my shin after he and two friends had held me up at gun point in the parking lot of a steak house in Tampa. I thought of my pal Stacey and wondered if there was any chance of finding her inside the warehouse. I should be so lucky.

I was around the corner in seconds, running along the side of the building as fast as I could. Just as I rounded the back corner a steel door next to the nearest loading dock crashed open and my guy jumped down the concrete stairs and up to the passenger door of the first truck. It was locked. I was about twenty yards away and he looked at me once over his shoulder and took off on foot, heading to the far side of the parking lot.

I should have identified myself as a policeman and called for him to stop but he knew who I was. And I wasn't feeling so much like playing by all of the rules at that moment. It took a lot to run hard like this in the heat of the day, running through but never catching the heat shimmers that distorted the air coming off the asphalt parking lot.

He was wearing big leather work boots and I was gaining on him. He made it to the weedy fringe off the asphalt just a few steps ahead of me. Through some more pine trees there was an eight foot chain link fence surrounding the property and when he got to it he started climbing. The rounded toes of his boots kept his feet from gaining purchase.

I leapt for the fence from five feet away and grabbed the back of his pants just as he was reaching for the top. The impact knocked his feet loose and the snatch force from our combined weight pulled his hands from the metal pipe running along the top.

He tried to scramble out from under me but I grabbed one wrist and forced it up high around his back while shoving him into the fence. This kept him from turning out of my hold and I jammed his face into the rough galvanized metal as he tried to force his way to his feet. I let him stand but kept the pressure going on his arm and used my weight and leverage to keep his face smushed into the metal links.

"Stop it!" I said, jerking his arm upwards to make my point. I had to do this several times before he stopped struggling. "Listen to me, you asshole, and you may get out of this."

"Fuck you!" he said, his lips pushed through the fence.

That bought him another arm twist as I used my free hand to work my cuffs off my belt. I clapped one bracelet onto the wrist I was holding and half turned him away from the fence. I gave his arm another hard turn up and he screamed and nearly went limp. I clipped the other bracelet around a link in the fence as high up as I could while keeping his body from turning around. As long as he stood close to the fence and on his toes, he could make the pressure on his arm a little bit lighter and keep his shoulder in its socket.

But not much. Sweat was dripping down from his forehead and mingling with the tears streaming from his eyes and he was muttering, "Goddamn, goddamn." With one hand on his outside shoulder I kept him pinned close to the fence and with the other I pulled his wallet from his back pocket. The driver's license in the plastic window said his name was Hector Ramirez.

I dropped the wallet on to the sand at his feet and said, "Listen to me, Hector."

He started to say "Fuck you" again but I was waiting for it and shoved him closer into the fence. He choked off his words and started saying, "Okay, okay...."

I let off some pressure and he got up as high as he could on his toes again. "Shut up and listen to me then, Hector. You assaulted me in a parking lot of a Tampa steak house with a gun. You know the 10-20-Life law, don't you? The one that says in Florida committing a violent crime with a firearm buys you an automatic ten years, don't you? 'Use a gun and you're done'? You read the billboards, right?"

"It wasn't me, man—"

"Save it. I was there, remember? And that's just for the one charge. I can do a whole lot better than that." I gave him another shove into the fence and this time he screamed. Part of me, a big part, wanted to give in to the moment and take all grief and stress and tension that had been such a part of my life for so long and work it out on his pathetic ass. But I wasn't ready to cross that line yet. Especially not with Burwell somewhere nearby.

"Last chance, pal. In about five minutes this place will be crawling with cops. You can get out of this if you talk to me right now." As I said this I looked back toward the warehouse and wondered how the sheriff was doing. The trees and long weeds were screening us from easy viewing although I didn't think there wasn't anyone else outside—yet.

"Tell me about this place, Hector. This is where you make the movies, right?"

"If you didn't know that already you wouldn't be here."

I started to shove him forward again but then stopped myself. "I'm not playing with you, Hector. You tell me right now how the website set-up works and I let you go over the fence. Seriously."

"Bullshit."

"You got any better offers? The clock is ticking. That sheriff comes out of there...."

We were both quiet for a few seconds, Hector probably considering his options, me listening for sirens. Nothing yet; Burwell must be keeping busy inside. I hoped he was all right.

"It's just a porn site, man. People fucking. What else do you need to know?"

I gave his body a shove forward that increased the pressure on his shoulder joint and was rewarded with another whiny scream. "Why do they blank the faces? Why do you need to be approved to join?"

"God, man, my arm. You're tearing up my shoulder."

"It's only permanent damage. Hurry it up. I'm not telling you again."

I didn't touch him, just let him half hang there, in clear pain, thinking about his options and waiting for the sheriff's troops to arrive. Finally he said, "It's not a normal website, man. It's a scheme, they call it legalized prostitution."

"What's that supposed to mean?"

"What's the difference between a hooker and a porn star, man? Huh? They both get paid to screw but one's illegal, right? What if you pay the bitches and the johns, call them both actors?"

"Who would do that, Hector?"

"You're not seeing it, man. Pay the hookers what they'd make on the street. Pay the johns a buck or some shit like that. Now make a movie of it and they're all actors fucking other actors."

I wasn't getting the whole thing. "Who's the money behind it all? Who makes the profit?"

Hector swallowed. His shoulder was going to be bothering him for a very long time. "To make it like legal porn, they have to sell something, a product. But no john is going to want to sell movies of themselves. So the website is like a club. You join, you pay dues, and you can buy these movies and watch them on your computer."

Now it was starting to making sense. That's why the faces were blanked out. Little Y acted like a secure pimp, setting up the girls—and apparently men—and filming the sex. As long as there was a product actually offered for sale somewhere, it was as legal as any other sort of porn operation.

We could hear sirens now, faint but growing louder. "What was the going on in the parking lot?"

His breathing was getting labored. I thought about cutting him loose before he passed out on me.

"I was just told to scare you, man. It didn't mean anything."

"Who told you to do that?" I poked his pec with a hard finger for emphasis.

"Shit, man, that hurts."

I lifted my hand again.

"It was Ralphie, Ralphie W, man."

That confirmed the set up in Stacey's town house. "One more thing," I told him as I dug my keys out of my pocket, let him see them. "Where's Stacey?"

"The chick that was with you? I don't know, man. Haven't seen her since."

Ralphie'd probably sent her away. Something else occurred to me: "Carlos Alcaro part of it?"

"Works with Ralphie. He drove the car. That's all I know, really. Me and Nando got dropped off after the steak house. Alcaro went away on his own."

I unlocked the cuff attached to the chain link fence and Hector collapsed to the ground with a groan, grabbing at his shoulder with his good hand. I took the bracelet off his other wrist then picked up his wallet. The sirens sounded like they were approaching the front of the warehouse. I slipped his license out of the case and held it in front of Hector's face.

"You're done in Florida, Hector. I'm keeping this. You can get another one in a different state. You won't want me to find you around here. Like ever."

He was still on his knees, clutching his shoulder. "You're really letting me go?"

"I said I would. Get out of here."

He looked up at the fence. "I can't do it, man. You fucked up my arm like I need surgery."

Aw, that was too bad. "Get up. Hurry." The sirens had entered the parking lot and even without looking I knew one was behind us at the trucks parked at the loading docks.

Hector pushed himself up and I made a stirrup for him out of my interlaced fingers. "This is going to hurt, man," he said.

"No shit. But you're a tough guy. I'd get going if I were you."

He put one of his work boots in my hands and stood, taking his free hand off his shoulder and grabbing at the fence. He was biting his lip from the pain. As he was pulling himself over the top, I said, "What were you doing with the trucks, Hector?" I'd forgotten to ask the obvious question.

"Shutting down, man."

"Why?"

He half fell on the other side of the fence, barely managing to land feet first, another stifled cry escaping from his lips. I could see his cheeks were wet.

"Ask Ralphie," he said as he ambled away through the weeds adjacent to the state road that ran twenty yards in the distance.

I watched him go as I wiped my hands on my pant legs. As I picked my way back through the undergrowth I thought about what he had told me. Legalized prostitution, he'd called it. Not quite, I thought, but close enough.

When I made my way back around to the front, Sheriff Burwell told me what had happened. After I'd taken off on the foot pursuit, he continued inside. Three other men were running toward the rear of the building where the trucks were. He identified himself and called for them to stop. They must have thought there were more of us than there were, because they did. One of them was carrying a gun with no permit. That was when he marched them back to the front of the building and out into the front lot where he used the radio in his cruiser to call for backup. He hadn't been wearing a portable.

"You lose your guy?" he asked in his usual dismissive tone.

"Got away. Went over the fence."

"Couldn't catch him, eh? I got three." He shook his head, losing interest already. "Looked like you was moving pretty good, too. Got all hot and bothered for nothing, eh?"

Burwell's deputies cuffed and pulled the three men up from their knees. They marched them over to their cruisers and guided them into the back seats. Sheriff Burwell told them to get their statements while we went back inside. One of the men looked like the second assailant from the steak house—Nando, apparently—but it didn't matter.

"This what you expected?"

Inside the warehouse area, fake walls had been erected to form a dozen or so different "rooms," each with their own décor. It looked more like a Hollywood sound stage than anything else. Different kinds of carpeting were on the floor, the furniture mostly leather and chrome and wood with oaken finishes. Quality stuff, actually.

A lot of it had been moved in front of the loading dock doors, and some was already into the trucks. I didn't need to see anything else. I'd gotten my answers.

"Looks like you got what you wanted, Sheriff," I said.

"How's that?" A touch of derision in his voice, like a city cop like me could never understand his rural point of view.

"You shut down a porn operation in your county. Congratulations." I took Hector Ramirez's driver's license out of my pocket and handed it to Burwell.

"What's this?" he said.

"Guy I chased dropped his license. If you come across him again, he may have had a hand in two murders." With that I patted him on the shoulder and left. Searching the front office area would have been nice but that would require a search warrant and more of the sheriff's cooperation and somehow I didn't think that either would be easily forthcoming, nor quite worth the effort.

Just as I reached the front door, Burwell, studying Hector's drivers license, called out, "And you let this guy get away?"

"At least you got three," I said.

Sheriff wins.

Chapter 29

Today had been a big day. So far I'd provoked a career criminal who quite likely possessed a photograph of me that would end my career in an eyeblink, if not actually land me in jail. I'd alienated my partner, a man who was perhaps my last true friend and who had been willing to go to great lengths to help me get my own mess of a life in order. I pissed off the wealthy and influential widow of a murder victim with pictures of a compromising scene between her husband, a strange woman, and another man, an additional action not designed to win me career longevity. Lastly, I involved the sheriff of Hillsborough County on an unauthorized, off the leash operation designed, if at all possible, to fly under the radar of both the Tampa and St. Pete police departments. If Lieutenant Greene got wind of any of this, Pope may not need to deal his little blackmail picture; I'd be done anyway.

In the larger scheme of things, Lori had left me and now I had no idea if I'd started something with my lawyer. With my lawyer. I'd expect her to know better. Clearly my judgment couldn't be trusted.

On the other hand, it looked like I'd found out what the Little Y porn site was all about, and possibly identified one of the killers of Randy Shawcross and Barry Schoenfeld. Now what I had to figure out was how I could use all this newfound knowledge to save my own ass.

I needed my partner for this. I'd gone off the reservation because I was feeling out of control and that other people and events had been steering my life and career in ways that went way beyond my own influence. I was still compromised but with my newfound knowledge, I may have enough on my side to pull myself off the firing line. And after that, well, it may be time to hang it up once and for all. See if there was any real chance of getting my wife and daughter back. It wasn't going to happen with all this shit going on with me.

I tried not to think of Leslie. She was married, too, wasn't she? Although if everything worked out right, Carlos Alcaro would find himself behind bars for a very long time. An image of Roy Lee Evans popped into my mind and I hoped I wouldn't find myself keeping Alcaro company up at Raiford on his account.

As I drove back toward my side of the bay, I began to regret letting Hector Ramirez go. Since the fingerprints from the gun I'd taken from him in Tampa hadn't produced a hit, I knew he didn't have any priors. If I'd popped him, Pope would have had him lawyered up immediately and without any proof of his involvement in anything else, the only realistic thing we could have gotten would have been from the steak house parking lot. It just felt wrong to have turned him loose, but really, I had no way of knowing if he knew anything about the photograph. I needed to keep a lid on that as long as possible.

Big deal, I thought. What I had really needed was a way to get him to give up Rudy Pope or Ralphie Wandorski but I didn't see what kind of leverage I had. Without a direct path to the heart of things, I'd have to work along the edges some more. Still, it rankled to let Hector go, even though he wouldn't be playing any tennis or softball for a while.

But I did find out about Little Y and that provided a motive for the two murders. Apparently Barry Schoenfeld, Tampa mayoral candidate, was one of many men who looked outside his marriage for sexual adventure. Maybe the lure was other men, maybe it was indulging some inner fantasy, or maybe it was just some other personal kink his wife couldn't or wouldn't satisfy at home. Maybe it was all of that. Clearly this was all a risky business, especially for a public figure, even with the anonymity provided by Little Y.

Maybe he'd wanted to quit, to get out. Maybe the requirements for quitting a Little Y membership were even more stringent than the ones allowing you to join. Or maybe Schoenfeld just wanted to rip off Rudy Pope's safe. Whatever the reason, he knew about Pope and his safe and wanted something out of there. And so he got Randy Shawcross, the King of Cats, to get it for him.

Randy creeped Pope's office and planted the camera, recording the combination over a wireless connection sent to a waiting video camera. But once he returned to recover the camera and actually open the safe, something had gone wrong. Pope's men found him and they killed him for it.

They had either gotten Schoenfeld's name from Randy before he died, or they'd found some other way to put the two men together. However they did it, they could have confirmed it by looking at the server logs for the Little Y site. They'd have seen different computers logging on with the same login name and password, and that may have been enough to nail Randy's coffin. Then they took out Schoenfeld.

I asked myself what they were likely to do next. They've compromised me but so far only exercised it as an unspoken threat. They've either shutdown or relocated their production "studio" but I had no doubt it was only temporary. Things were moving fast and the only hope I had to save my own ass was to move even faster, to get to Pope on the murder beef before he finally flushed my career, and possibly my freedom, into the sewer.

Eventually finding my way back in St. Petersburg I pulled into the lot across the street from the station and automatically looked for the bright yellow smear that would be Moran's Monte Carlo. It wasn't there and part of me was relieved.

Inside, on the way to my desk, I passed the break room which was standing room only, the TV in the corner tuned to a local news bulletin. "What is it?" I asked Fred Hoying, another detective, who was standing just inside the door.

He raised his eyebrows in exaggerated surprise. "You haven't heard? Rudy Pope just bought it in Tampa. At one of his restaurants."

"What happened?" I said, my mouth suddenly going dry.

Hoying shrugged. "Don't know. Someone blew his head apart with a shotgun." He looked at my face. "You okay?"

I didn't answer him. I walked down the hall and dropped heavily into my chair. Moran's desk was clear; with his car gone I knew he wouldn't have been in the break room.

Who had killed Pope? And after all these years of outlasting his contemporaries, why now?

My mind was reeling. All I could think of was that I might have caused this somehow, that the questions I'd been asking and the people I'd been seeing had led to this new execution, but I couldn't see how. Until an hour ago they had to think they had *my* balls in a vise, not the other way around.

Christ, I really needed to speak with Moran. If everything was hitting the fan, it would be coming my way next. I had to get out of there. I looked at my watch; it was nearly the end of my shift anyway. I took off in a hurry, this time not stopping at the break room. Behind me I heard Greene's voice booming but I didn't hear my name and I didn't look back.

Outside I called Moran's cell phone from mine. When it went through to voice mail I hung up.

Where the hell was Terry Moran?

I pulled out of the parking lot and drove slowly in the gathering traffic toward the bay and pulled into a no parking zone in front of an office tower a block from the water. I pulled out my notebook and found Ding Dong Marquez's desk and dialed but there was no answer. I wondered if she was out working the Pope murder.

Rudy Pope was dead. Senior citizen, last of the old time Mafia bosses, more recently operating on the fringes, was gone. He had survived for decades, longer than nearly all of his contemporaries, and somebody finally got to him just now, today. But why? How can a man in his line keep himself going for so long and then suddenly, bam, get himself blown away in one of his own restaurants? What happened to his security, his bodyguards?

I pulled away from the curb and drove a few blocks to a public parking ramp near the minor league ball park and found a spot. I couldn't sit where I'd been in that loading zone, melting in the greenhouse effect of the Jeep interior, but I didn't know where to go or what I should do. I drove slowly to the rooftop level and got out and walked to the low wall along the eastern edge. There were a number of small sailboats on the water, probably a class from the marina in front of the St. Petersburg Yacht Club. A helicopter was descending from the north and I turned and watched as it headed towards a landing on top of Bayfront Medical Center, roughly at the same altitude as I was now.

I couldn't concentrate, couldn't focus, couldn't process everything going on around me. Events were burying me and I had no idea what they meant, how they all fit together. I made sure my cell phone was clipped to my belt and I started for the nearest stairwell. Motion.

For all the progress I'd made on the case today, it had likely come at great cost. In order to keep Terry Moran's reputation as unblemished as I could, I hadn't told him about my visits to Rachel Schoenfeld or to the warehouse in Brandon. If I was going under the son of a bitch would be trying to hold me up so hard he'd get sucked right down along with me, and I wouldn't do that to him.

Although maybe I already had. Maybe Greene took it to him when I was gone because Moran couldn't account for his partner's whereabouts. The more I thought about it, the more I thought that I couldn't go on with this anymore. I wasn't even sure what "this" was. I didn't know if I was just going through the movements, playing at being police, a make believe homicide detective. Was I really trying to take down Pope, a man who'd literally eluded the law for decades? Or was I looking for justice for Randy Shawcross, a convicted thief I barely knew, or even Barry Schoenfeld, a man I'd never met, and probably wouldn't respect if I had?

I'd reached the ground level and pushed on the crash bar to get outside and back into the sunshine. It took me a moment to orient myself and I headed down the sidewalk to my left. I could smell a combination of salt water from the bay and fertilizer from the outfield grass in the baseball field.

Maybe it was the truth I was after. That would be good. I could tell myself that. It would actually be noble. I was just searching for the truth.

But I knew what I was really doing, I just hadn't thought about it enough to be able to admit it to myself. I'd been running away, and quite poorly, from the shards of my own life. A mess of my own making.

You can't run away from something without running toward something else. And sometimes you can only do that when you don't look ahead at what that is. Was my inability to deal with my wife's leaving enough justification to trample anyone who got in the way? All in the name of "seeking the truth"? Who really cared about the truth? Then there was Leslie Alcaro: was I running from Lori and running to Leslie instead? Would that really be any less complicated?

The fact is that wherever I found myself was the result of the flaws in my own decision making. I had made choices, the hardest ones, to protect the people I loved and while it probably worked, I drove those same people, my family, away in the process. I had made a decision to decry a legal system that would allow a murderer to walk free because an incautious cop looked over *here* when the search warrant said he could only look over *there*. It was of my own making that I got run out of Tampa and had my every move scrutinized in St. Petersburg.

Now I had to wonder what I was doing to Terry Moran. I'd slipped so far I could justify bending not only the rules but the established procedures of two police departments. I'd gotten into a compromising situation with a hooker, and I'd deliberately left Moran in the dark about my recent actions on both sides of the bay. So I knew what Little Y was about and I knew why Barry Schoenfeld would acquaint himself with the King of Cats.

But that was just more truth and I wasn't sure who really gave a damn. Everything I did was because I thought what I was doing had been *right*, yet everything I touched kept turning out so *wrong*.

I'd crossed several streets until I was walking along the marina at the base of the Million Dollar Pier, St. Pete's biggest tourist draw. I turned the corner and kept walking towards the structure, built at the end of the road a few hundred yards over the water. Brown pelicans eyed me sideways as I walked past them, perched on the balustrade, waiting for fish guts to fly out of my pockets in their direction.

I had no right to mess up Moran's life. He had been unlucky enough to get paired with me in the first place. There was a corrosive feeling of guilt building up in my stomach that could have been coming from oh so many places. Guilt is the dark side of an unheeded conscience. I could destroy my own life, put my own family through pain, but I had no right to do that to Terry. He thought he was my friend. So what was I?

I thought about telling him everything. I figured I didn't have anything else to lose.

Why did I always have to keep making everything about me?

I could tell Moran about Roy Lee Evans, the whole story, top to bottom. He could guess for himself why Lori and Roxy left then, and he might understand why I'd been doing the things I had.

There'd be no strings. He could have the information free and clear, to do with as he saw fit. He could follow the letter of the law, or seek justice, seek his own truth, whatever ideal he might think would be important at the time.

I was ready to be done with it. All of it. He could have my story and my badge and the rest of it all be damned.

The tightness in my stomach eased noticeably as I came to this decision. I stopped at a cart on the sidewalk and bought a cherry snow cone from the sweating vendor. It was cold and tasted sweet and tart and delicious in the burning glare of the late afternoon sun.

White noise filled my conscious mind as I turned and headed back toward the parking ramp. Everything I was keeping in my head seemed quieter than it had for months. The snow cone was already dripping red streaks down the paper holder and onto my hands.

My phone rang and the interruption was jarring. I took it from my belt and checked the display before I answered it. It was Moran. Finally. I poked the talk button with a sticky thumb and said, "Where the hell are you?"

There was no response. I pulled the phone from my ear and checked the signal strength: four bars. I put the phone back to my ear and said, "Hello? Terry?"

"Jeff?" came Moran's voice.

"What's wrong? You okay?"

"No, everything's fine. I need to talk to you."

I dropped the rest of the snow cone into a garbage can. "I want to talk to you, too. Where are you?"

There was another odd pause. "I'm at home. Can you come over here?"

"Sure," I said, licking red stains from my free hand, distracted. "Give me about twenty."

"Okay."

It was a strange call. Moran sounded stressed and I hadn't had the sense the conversation was over until he hung up. At the end of the pier I walked down to the parking area and hung my hand over the sea wall. Salty brown bay water was better than sticky red syrup.

I stood up, shaking my hand clean then wiping it on my pants leg, and started again for the Jeep. I didn't feel good, exactly, but I was better somehow as I walked. Dumb bastard, I told myself. I was still thinking in terms of me.

Things would change very soon, though. They might even get better.

Chapter 30

Moran's banana yellow Monte Carlo was in his driveway as I pulled up to his house. I parked at the curb in front and walked around the Jeep and up the short walkway to the front door. I was still feeling that indistinct sense of relief, illusory though it may be. It would be good to talk to my partner about it.

The front door was wide open behind the screen and I rapped on the security door frame with my knuckles. "Terry?" I called through the screen.

I heard something like a cough and then a "Back here!" from somewhere in the house. I pulled the door open and walked back toward the kitchen, which was empty, and then turned down the hall leading to the rest of the house. "Terry?" I called again.

"In the bedroom."

Probably changing clothes after work. It might have been nice if I'd stopped at my house for a pair of swim trunks. A dunk in his pool and a few beers would be good things while we talked. I turned the corner into the master bedroom and stopped cold. Terry was lying on the bed, fully dressed, hands cuffed in front of him; his face was bloody and swollen from the beating he'd taken.

Ralphie Wandorski stepped out from behind the bedroom door, a gleaming 9 mil held forward in his left hand, the barrel pointing clearly at my forehead. His bandaged right hand hung at his side.

"Hands up, Prentiss!" he hissed.

My hands rose slowly into the air. If this was a straight assassination, he would have shot me where I stood. I did what he said, keeping my eyes on the gun barrel.

"Now get down on your knees! Slowly! Put your forehead on the floor and your hands up in the air behind you, high as you can."

Ralphie stayed two steps away from me as I assumed the position he demanded. I felt like a statue of a swimmer on a starting block. Ralphie moved up behind me and unsnapped the cuffs from the back of my belt.

"If you move, asshole, you're dead first, then your partner."

I didn't answer. Ralphie snapped the cuffs over my wrists with my arms still held as high as I could manage. When he was done there was a definite note of triumph in his voice as he pulled my gun from the holster on my hip. "There we go now. Shit ain't easy with a pin in my finger. All right, Detective, lower your arms and sit up. Make yourself comfortable. Just don't try to get off the floor."

My shoulders had already started aching as I sat up and pivoted on my butt so that I could face the bed. I wasn't tall enough to see much of Terry but I could hear his breathing. It sounded moist and difficult.

"Where's Sandra?" I asked.

"Who?"

"His wife, Ralphie. She lives here, too."

He looked over at the bed. "How about it, bud? She going to be a problem?"

Moran said, "She won't be home till seven. Around there."

"Okay," Ralphie said, grinning. "We'll be out of here by then."

"What's going on, Ralphie?" I asked. "What'd you do, lose your copy of the picture you had made to blackmail me? You could have mine but I burned it."

"You burned a picture of a chick with an ass like that? I'd keep something that sweet in my wallet, I was you. That wasn't even my idea, but I liked it." He pulled a chair out from the wall behind him and sat down. "Things have been happening, my friend. I just wanted to see you get your ass canned, dickhead, but now you've fucked things up so bad I've got to take things to another level."

"So what? Somebody offed Pope and now you're running away? You don't need me for that."

He laughed loudly, like some drunk had just told him a joke in a bar. "Somebody offed Pope?" he repeated. "Well, who the hell do you think did that?"

It took me a second to understand what he was saying. "You blew away your boss?"

"Thanks to you two assholes I had to. I didn't have much choice after you told him about that tape of the combination to his safe."

"What?"

"If he knows his combination isn't a secret anymore, he's going to change it, isn't he? Would make it a bit harder for me to get inside it, wouldn't it?"

At least something was coming clear in this mess. "You were going to rip him off."

"Ding ding ding," he said. "We have a winner."

"What did you do to my partner?" I asked. Moran was still breathing noisily on the bed, not participating in the conversation since the question about his wife.

"You're not an idiot, you saw him."

"Terry?" I called. "You doing okay?" It sounded asinine as I said the words but I needed to hear his voice.

"Don't let her find me like this," he said. "Don't let her." He sounded like he was sobbing.

"You're a punk ass son of a bitch, Ralphie," I told Wandorski with feeling. He wasn't bothered. "What do you want with us?"

"I need you to get into Pope's safe."

"And you're a crazy bastard, too."

"No, seriously. I can't do it now. They're looking for me."

"I don't know why you think we can do it, either."

"Not the two of you," he said, pointing the barrel of my gun at my head again. "Just you. Your partner's the reason you'll do it. That picture would have been enough to get your ass fired but knowing you it's probably not enough to get you to steal for me."

He was right about that. And now he thought he could force me to do this by threatening my partner. He's probably right about that, too, I thought. "What's in the safe?"

Ralphie Wandorski nodded his head as though I'd already agreed to do the job for him. "A notebook, about the size of a paperback book, brown leather covers."

"What's in it?"

"Your partner's life, I'd say. The fuck you care?"

"Don't do it, man," came Terry's weak voice from the bed. "All he can do is run away no matter what he does."

He didn't sound any more convinced than I was. Ralphie may be on the run but there were a few things he could do on his way out of town that neither of us would like.

"How'd you pick up Terry?" I asked Ralphie.

"That was awfully easy. I just called him up, said I had some info about my buddy Roy Evans that he might want to hear. Told him to meet me at ol' Roy's house and he trotted right over."

"Prick followed me home from there," came Terry's voice.

"What do you expect, driving that bright yellow car. You're asking for it. Anyone could follow you from half a mile back if they wanted to."

I was tempted to tell Wandorski to go straight to hell. I wanted to drive myself up from the ground and head-butt that cocky grin off his face, smash it into his puny mustache. He couldn't shoot me, he needed me to steal Pope's book for him.

But he could shoot Terry. Or he could wait for Sandra to come home and do something to her. God damn it, I thought. And the only reason Terry would have listened to someone about Roy Evans would have been if he thought he was doing something to help me out.

Ralphie could see the indecision on my face. He took two steps further back from me and held the gun out in front of him. "There's another reason you'll help me," he said.

I just looked at him. Perspiration was forming on my forehead and my shoulders were beginning to ache.

"Talk to your wife lately? She told me you lost contact after her recent move."

At that I did spring off the floor and instantly he turned, stepped to the side of the bed and jammed the barrel of the gun to the back of Moran's head. Ralphie looked at me, eyebrows raised, daring me to keep coming.

He'd done the right thing. If he'd pointed that thing at me I wouldn't have stopped. He shoots me and everything's over. He'd have no reason to hold Terry or see Sandra or even have any further contact with Lori.

I pulled back as quickly as I could.

"Sit your ass back down," Ralphie said. At least that infuriating grin was gone. "Now!"

Slowly I reversed myself into the corner and slid my back down against the wall. "I told you what I'd do to you if you ever mentioned her to me again."

"You really want to keep threatening me, big man?" He pulled a cell phone out of his front pocket. "Tell you what. Let's call her. I need to tell her what a good time I had with her at dinner the other night."

I was actually a lot calmer than I could have been. At this point I wasn't taking him that seriously; he wouldn't know where she is any more than I did.

Wandorski speed dialed a number and said, "Hush, now," as he activated his phone's hands-free speaker.

She answered on the third ring. When she said the word "hello" my throat spasmed and I had to swallow hard before I could breathe again.

"It's just Ralph, Miss Lori. I wanted to tell you what a fine time I had with you at dinner the other night." His grin was creeping back but his eyes were cold, his pupils small, the gun still at the base of Terry's skull.

"What about Roy?" Lori asked. "Did you find out anything more?"

"Not just yet, but I will. And soon, probably. Oh, wait a second, I have another call coming in. I have to go, I'll let you know. 'Bye, darlin'." Without giving Lori a chance to say anything more, he killed the connection with his thumb. "What do you think, big man?" he said to me. "Who's full of shit now?"

"What are you playing at, Ralphie? Why are you involving yourself with my family?"

He lowered the gun and leaned against the wall, arms crossed in front of his chest but with the gun still held in front of him. "I'm doing what I learned from that old fuck Pope. You know why he stayed around all these years? Why the big boys in New Orleans and Miami and New York left him alone, why the feds and the cops can't never prove he's dirty? That motherfucker covered all his bases, man. He didn't sneeze unless he was holding three boxes of Kleenex and had a handkerchief in his pocket. He never had just one way to screw anybody. Bastard always, always, had three or four."

He stepped closer to me, looming high so that I had to tilt my head back in order to see his face.

"You will do what I say," he told me. "And you know it."

I looked down at his feet. I didn't want him to see my face; I didn't know what would be on it.

"You know," he said. "You've got some good people looking out for you. I can't think why else your partner would care about my buddy Roy. And your wife, she's desperate to find that boy, did you know that?"

I didn't answer.

"You know why she wants to find her ex-husband so badly when she wanted nothing to do with him just a few months ago?"

"Go to hell, Ralphie."

"I'll tell you anyway, though I think you already know. She wants to make sure you didn't have nothing to do with him disappearing like he did. You think that's right?"

I could hear Terry's breathing grow deeper but I didn't say anything.

"I told her I might be able to find him. After all, I had some money for my old partner and he needed it. I was sure I could track him down."

My eyes were watering as I was staring at a spot on the floor in front of my knees.

"But now I'm not so sure I can find him," he went on. "Now I'm thinking maybe only you can do that, big man. Would I be right in thinking that way?"

"You win, Ralphie," I said weakly, and I meant it. No matter why I'd done what I had, no matter how much I had been trying to do what I believed was *right*, was necessary to protect my family, all I'd ended up doing was causing pain to others while destroying myself and everything good about me. It was time to stop it all. The first step was to get Terry out of all this. "Tell me how you think this works."

Ralphie went into what he thought could happen, including the exchange of Terry for the leather book from Rudy Pope's safe. We both had our cell phones so we could talk to each other, adjust things as necessary, so we didn't have to nail down every detail. When I agreed to his plan he dug the keys to my cuffs out of my pocket and dropped them behind the mattress near Terry's head; I heard them clatter to the floor. He prodded Moran to his feet where he stumbled badly, fighting for balance. For the first time I saw my partner's face clearly, and it was a mess. One eye was swollen completely shut, and his lips were three times their normal size. His teeth were stained pink with blood and there wasn't a spot on his face that didn't look bruised or damaged.

"I'm sorry, Jeff," he mumbled.

He was sorry? I looked away from him and was ashamed for it.

"Give us a few minutes before you go for those keys, eh, big man?" Ralphie said as he herded my partner out the door ahead of him; Moran's hands were still cuffed behind his back. "I don't want to have to come back and make things even more difficult for you."

"Just leave," I said, but there was no force behind my words.

"Talk to you," Ralphie said, and went.

Motherfucker, I swore to myself but who it was directed at I had no idea. There wasn't any shortage of appropriate candidates. I heard the kitchen door slam shut and sat my weight over my legs and levered myself against the wall until I was standing.

Chapter 31

It took me fifteen minutes to dig the keys out from behind the bed and actually get myself free. There was a bloody patch on the pillow where Terry's head had been. This stopped me for a minute. Whatever this thing was, it was no longer about Randy Shawcross or some asshole politician in Tampa. It wasn't about Rudy Pope or me or Lori or Roy Evans or my daughter or blackmail pictures or my joke of a career. It was about saving Terry Moran.

I put the bed back together as neatly as I could then found some replacement linens in the closet in the hall. I changed the sheets and pillow cases and balled the bloodied ones into a bundle I left in the laundry room stuffed between the washer and dryer. Then I went to the kitchen and wrote a note to Sandra telling her that Terry was going to be late getting home. I signed my own name and hoped she'd understand; she may be puzzled as to why Terry hadn't called her but it shouldn't worry her. Much. At least for a while.

Like I knew what the hell I was doing.

Then I climbed into my Jeep and finally got out of there. The yellow Monte Carlo was gone from the driveway. Sandra would assume I was driving with Terry and for some reason we'd needed to make a stop at their house.

Once I was on the road it hit me just how clueless I'd been about everything. I may have gone off trail and been able to figure out some of the details of Pope's porn site operation, but I'd missed the most important thing: I hadn't identified the real enemy, the guy with the power to bring the actual hurt. I had dismissed Ralphie Wandorski as an uneducated punk and now that I looked back at everything I thought I knew, I could see how it all added up. It was shocking to realize how distracted I'd allowed myself to become. And it was hurtful to realize that I hadn't been able to avoid it.

Ralphie worked himself up from boosting cars to a position close to Rudy Pope, the head man himself. He had to be bringing something to the table. He'd been involved to a large degree with the Little Y operation, a form of "legalized prostitution" as Hector Ramirez had described it, and it was clever as hell. He knew Roy Lee Evans, which wasn't a positive endorsement of any sort, but it made him curious when Evans disappeared after asking him for money. That prompted him to make contact with my wife. Apparently more than once. Then he set me up with the blackmail photo, only he said it wasn't his idea....

Now he'd murdered his boss. And beaten and humiliated my partner in his own home.

I felt as if I'd just finished a hard run; my pulse was racing and my breathing was rapid and uneven. There was too much to do, and I didn't know if I was capable of pulling it off. Not without giving myself away.

I had to find a way to calm down. I didn't trust myself to be able to make this work the way Ralphie wanted. Taking out my cell phone I called Leslie Alcaro. It was the only thing I could think of. Someone needed to know what was going on if this thing didn't come out right.

"Jeff?" she said when she answered. "I—"

"Leslie, I need you to listen to me." She stopped talking.

"Are you all right?"

"In no way am I all right." And I told her everything I'd done at the warehouse in Brandon and kept going until I caught her up with Ralphie Wandorski and what he was doing with Terry Moran.

"You have to stop this, Jeff. Now."

"I'm trying," I told her. "It's all I can do."

"No, that's not what I'm saying. You have to call Greene, the FBI. You have to let your own people take care of this now."

"Leslie, I— I can't."

I could hear the disbelief in her voice. "You don't have a choice! You can't stop Wandorski! What about Terry?"

"Terry's okay until I figure out if I can get Pope's book back or not. After that, there's time to make that call."

"You need to do it now. I'll do it—"

"No, Leslie! You can't. Right now Terry has a gun to his head and Ralphie told us both he'd already killed Pope. Ralphie's got nothing to lose anymore. I've got to get Terry back."

"How, then? Why did you call me?"

I shook my head. "I don't know. I just—I just wanted someone to know, that's all. Ralphie has a plan. If it works, it works, and Terry could walk away. If it doesn't—"

"Well, what if you don't walk away? Have you thought about that?"

I almost laughed. "I've already thought too much about what could happen to me. You don't even know. All of this is my fault. It's my fault."

She sounded disgusted with me, like she didn't believe what I was saying. "So you don't get to get out of this yourself, is that it? Is that what you're saying?"

"I don't know yet. Thank you for listening. I mean it." I put my thumb over the "end" button and said, "Goodbye, Leslie." Then I hung up.

She tried calling back once but I didn't answer. I didn't want to argue and I already had enough fights going on.

The best thing that could happen now was that Pope's office would be unguarded. I'd expect it to be sealed but not necessarily watched. It might depend on how much the Tampa cops thought Pope's murder tied into other cases, especially the Barry Schoenfeld murder. Terry and I had planted that seed with Isabel Marquez ourselves and if she had listened she'd be concerned with gathering as much evidence as she could from that office. Which would include the contents of the safe, I knew. But according to Ralphie, she'd have a hard time finding the combination, which would mean a court order to get someone to open it, assuming she could convince a judge she needed access. It was a matter of time, in any case.

I got off the interstate and headed south into Ybor and drove as slowly as I could past the Casa Amarilla. There was a single patrol car parked out front in a no parking zone. That didn't help things. I swore out loud several times as I drove down Seventh and took a right at the corner. I had to get in there. My fingers were aching as I gripped the wheel.

I drove to the same loading area where Moran and I had parked when we paid our first visit to Pope and Wandorski. I looked up through my window and could see the rusting steel fire escape that had saved Ralphie's ass when I'd thrown him through the picture window. It would have cost me mine but Terry wouldn't be going through this hell right now.

There was no time to feel sorry for myself. I had the combination to Pope's safe in my pocket, straight from Ralphie, and I had to find a way to get inside that office. The cop on duty was probably sitting right outside that door. Could I bluff my way in? I thought about it but I didn't see how. If he or she didn't buy my excuse, one call to Marquez or whoever was in charge would shut me out for good.

Could I bluff Marquez? I checked my watch. Ralphie said he'd call in ninety minutes; I had a little more than half that time left. I needed to figure out something soon. I didn't want to talk to that prick without Pope's book in my hand.

I looked up Marquez's number in my notebook and picked my phone off the passenger seat. As I dialed I restarted the Jeep and took down the window as I worked the accelerator for background noise. While the phone was ringing I took deep, long breaths; she was going to hear my stress regardless but if I could keep the panic out of my voice I'd be more convincing. She just had to be there....

"Isabel Marquez," she said. Finally.

"This is Jeff Prentiss, Isabel," I said. She'd taken the company line when it came to my expulsion from the Tampa PD and without being overly familiar found it most convenient to decide she didn't like me. My impression was she didn't approve of anyone who became bigger than the job; didn't matter whether they sought it out or had it thrust upon them by someone else, including the media. It could be she resented the fact it hadn't happened to her.

I might be about to change that.

She was hesitating before responding. "I've been dealing mostly with your partner," she said.

That stopped me for a moment before I realized she hadn't meant in the last hour or so. "I need to get into Rudy Pope's office," I said. "Right now. I need to know if you have a problem with that. I don't have any time." As I spoke I pumped the gas pedal up and down, nearly to the floor each time.

"What do you need that for?" she asked. "What do you guys have going on?"

"Look, I don't have time to explain. Terry's got a package for you that will wrap up Schoenfeld with a bow. You can cap it off with the King of Cats and the Rudy Pope killing. All yours. He'll be there in ten minutes but you've got to get me into that office right now." I wanted to get the drool flowing and then blitz past her before she could reconsider.

"Where are you now?" she asked. The tone of her voice had changed.

"I'm almost to Ybor," I said. "You got a guard posted? Can you radio them to let me by?"

"What are you—" She stopped, probably checking her watch. "If I'm going to meet your partner downtown I have to get moving. What do you need in Pope's office?"

"There may be more bodies," I said, winging it. "We got a tip from someone in Pope's organization. Terry's package will explain everything. I've got to get a look at what's in Pope's desk drawers. Timing's important here. Pope's guys are still out there."

I could hear her moving, then another voice was speaking in the background. Something to distract her, I hoped.

"Okay, I'll call ahead for you. But you don't take anything, you hear me? You just look. I'll meet Moran at my desk and we'll call you." She exhaled loudly into the phone. "We really got more bodies out there?"

"I don't know, could be," I said. "Pope was an old man. This thing could go back a long way."

"Okay," she said, a different person than the one who'd answered the phone. "Keep your cell handy."

"Got it," I told her. "I'm almost to the restaurant. Talk to you in a bit." Then I hung up without giving her a chance to reconsider or ask more questions. I killed the engine and got out of the Jeep. By the time I got around to the front of the building and found the police guard, Marquez should have made her call.

When I found him with his ass parked on a chair outside a strip of yellow barricade tape in front of Pope's office, the cop looked up and asked, "You Prentiss?"

"Yeah, that's me," I said.

"I need to see your ID."

"Jesus Christ," I swore, grabbing my badge wallet out of my back pocket and flinging it into his lap. He looked at it then calmly handed it back to me and I knew what was going on behind the look he was giving me: *Just doing what I'm told, asshole.*

He stood up, found a key on a ring with a dozen others, and reached around the tape and unlocked the door.

"It'll just take me a minute," I said.

"I'm supposed to go in with you."

"Fine, but I'm in a hurry."

He took a step back into the hall. "After you, then," he said.

I ducked under the tape and entered the late Rudy Pope's office. I hit the light switch and stopped just inside. It stunk of damp iron, the smell of old blood, not all the way dried. There was spatter along the wall to my right, a larger stain in the carpet on the floor in front of it. Rudy Pope's last stand. That was something I didn't need to see.

Across the room in line with the door was the desk, a large carved affair with a leather blotter and a set of antique looking accessories: letter opener, a small box, pen holder, stamp tray, and a lamp with a cracked ivory shade. The small bookcase behind the desk was just as it was in the Shawcross video.

I went to the desk, moved the chair aside, and made a show of going through the drawers. The cop stood on the other side and watched. When I turned and started to slide the wheeled bookcase away from the safe, he came around and said, "You were only supposed to look at the desk."

I wanted to hit him. I resisted the impulse to look at my watch. "And what I'm looking for isn't there. Now I'm going to look in here." I finished moving the bookcase and took out my notebook as I kneeled in front of the safe.

"Marquez didn't say anything about this," the cop said.

I didn't stop. "I'm trying to solve a crime, pal," I told him. "What are you trying to do?"

He didn't say "be a kiss-ass toady." "Isn't this what got you run out of Tampa PD?"

That almost made me spin the dial past the last number of the combination. "You know what you're talking about, do you?"

As I swung the door open, I could hear him moving behind me. Trying to get a better view at what was inside. I heard the crackle of his shoulder radio and knew he was calling in to Marquez.

There were two shelves in the safe; the brown leather book was covering a steel box on the upper one. With my body shielding the contents, I slid the book off and underneath the steel box as I pulled it out and, still kneeling, turned around to face the desk. Before the cop could move closer to see what I was doing, I slid the book under my jacket and held it next to my body with my upper arm.

"Bring it up here," the cop said. His arm was crossing his body, his fingers on his radio. "Let me see."

Holding my left arm firmly against my side, I picked up the box with my right hand and set it on the blotter on top of the desk.

"It's locked," I said.

He began talking into his shoulder set as he came around the desk to be closer to the safe. I edged around the other side and headed for the door, breathing shallowly and not looking at the gore by my feet.

A burst of static and some low chatter. "Where are you going?" the cop called as I got to the door.

"To get the key," I said, which was nonsense but if he was charged with watching that room and its contents, following me outside wouldn't help him, especially if he thought I was coming right back.

I made it to just outside the door when my phone rang. I snatched it from my belt and flipped it open, thinking it was Ralphie but the number on the display was Isabel Marquez's. I almost answered but my bluff was over. Her boy upstairs must have reached her on the radio already. Only he wasn't upstairs anymore.

He came out of the door behind me while I stood on the sidewalk holding my phone. "Prentiss," he said. "Detective Marquez would like you to wait here."

The phone stopped ringing, probably kicked over to voice mail. "What the hell for?" I said.

He just looked at me. What exactly did she expect him to do? Arrest me?

"Tell her I opened the safe for her. What I was looking for wasn't there. Now I have to go."

I turned and as I was putting my phone in my pocket he stepped forward and grabbed my arm.

"What are you doing?" I asked him, staring him in the face. My patience was about gone. There were other things I needed to be doing. His fingers opened though he kept his arm extended toward me.

"You are coming back with the key to that box?" he asked. "She'll want to know."

"I will if I can find it," I told him and walked away again. This time I made it to the corner and then around to the alley where I had left the Jeep.

My phone rang again and I pulled it out to check the number. Marquez again. I put it back in my pocket. I flicked through the pages of Pope's book: lists of names and numbers. I didn't have time to study it now.

There was a group of four or five men coming out of the alley as I got there. They had been laughing and talking but when they saw me they quieted down. Not a good sign, not in this part of the city. The missing weight of the gun from my belt was noticeable.

We were only about ten yards apart and of course they could have quieted down out of their own nervousness. But they outnumbered me too much for that. I took out my badge and held it out to them as we closed.

"You guys seen a Latin girl, wearing a purple tank top shirt and carrying a bag?" I asked.

This stopped them, made them think of something else. Their postures got a little straighter and they hustled past me with a chorus of "no's," "uh-uh's" and "not me's." One of them said, "Hope you find her, man."

Crooked loading docks and stacks of pallets kept me from seeing my car. If those bastards had done something to my Jeep, it would make it more difficult for me to get to Terry when I heard from Ralphie. It looked like there was a car parked next to mine, one that hadn't been there before.

Something hit me in the back, hard, and I dropped to my knees, half turning toward the dumpster I had just passed. A figure was moving, swinging something.

Everything exploded into a brilliant white mass of something something something....

Ralphie Wandorski stood over me, wooden baseball bat at his side, his crooked-toothed grin leering down at me. His right hand still bandaged, in his left he held Rudy Pope's leather bound notebook. My head was pounding but I didn't think I had a concussion. Not a serious one, anyway. Otherwise I wasn't even sure if I'd be able to consider the question. I tried to move and felt a sudden sharp pain across my lower back.

I had to try twice but I finally managed to ask, "Where's Terry?"

"Your partner's in his car, next to yours." He let the bat fall to the pavement and he kicked it behind him. From somewhere he produced a gun and he held it out so I could see it. "Recognize this?"

It grew bleary the longer I tried to stare at it but it looked like my gun, the one he had taken from me at Moran's house.

With his broken finger pointing up in the air, Ralphie ejected the magazine and tossed it into the dumpster at his side. Then he jacked out the shell in the chamber and kicked it away, too. "Nice gun," he said. "Shoots straight, too. Even left handed." He dropped it on the ground next to my head and I flinched, expecting it to hit me.

He laughed, and it sounded vicious. "You came into my world, you dog shit, and you pissed on me in front of my boss. It's your life that's getting fucked up now, asshole. It's your life." Ralphie pulled Pope's book from under his arm and rifled the pages, probably checking to see if they were all there. I wished I'd thought to pull out a few.

"I got my ticket now, big man. Thanks to you."

From the quick look I'd had of the book, my guess was that it contained the list of names and details belonging to the clients for the Little Y website, the member roster of the men involved in Pope's "legalized prostitution" ring.

"Going into the blackmail business, Ralphie?" I asked.

"I don't have much choice, do I?" he asked. "You've pretty much ruined everything else for me here. Pope's shit is finished."

I turned my head to follow him as he took a few steps back and picked up the baseball bat. I rolled on to my side so I could push myself up but Ralphie was there and he kicked me hard in the shoulder and knocked me flat back on to the filthy concrete.

There were footsteps coming down the alley and I saw Ralphie look up, toward the corner. "I'm not finished with you, cocksucker," he said. "Remember that." He ducked away behind the dumpster and a second later I heard a loud steel door clang shut.

I had gotten to my knees and was fighting a wave of nausea as Isabel Marquez ran up to me. "What the hell are you doing?" she asked. "Who was just here?"

I almost threw up on her shoes when I rolled over and tried to answer. Instead of standing, I sat back on my knees and let my head droop down. "Ralphie Wandorski," I managed.

"We want him for Rudy Pope," she said, pulling a hand held radio out of a purse slung across her shoulder.

She started speaking into it and I tried again to stand up, this time using the dumpster for something to hold on to. Apparently Marquez wasn't going to help.

I made it, but I had to stop at achieving something only approximating vertical. I was leaning on the front edge of the uncovered garbage bin with my forearms, staining my shirt with a brownish-green slime. It had to stink, too, but just then I couldn't smell it.

Marquez appeared at my shoulder. "Get Terry," I said. "Next to my Jeep."

She looked down the alley, said, "Is that why he didn't show?" and trotted off. She was back a minute later. "There's no one there," she said.

I didn't believe her. "Help me," I said.

"What's going on, Prentiss?"

"Oh, hell," I said and pushed off the dumpster. I could walk but my head was pounding with each step and I kept blinking my eyes and squinting ahead. Marquez stayed at my side, again not bothering to help.

Terry's yellow Monte Carlo was parked on the other side of my Jeep. Like Marquez had said, it was empty. I didn't understand. Why would Ralphie keep Moran after he had gotten the book?

Isabel Marquez walked around the other side of the car and pulled open the passenger door. She ducked her head inside, something I didn't think I could do at the moment, and said, "There's blood on the upholstery."

That wasn't a surprise. "Open the glove box," I told her. "Pop the trunk."

"What happened here?" she demanded. "Should I be getting a team down here before we—"

"Open the damned trunk!" I said with as much force as I had left. The rush of pain made me want to scream and I clamped my eyes shut as I heard her fumble with the glove compartment door, followed by the release of the trunk itself. I pushed away from the car and made my way to the trunk. Marquez was next to me as I pushed up the lid.

"Holy shit," she said.

My partner was in there but he couldn't see us anymore. I turned away and threw up at last.

Chapter 32

Ten minutes later the entire block was swarming with uniforms and plainclothes officers. Ralphie Wandorski had disappeared but clearly he had planned this all out. Isabel Marquez wouldn't leave my side and for a while I didn't care but now it was starting to get to me, especially when the medical examiner's crew lifted Terry's body from the trunk of his own car. I had to get away. The man may have been my only friend and I felt as though I'd barely started knowing him.

"Where are you going?" Marquez asked, catching up to me as I walked down the alley. Reluctantly, I stopped.

"The murder weapon," I said. "It's in that dumpster."

"How do you know?"

"It's my gun," I said, closing my eyes against another flash of light and more stabbing pain in my head.

"You should sit down," Marquez said. She called for a crime scene tech and I watched as he climbed over the dumpster's side and lifted out my weapon.

I sagged against the wall and told Ding Dong about the gun, the ejected magazine, and the shell Ralphie had let bounce away on the pavement. I also pointed out the baseball bat.

"Anything you can tell me about how to catch this douchebag? Where he could have gone?"

I tried to shake my head. That was a mistake.

Marquez led me to an ambulance and an EMT started looking me over. Large contusion, possible fracture, possible concussion. The last thing I wanted to do was get out of that ambulance but I did it anyway. All I wanted to do was sit back and close my eyes....

The EMT said I needed to go to the hospital.

Not gonna happen, son.

Marquez saw this, came over and told me to stay in the ambulance. And not out of concern for my health.

"Where the hell do you think you're going?" she asked.

It was still hard to think clearly for more than a tiny burst at a time. "I'm not sure," I said. Something was rattling around in my mind and I had to get out of there so I could figure out what it was.

"You're a witness now, Prentiss. Maybe something more. You need to tell me exactly what you know. If you don't need to go to the hospital, you can talk to me now."

I looked at her and my eyes spontaneously filled with tears. "You're a tough bitch, aren't you, lady? Look over at Terry's trunk, why don't you? Look at Terry. Then just shut the hell up, why don't you?" I wasn't crying, my eyes were just wet. I blotted them both with my sleeve until they were dry. It didn't happen again.

Whatever Marquez would have said next wouldn't have been nice. I told her to take out her notebook and start writing. She did. I ran down everything from the Little Y "legalized prostitution" operation to Schoenfeld's apparent involvement, the business relationship he must have formed with Randy "King of Cats" Shawcross, and how it led to the brown leather book in Pope's safe. By the time I told her about Ralphie's rant in Terry's bedroom, she'd filled a half dozen notebook pages.

"And now Wandorski's got the book?"

"He does."

I looked over at the yellow Monte Carlo, the source of so much casual joking but still and always Terry Moran's pride and joy, one of those silly symbols that tie us to our past and make us who we are today. Or were. They had his body zipped into a bag now and were loading it onto a gurney. For some reason I was shocked to see Lieutenant Greene standing next to the car, somber and gray. The last thing I would have expected from him in this situation was quiet. Part of me felt ashamed at my surprise.

Marquez, too, seemed to be coming down from the manic rush of the initial activity. She read over her notes and asked me a few more questions. "And that's all of it?" she asked.

I realized I hadn't mentioned Roy Lee Evans or Ralphie's contacts with my wife. That hadn't been on purpose. It got me thinking again. "Do me a favor," I said. "Go run it down for Greene, will you? I think I do need to sit down."

Her eyes were growing bigger by the minute as she began to grasp the true size of the case here, beyond Barry Schoenfeld's assassination. She went off to confer with my boss.

I stood where I was, watching two technicians load my partner's corpse into a white medical examiner's van. The daylight was waning but everywhere in the alley the colors were brighter than they should have been.

Slowly I walked away from the scene along the buildings and the lines of uniforms and techs that were combing the alley for more evidence. At the mouth of the alley a small crowd had formed, held back by a single cop who was using his arms and attitude to keep the right of way clear. I stepped past him onto the sidewalk and disappeared in the crowd, the pain in my head a bit better, relieved to not hear Greene's voice bellowing after me. That wasn't going to last, I knew. I had to move, and the first thing I needed was a car.

On Seventh I caught the trolley heading into downtown. I got off and flagged down a cab near the Aquarium. I told him to take me to the airport, another fifteen minute drive. I rented a car at the counter with the shortest line.

The sun had gone down by now and the sky was filled with its normal smear of artificial colors. My head throbbed every time I moved it and I became a mirrors-only driver when I changed lanes.

I'm not finished with you….

I kept hearing Ralphie's voice, over and over, repeating the last thing he said to me: *I'm not finished with you….*

I drove too fast and too sloppy but I got to Ralphie's house in Tampa in one piece. I remembered his bandaged hand and me throwing him through a window and for the first time I realized that Ralphie could have been a lot more wild and out of control than he had been. He was colder and more calculating and right then I should have realized what or who I was really dealing with.

The fog in my head might have been a good thing, in a way. It kept me from reacting to the deep rooted fear in my gut, which in turn helped blot out the image of the damaged and lifeless face of my friend and partner, shot to death with my own gun. I was aware that there was no way I was thinking clearly but I also knew I didn't know how to tell the difference.

I turned up Wandorski's driveway and managed to stop the car just before crashing through his garage door.

The house was dark, as I'd expected. He wouldn't be here, probably not ever again, but the Tampa cops certainly would be. I needed to get in and out of there quickly.

I walked around the back of the house to the pool and lanai area. With the key from my rental car I jabbed a hole in the screen and ripped a two foot gash above the door handle. I reached in and unlocked the door and went in.

I stayed away from the thick, hurricane rated sliding doors. There were a number of windows to choose from and the easiest to access was one that looked into a bedroom. I did the key trick on the screen again then ripped it out of the frame. I picked up my foot and kicked my shoe through the window glass. No alarm went off, which wasn't a surprise. Almost every honest person in Florida had a burglar alarm and response service. Guys like Ralphie figured they either didn't need them or they could take care of their own security.

A quick look into each room showed a desk in one of the other bedrooms, a stack of mail on top. What I was looking for was in there, already opened and close to the bottom of one stack. I pulled the sheets of paper from the envelope and scanned the list of numbers. There it was: a Gainesville number, dialed three times during the billing period that had just passed. I shoved it in my pocket and left the same way I'd come in because it never occurred to me to unlock the front door.

I'd beaten the cops to Ralphie's place but what about to my own? I sped down the highway, across the bay and onto the St. Petersburg peninsula. I couldn't guess what was in Greene's or Marquez's mind about where I'd gone, or what they'd do about it, but I knew they'd want to bring me in. If I was really lucky they'd assume I might be wandering about in a concussed daze, and not think I was up to anything unexpected on my own. That was probably a longshot. All I knew was I couldn't let them catch me yet.

There was no one at my house when I drove by but just to be safe I left the car on the street a few houses up. I didn't want to get pinned in my own driveway if the timing went bad. I ambled down the sidewalk the best I could and moved across my yard to the front door. It didn't take long to get what I needed: a charged battery for my cell phone and my spare gun. I took the extra few seconds to put its box back on the rack in the bedroom closet, and covered it again with the stack of sweaters that I never wore. I didn't want to leave Greene any unnecessary clues.

Back in the rental car, a marked St. Pete patrol tore past me, no siren but with light rack flashing, and I watched it turn onto my street in the rearview mirror.

Good, I thought, relieved. I was free for a while now. The cops weren't going to find me or stop me or talk to me or reason with me. Nobody was.

I'm not finished with you....

You damned well better not be, Ralphie, you son of a bitch. I'm not finished with you, either.

Chapter 33

My phone rang again as I drove. I checked the number, the way I had been doing, and saw that this time it was Leslie. A friendly voice, I hoped.

"Jeff!" she said when I answered. She sounded terrified.

"I'm here."

"How are you doing?"

I told her about getting my head smashed with a baseball bat and the fireworks still popping dully inside my skull.

"Where are you?"

"On my way to finish this thing."

She was smart enough not to say anything to that. She may know me better than I thought she did. When she spoke again, it was in a quieter voice.

"I have Carlos's computer."

"Your husband?"

"There's a memory card in there," she continued. "It— it has that picture on it."

I didn't know whether to be relieved or not. "I'm sorry you had to see it," I told her.

"That doesn't matter. I went to his house, talked to those girls. Do you know what they're doing?"

"I have a good idea."

I didn't really need to know but Leslie went into the details of how Carlos would post "Free Flights to Florida" ads online, and about what that meant for the girls that responded. They knew what they were getting into. What they hadn't know was that the average "career" of a girl that made those scenes was only three months. Their average fee was eight hundred bucks, and out of that they had to pay their agent, in this case Carlos Alcaro, travel expenses, and get tested for disease every two weeks. Other than being eighteen years old, there were no other federal laws.

"Is this what you deal with every day?" Leslie asked.

"That's more on the vice end," I told her, "but I see it." Or saw it.

"At the end, when they're through, most of them barely have enough money to go home and buy new clothes."

"Did they talk about the set up with Pope?"

"Only that there was a special project that some of the girls would get to work on, but they had to be chosen first."

"By who? Your husband?"

"Don't call him that. Please." I apologized. "They didn't know. They were treating the other shoots as auditions for the Big One."

I didn't know what to say. After a pause, Leslie said, "Why do they do that to themselves?"

"There are probably dozens of different answers, Leslie. It's a big country."

"And every day another girl turns eighteen."

"Every single day."

"Are you going to tell me where you're headed?"

"I don't think that would be wise." I felt that I was hurting her by saying that and it made me sad. "Where is Carlos now?"

"I don't know," Leslie said. "The girls said he hasn't been around since yesterday."

"If you see him, stay away," I told her. "Far away. This whole thing with Pope has crashed around their ears. I don't know who's trying to do what to who right now."

"I will," she said quietly. "And Jeff? I'm sorry about your partner."

It took me a moment to realize she'd never actually met Terry Moran. "Me too, Leslie," I choked out. "Me too."

Maybe if my head hadn't been ringing since Ybor City, or maybe if Leslie hadn't called and distracted me so much, or maybe if I'd been able to turn off my thoughts and drive with as much attention as I should have, I'd have been aware of what was happening behind me. By the time I did, it was way too late.

Maybe, maybe, maybe. I lived in a whole world of maybes.

I was waiting for him when he came into the house. Lori had to be there, of course, to let him in. He was far too cagey to have fallen for anything else. She was the bait, after all. For both of us.

The question now was what to do with her.

I had to dial her cell phone eight times before she finally picked up and would listen to what I had to say. She only did it then because I told her voicemail that I had her address and was already on my way up there. The distress was clear in her voice but I told her this wasn't about us. I asked if Ralphie Wandorski had contacted her.

"What's this about, Jeff? Really."

"He's trying to get to me, Lori," I told her.

"What are you talking about, Jeff? What he and I talk about doesn't have anything to do with you."

But I knew it had everything to do with me. "I may be wrong, Lori, but I don't think so. I need to be with you right now. If it wasn't important I wouldn't be calling."

"What are you talking about? I told you I need space right now, I need time, Jeff, time away from—"

I didn't want her to say it. "Please, Lori. Believe that I think you may be in a dangerous situation. Trust me. Just one more time. Life or death, Lori."

When she finally told me she'd see me it sounded like something else. It sounded like a different way to say goodbye. I could never have imagined there would be so much distance between us.

While Ralphie had her phone number, he did not know her address. Just the same, I wanted her to get Roxy and get the hell away for the night, at least until I got there. I wanted to be sure I didn't underestimate Ralphie Wandorski ever again.

"What if he doesn't call?" she asked.

"He will," I told her. "He knows I'll come for you. And if I'm gone, he has a better chance of pulling off his—" I almost said blackmail scheme but finished with "future plans." I knew Ralphie was banking on the idea that if both Terry Moran and I were out of the way, he could start milking Pope's Little Y clients.

As far as Ralphie was concerned, with the brown leather book in his possession and with Pope gone, other than Terry and I no one else that mattered had any idea of who his future victims were going to be. Terry and I had never gotten that far but Ralphie couldn't know that, and he had to be careful. He'd need help, too, because now he'd made himself a wanted cop killer. It might have been a long chance but it was all he had left and I didn't think he was going to let it go.

Roxy had been gone when I'd arrived at the house; Lori said she was staying with a friend, but she didn't elaborate and I didn't push. Lori let me in, said a few words and retreated to a bedroom. She didn't want to talk to me. I spent a restless and lonely night on the living room couch.

He finally called while Lori and I were eating a speechless breakfast in her kitchen the next morning. It felt like we were strangers and she wouldn't meet my eye but at that moment I had to focus on Ralphie Wandorski. Lori sniffled when she answered the phone, as though she had a cold, and when Ralphie told her he needed to see her, about Roy Evans of course, she gave him the address and told him to come over to the house she was renting. She was ill and didn't feel like going out.

Perfect, he had told her. I felt the same way.

When Ralphie arrived at the house, Lori let him in, a tissue to her nose, and walked away across the living room as quickly and as naturally as possible. I hadn't known if I could count on her to do as I'd asked but she pulled it off perfectly. I did not want him to get close to her and I did not want her to be between us.

Ralphie entered and carefully shut the door behind him. Lori called out that she was getting some coffee and headed into the kitchen at the back of the house before Ralphie was all the way in. When I heard the latch of the door catch, I counted to two then stepped into the room from the hallway that led to the main floor bedrooms.

"Hands up, Ralphie," I said. His face turned white and then red as I watched him through the sights of my gun. When Lori came back into the room she was almost as pale as he'd been. I wanted to study his face, to see if there was any recognition of the damage he'd caused to the people I'd cared most about. I didn't see anything like that. He gathered himself and after a few seconds, a twisted grin formed beneath that ugly wisp of a mustache he refused to shave.

"I didn't think they'd let you get away so quick," he said.

"Clasp your hands behind your head, Ralphie. Now."

"Can't do it, Prentiss. Remember, you busted my finger." He held up his damaged hand but moved it behind his head anyway. He did it slowly, the grin never leaving his face.

"Now down on your knees. You move your hands past your ears and you'll have nothing to hold your head together after I blow it wide open."

I stepped behind him and parted his hair with the barrel of my gun. I wanted him to feel that I was there. I wanted to smell his fear. With my free hand I brought out my handcuffs and closed one of the bracelets around his left wrist, the one that was unbandaged.

"Where's y'all's daughter at?" he asked. He seemed to be speaking more to Lori than to me. "Don't you think she'd like to see her new daddy act like a policeman one last time? After the mess he left down south he may not be carrying a badge too much longer."

"Shut up, Ralphie."

"Sure, sure. By the way, your boss is gonna get a kick out of those pictures I sent him yesterday. What time does the mail usually get to your headquarters, Prentiss? You want me to get a copy made for your wife here? There's one out in my car."

Lori made a sound but I kept my focus on Ralphie and didn't look at her. I moved the gun off the back of his head so I could take hold of his other wrist and fasten the second bracelet when he whipped his hand down and to the side. A searing pain cut across my right calf.

He scrambled forward, getting to his feet after pushing up from his knees, and threw himself toward Lori.

I had almost fallen after he'd cut me. I didn't have time to set myself and I had to aim high as I squeezed the trigger with a prayer that I could stop him without shooting my own wife.

The bullet went high and Lori screamed as Ralphie threw his left arm around her throat and whipped her body in front of his own. I slumped to the side, against the wall. Lori's face was turning red.

"Take it easy, Ralphie."

"You first. Drop the gun, Prentiss."

I shook my head. He held his bandaged hand against the side of Lori's neck and I could see the tip of the thin blade he'd wrapped up inside his bandages press against her flesh near her carotid artery. There was only about half an inch of metal exposed but it was enough to slice open my leg and do something even worse to my wife.

"You hurt her and you die, Ralphie." I lowered the gun so he wasn't staring at the barrel but that was all. "You know this."

He didn't lose his swagger. "I don't want to die, you don't want to die, Lori doesn't want to die," he said. "You got any suggestions?"

"Let Lori loose and I'll put a bullet through your heart."

A drop of blood formed on Lori's neck where he applied more pressure with the tip of his blade. "I just don't see that happening," he said as I brought the barrel up in line with his eye. "How about this? What if I told you I lied about sending that picture of you to your boss? I've got a print in the car, sure, but I haven't sent it yet. The memory card is in there, too, the one that came out of the camera."

"And?"

"You let me walk out of here and your career is safe, at least from me. I get it, you figured I was coming here, you got here first. You're a smart man. I'm smart, too. I know when to walk away."

The blood flowed in a crooked stream down Lori's neck. My head was pounding with little concussive blasts exploding behind my eyes.

"How 'bout it, Prentiss? We going to make this work?"

The call I'd had from Leslie played over in my mind. She said she had Carlos Alcaro's computer. And the memory card.

I lined up the front and rear sights. I hoped Lori would forgive me.

There was a crash of glass from the living room window. Ralphie instinctively ducked down, whipping Lori between himself and the sound, almost knocking her over. I moved the gun and shot low. Ralphie screamed as a bloody hole blossomed on his right thigh. Lori threw herself forward, Ralphie's blade raking her neck, leaving a long line of dripping red.

A shot came through the window and entered the sheetrock next to my ear. I dropped and backed against the front door. "Move to the kitchen!" I yelled to Lori, who crawled out of sight, leaving a blood trail on the floor. I had no idea how bad Ralphie had cut her.

"Who's out there, Ralphie?" I asked.

He gritted his teeth and didn't answer.

"I want that book!" came a voice through the cracked glass.

Ralphie looked at the hole in his leg, then at me, and tried to smile when he called, "Come and get it, you prick!"

Another shot came through the window, then three more. At least two of them hit Ralphie as he was pulling his own nine mil from under the front of his shirt. I had no idea who he was planning to shoot.

I couldn't wait to see if I'd be caught in a crossfire between whoever was outside and the injured Ralphie. I almost shot Ralphie again but then I hoped he could keep the other guy busy as I reached behind me and turned the knob on the front door, tumbling backwards onto the front stoop.

The figure at the window turned at the opening door but I was on the ground and before he could adjust I put three through the center of his chest. I rolled behind the front door and called Ralphie's name.

"What now?" he called back. His voice was wet and raspy.

"Throw the gun out, Ralphie, or I'm coming in shooting."

Ralphie coughed and it was ugly. I'd heard that sound before.

"Do it now." I needed to get to Lori.

"There...." I heard the clattering of metal on the hard floor.

He was laying there, on his side, leaking life from too many places. I kicked the gun away and shouted for Lori.

"In here," she called from the kitchen. "I'm okay. I'm just bleeding."

Thank heaven. My knees felt weak and I almost went down. I picked up Ralphie's gun, then placed my foot on the wrist of his bandaged hand as I checked for anything else. He was clean. "Stay where you are, Lori."

I went outside to finish with the second gunman. He was on his back on the ground, not moving and not bleeding. His gun was next to his out-stretched hand. I understood he must have followed me all the way up here, starting with the trolley ride from Ybor.

It was Carlos Alcaro.

Lori's cut was long but thankfully not deep. It produced a lot of blood and would leave an impressive scab, but probably not even scar.

Rudy Pope's brown leather book was in Ralphie Wandorski's back pocket. I looked through it once then put it into my own. I went outside to his car and found the glove compartment open, its contents scattered across the passenger seat. Alcaro had to have come for the book. He, too, was trying to climb over the bones of Pope's corpse.

I found one copy of the photograph of Stacey and me but there was no computer or memory card. I took the photo to the backyard and burnt it on the grass. There wasn't much more I could do.

The local cops started to appear just as I finished checking Alcaro's pockets. He had nothing on him. I could only hope Leslie had been right about what she'd taken from his home. Hope was all I had left.

The local captain gave me some leeway when I told him who Ralphie Wandorski was, that not only had he just killed Rudy Pope down in Tampa but also my partner, a homicide detective from St. Petersburg.

He blew a long, slow whistle through his cheeks and said they didn't get much of this kind of stuff up in horse country but was happy it ended the way it did. For him it was over. For me, it would never be. I didn't try to correct him.

I asked him to contact Lieutenant Greene at St. Pete and Isabel Marquez at Tampa PD. Both would be interested and they'd give him the whole picture. Lori and I spent a half hour giving them statements as an ambulance responder bandaged the cuts we'd received from Ralphie. Mine was deeper and they asked if I wanted it stitched, said it could go either way. I asked him to butterfly it and I'd take care of it later. When we told the captain about our daughter he let us go so that we could pick her up. His department's role was about finished; he'd hand everything off to Tampa, most likely, and be done with it.

My situation, though, was something altogether different.

Chapter 34

Eventually Lori had calmed down and was able to give me directions to the stables once I had gotten her into my rental car and away from the house. I had called Greene at his desk and told him where to find Ralphie's body, Carlos Alcaro's, and told him to expect a call from a Captain Bradshaw.

"Where are you right now?" he asked.

"I'm going to get my daughter."

He began to shout but I didn't hear any of it. I broke the connection and powered down my phone. I wasn't sure how I could make anything actually worse for myself.

After a few minutes, my wife and I watched our daughter from a hundred yards off, partially shielded by a fence, as she worked with a trainer to exercise a horse. Lori didn't want her to see me.

"Why the hell not?" I asked.

She looked away. "Because you'll make the goodbye that much worse," she said.

So we stood there in awkward silence until I began to feel that I either had to grab Lori by the shoulders and hold her in front of me until she *saw*, until she knew why I'd done what I had, or else pound my head into the rails of the fence.

Instead I just said, "I love you, Lori."

"I love you, too," she said almost absently.

"What's going to happen now?"

She gathered herself with a long breath, then turned toward me, but kept her eyes on the ground between us. "I don't know," she said. "Will you tell me what happened to Roy?"

And there it was again. What was I supposed to say to that? Would she, or Roxy, even be here to ask that question if Roy Evans had stayed in their lives after he'd come out of prison and found them again? Or would they be two more people I had to mourn?

"You know what happened to Roy," I said.

She turned away again, watching Roxy while I stared at the side of her lovely face. "I think I do, Jeff. And I know why, and I know what it means, and I know that it's probably the only reason Rox and I are still—" She searched for the word. "Unhurt."

Now she did turn and look at my face, into my eyes. She reached forward and took my hands and for the first time in too many days I saw and felt the love that we shared between us. But something else was there, too. "Right now, Jeff, right this very minute, all I see, every time I look at you, is the face of the man that made Roxy's father—"

"I'm Roxy's father," I blurted.

"I know, I know. She wouldn't have it any other way. But how can I look at you, or talk to you, be with you, and not think about how Roy has just—gone away."

There was nothing I could say to that.

"He's not coming back, is he?" Despite that she said she *knew*, she'd always have the question.

I tried one more time. "Please don't run from me," I said. My eyes were moist and I didn't want to break contact with those hands.

"Please don't make me," she said. She held on a moment longer, searching my face, then let go. She turned back to the fence.

We stood like that for another quarter hour, quietly watching our daughter, anchored in our pain, until I bent over, kissed her on her cheek, and walked back to my car. She had said she could call a friend for a ride home and I reminded her that she may not want to go back there right away. She nodded then, aware that I'd brought that much more pain into her life.

Courtesy of me, her one true love.

I drove back to her rented house to throw myself into the fire.

Chapter 35

I sat down on the edge of my dock and let my feet hang over the surface of the water. It's funny how brown it is, how people think it's dirty when it's actually just filled with too much life. Lawn fertilizers and chemicals wash and seep into the bay through the ground and storm drains. Algae thrives, and blocks the sun from the lower depths. It's the clear water, like in the Caribbean, that is the dead stuff. Or at least less alive. Transparent as glass, but supporting only minimal life, there's no place to be born, to grow, to be safe from predators.

Being alive doesn't mean being healthy. Too much algae near the surface prevents sea grass from growing and without that, there's no shelter for the littler fish. Which then can't grow into bigger fish. Or serve as food. Another side of the coin.

I could feel the presence of the gun on my belt. I took it out of its holster and laid it on the faded wood next to me. My badge was poking into my leg so I took it out of my pocket and laid it next to the other.

Terry Moran was buried yesterday. I went to the service but I didn't speak to anybody. Once I had begun to walk over to Sandra but she stopped me with a look. I went back to my place in the church and stared at my shoes. I kept thinking over and over about the note that I had left her, saying that Terry was working late. Like I was vouching for him, keeping him safe, when he was already in Ralphie Wandorski's hands. I wondered if she'd viewed the body and hoped she had not.

The department was playing every note by the book. I had finished all my statements and been sent home on mandatory leave. We all knew what was coming next. Leslie wanted to be there with me but I told them I didn't want her or anybody else I would choose as part of that.

Lori and Roxy moved on again, which has to be hard on the kid, I thought. At least she's young, I tell myself, but I don't know what that means. I also think that if I stop trying to take care of them they can settle down and Roxy can stop being dragged to a new town or new state just so Lori can keep from seeing me. Few things can turn as bitter as true love.

A few yards from my feet a mullet propelled itself from the water at a low angle and sailed, its body a quarter turned, and hit the water with a sharp slap and a splash six feet further on.

I picked up my gun and looked at it in my hand. It was a Glock 26, a smaller version of the model 17 that Ralphie had taken from me. I kicked out the magazine then slammed it back into the grip. The exact same bullets came out of either weapon.

Randy Shawcross was gone, his wife Darlene finally moved to San Diego. There had to be some part of her that was happy to be free from her husband's notoriety and reputation, no matter how much she may have loved or missed him.

The widow Schoenfeld is threatening a lawsuit against anybody whose name her attorneys can spell. I wasn't surprised when they told me. She was trying to keep her husband's image clean, or maybe just her own, really. She wouldn't be able to do it, though. Hidden sex, politics, organized crime: that mixture will draw too many flies every time. And those movies are still out there, somewhere. The thought that digital copies never degrade popped into my mind, and I smiled over the double meaning.

And then there was Pope's book. Nobody'd ever found it, but that was because I'd never turned it in. I checked my watch. Leslie should be here soon. When she came I'd give it over to her. If the right names were in there maybe she could use it to make a deal. Or maybe she'd barbeque it on my grill. The decision would be up to her.

I couldn't get my partner's face out of my mind. When I closed my eyes I could hear the laugh in his voice, see the yellow flash of sun off that ridiculous yellow car left over from his high school glory years. I could feel the warmth of his concern for me, in that brief time we'd spent getting to know each other, the belief he had in me. All the way to the end.

My whole life I had only done what I thought was right. What I thought had to be done to protect my family, the public, the victims of violent crime. God help me, despite all evidence, I still couldn't *feel* how wrong I must have always been.

Rudy Pope's gone, along with his "legalized prostitution" set up, but his bolita operations would go on for a while: his bookmaking, his girls, whatever else he was into. The cops would be looking at it more closely now, but so what? The business wouldn't survive without a head, or else it would be taken over by someone with even more juice.

Ralphie's gone but I couldn't feel anything but a warm satisfaction for that one. I took the gun into my hand and flicked the safety off, then on. Off, then on.

I wondered if I would ever be with my family again. Lori said she loves me still but she can't bear to look at me. Roxy doesn't understand what happened and hopefully never will.

And what about Roy Lee Evans? What if I was wrong, what if he was only following the deadly pattern up to a point? What if he was really just trying to scare Lori and Roxy and wouldn't have crossed that line from stalking to physical violence? And then worse? What if the stalker had turned out to be just a stalker?

Bullshit, I told myself. I had to. It goes that way every single day, somewhere.

With my free hand I picked up my badge and held it next to my gun, weighing one against the other. I didn't think there would be any chance of saving my job this time, no matter what Leslie said, or what she might be able to do with Pope's book when she had a chance to study it. Not without some monumental effort made by someone I didn't know on my own behalf. Yes, I'd broken the rules while I was working on this case. At the time I justified it by telling myself I had to, that after my time in Tampa I didn't have the backing, the respect, of an organization that contained cops like Terry Moran. He wasn't pulling the kind of baggage I had been since the day I stepped into the St. Petersburg PD but he and his brother officers weren't like me, they hadn't earned the hardship and I had.

They tell us the ends never justify the means and they may be right. I don't really know. My wife and daughter may not be with *me*, but at least they're *somewhere*. I have no family but they still *exist*. That had to mean something.

Somewhere in my mind I lumped Schoenfeld, Pope, Ralphie and Carlos Alcaro together in the same trash bin, and I was fine with that. The death of Randy "King of Cats" Shawcross was a tragedy to his wife but not an altogether unexpected end for a person who'd chose the career and lifestyle that he had.

But Terry Moran? I had no words. I was emptied out.

There was also the loss of a detective, formerly of the Tampa PD, more recently working this side of the bay, but it wasn't likely he'd be missed by many. Maybe that's the right thing, too.

The grill needed to be fired up, the meat taken out of the freezer. A semblance of life must go on. Leslie was on her way. I wondered what she really wanted from me, and, not for the first time, what I really wanted from her.

I chucked what was in my left hand into the bay where I'd last seen the mullet splash. If anyone ever wanted it again, I could tell them just where to find it.

Silted over, discolored. Tarnished.

I did make the right decisions. I did do the right things. I kept my wife and daughter safe and I took a murderer off the board. I did some good, right? Didn't I?

I dangled my feet over the water, listening to the fish jump, and played with the safety on my gun.

THE END